MARVEL

For Max, who is very funny

SHADY OAKS NAMED LEAST DESIRABLE PLACE TO RAISE A FAMILY

Litter, graffiti, thefts, and packs of feral dogs helped land our township in last place in the annual *New Jersey Today* poll.

MYSTERIOUS TAILED GIRL SAVES BABY

"She tore that car door right off," said a local man. "Saved the baby from the backseat of the stolen car and caught the carjacker to boot. I tell you, I've never seen the like."

"SQUIRREL GIRL" SAVES THE DAY!

An amateur Super Villain headed to jail after Shady Oaks's local Super Hero Squirrel Girl foiled his nefarious plot.

SQUIRREL GIRL STOPS CONVENIENCE STORE ROBBERY

"I didn't know what hit me," said the alleged thief. "Turns out it was a giant squirrel tail. Man, I'm telling all my buddies to avoid Shady Oaks. This neighborhood is protected now."

ALLEGED CAR-RADIO THIEF RESCUED FROM EXTREMELY TALL TREE

When asked why he was in such a tall tree, the suspect responded, "Squirrel Girl told me to spend some time up here thinking about my life choices."

COUPON COUNTERFEITING OPERATION SHUT DOWN

County police discovered a coupon-counterfeiting gang when the alleged criminals made a panicked 9-1-1 call: "They're everywhere! They've taken out the lights! Hundreds of small black eyes staring at us! Now they're throwing acorns! Save us! Save us!"

SHADY OAKS CRIME AT ALL-TIME LOW

Local residents credit their own neighborhood Super Hero, the unbeatable Squirrel Girl, and her squirrel friends for the sudden drop in crime.

SHADY OAKS TO GET A SHOPPING MALL

With crime low and consumer confidence high, businesses are starting to invest in long-overlooked Shady Oaks.

1

SQUIRREL GIRL

*T*he night was as cool as glass. Streetlamps cast orange cones of light onto the pavement, but everything in between them was darkness. Darkness so thick, you could gnaw on it.

Squirrel Girl perched atop a streetlamp, twelve feet above the quiet suburban street. Not the kind of place where you'd expect to run into a laser-blasting maniacal villain. Squirrel Girl's bushy tail twitched. Her keen eyes raked the darkness for any sign of that dastardly ne'er-do-well.

Then her phone buzzed.

Finally! All this waiting was getting super-boring. She went for the phone, scooping it out of a pouch on her utility belt. But a bunch of loose cashews spilled out of the pouch, and she fumbled the phone.

"Dang it," she said, diving headfirst off the streetlamp. She caught the cell just before it could crack against the sidewalk, twisting to land on her feet.

On her phone was a text from Ana Sofía Arcos Romero, her BHFF.[1]

> **ANA SOFÍA**
> Are you hidden?

Squirrel Girl checked her surroundings in a super-sleuthy sleuth way. She was standing directly under the streetlamp, orange light falling over her as bright as a fire.

She leaped up into the shadowy branches of an oak tree in someone's front yard.

> **SQUIRREL GIRL**
> Yep of course I'm the most hiddenest. Soooo sleuthy. Very stakeout

> **ANA SOFÍA**
> Good cuz u know sometimes u forget to hide and the bad guys see u and no more element of surprise

---

1 That means Best Human Friend Forever. By the way, this is me, Doreen Green, aka Squirrel Girl. I'm just gonna read along with you and let you know my thoughts down here in the footnotes, deal?

SQUIRREL GIRL

Who me?

ANA SOFÍA

Anyway the Squirrel Scouts on the north end of the park saw Laser Lady going down Bungalow Row so she might be coming your way

SQUIRREL GIRL

Ooh is that what we're calling her cuz i was thinking maybe Light Emitting Desperado? You know, cuz it would be LED? Or Smashlight maybe? Zap Mama?[2]

ANA SOFÍA

She kinda named herself already. In the way that she's running around shouting I AM LASER LADY

SQUIRREL GIRL

Good way of making sure no one messes up your name

ANA SOFÍA

Maybe I should try it. Mr Hanks calls me Annie Sophie. The pain is real

---

2 Or Luster Lass, Lumen the Undying, Captain Incandescent, Flicker Filly, the Inexcusable Glare, Sun Bunny. . . . If it were me, I would just go as "Shine," but I would also pretend to be Australian, because with the accent people might think my name is "Shoin," which would confuse and discomfit them, and that's what crime is all about, right?

SQUIRREL GIRL

> I'm so on board with u walking into first period
> and shouting I AM LASER LADY and u know
> what that's a pretty good name now that I think
> about it

A voice cut against the cool-as-glass night, sharp as a diamond. Squirrel Girl wasn't sure if normal humans would be able to tell what the distant voice was saying, but her slightly-better-than-your-average-person's hearing most definitely identified the words "I AM LASER LADY! FEAR ME!"

Squirrel Girl leaped from the treetop to the next one, and from there to a streetlamp, but the shouting faded. She sniffed the air but smelled no trail. In the next tree over, someone was waiting. A small, furry brown someone with a fetching pink bow tied around her neck. Tippy-Toe, her BSFF.[3]

"Chkkt-tik," said Tippy-Toe.

"You got that right, Tip," said Squirrel Girl, landing on the branch next to her. "Wandering around a neighborhood pointing lasers at people *is* super annoying. Laser Lady might hurt someone."

"Chukka chik-chet."

"Yeah, Laser Lady is a pretty cool name. Per usual, we agree in all things."

---

3 Best Squirrel Friend Forever, of course.

Squirrel Girl lifted up her human fist. Tippy-Toe tapped it with the knuckles of her tiny squirrel fist.

A call began to ululate, growing louder and louder. A message was traveling down the chain of squirrels: Laser Lady had been spotted near the park. Tippy-Toe scurried up to perch on Squirrel Girl's shoulder.

"It's clambering time!" said Squirrel Girl as she clambered out of the tree and onto a roof. "Did you get that joke, Tip?"

Tippy-Toe shrugged.

"'Cause I was clambering?" said Squirrel Girl, who was in fact still clambering, this time up a chimney.

"*Chkt-chikka kit coff,*" Tippy-Toe said, which meant, "But clambering implies climbing in an awkward manner, and you're much too graceful for that."

"Aww," said Squirrel Girl, as she jumped off a roof. "Your compliment really takes the sting out of my failed joke."

And suddenly, there she was. The nemesis of the night. The hoodlum of the hood. The mysterious Laser Lady.

"Aha!" said Squirrel Girl, landing on the sidewalk directly in her path.

Laser Lady swerved her bicycle to miss Squirrel Girl. Because Laser Lady was riding one. A bicycle, that is. Squirrel Girl had never battled a villain on a bike before. Firsts were always a plus.

The bike crashed into a tree. Squirrel Girl managed to grab hold of Laser Lady's cape to keep her from crashing into the tree as well. Because Laser Lady was wearing one. A cape, that is.[4]

"FEAR ME!" said Laser Lady, tugging her cape from Squirrel Girl's hand.

She looked about forty years old, white, with brown hair in a trim bob. She jumped to one side, flipped her purple plastic cape back with a cracking sound, and pointed her laser directly at Squirrel Girl's face.

"Laser shot!" she said, firing a red beam into Squirrel Girl's eyes.

Squirrel Girl squinted. "Ugh, stop that! It's really annoying. And could possibly cause retinal damage—I mean, I'm not an ophthalmologist, but you just never know."

"Laser shot!" said Laser Lady, aiming the laser beam at Ana Sofía and the Squirrel Scouts, who were running toward them up the sidewalk.[5]

"She's been shining her laser-pointer thing at people in the park," said Ana Sofía. "She even shined it at cars."

Squirrel Girl gasped. "That could distract a driver and cause an accident!"

"That's right!" said Laser Lady. "I *could* cause an accident! So you should FEAR ME!"

---

4 In my experience, capes are a lot more common among the Super Villain lot than bicycles. Which is a shame because bikes could totally be evil with the right look. SPIKES! CHAINS! EVIL HANDLEBAR STREAMERS IN SHOCKING COLORS!

5 Squirrel Scouts are basically people who think Squirrel Girl is pretty awesome and wants to help me stop evil. This group was mostly students from my school, but you can be a Squirrel Scout, too; it's not an exclusive club or anything.

While she said it, she was trying to climb back onto her bicycle, but her cape kept getting caught on the chain ring.

Squirrel Girl picked up the bicycle. Laser Lady tried to grab it, so Squirrel Girl held it over her head.

"Look, Laser Lady," said Squirrel Girl, "I'm sure it's fun to ride around on a bike and shine a laser pointer at people and shout *FEAR ME* and all—"

"It isn't about *fun*," said the would-be villain, jumping up and down, trying to reach her bike. "Sometimes you . . . you just want someone to . . . *fear* you . . . you know . . . what I mean?"

Squirrel Girl smiled as a way to show understanding but not answer directly because, no, not really interested in being feared, thanks. For one thing, she wouldn't get invited to parties.[6]

"Let's get down to the nuts and bolts of this," said Squirrel Girl. "Why do you want so much to be feared?"

Laser Lady lifted her laser pointer at Squirrel Girl. "LASER SHOT!"

But before the beam of red light hit Squirrel Girl's face, Tippy-Toe leaped through the air, seized the laser pointer in her valiant jaws, and landed on the sidewalk.

Laser Lady's shoulder's drooped. Her bottom lip quivered. "No more laser! Now what am I going to do?"

"What do you think you should do?" Squirrel Girl asked.

---

6 Even so, I haven't been invited to that many parties in my life. Yet. Probably the invitations will start rolling in soon. But I was trying to empathize with Laser Lady's feelings first so she'd take my advice after. You know, like parents do.

Because it was what her dad often said when she went to him with a problem.

"Stop . . . shining laser pointers into people's eyes?"

"Well, yeah. That's a really good start," said Squirrel Girl, still channeling Dad. "But back to the nuts! You want to be feared because . . ."

"I don't know." Laser Lady jumped and reached for the bicycle, jumped and reached. "I guess . . . it's better . . . than being ignored. I'm sick of being . . . ignored!"

Squirrel Girl nodded encouragingly. "I hear you, Laser Lady."

"You do?" Laser Lady stopped jumping. "Because today at work we were in a meeting and I kept trying to give my input, but every time I spoke, Todd talked right over me just like always. I'd say, *Maybe we could minimize the negative publicity . . .* and Todd would say, *WE SHOULD MINIMIZE THE NEGATIVE PUBLICITY* while pointing his laser pointer at the board, and everyone would say *Good idea, Todd! Great input, Todd!* till I just snapped! I grabbed Todd's stupid laser pointer and ran!" Laser Lady sniffed. "The cape was from last year's Halloween costume. . . ." She sniffed again. "Bride of Frankenstein."

"Todd sounds like a real gem," said Squirrel Girl.

Laser Lady looked up in surprise, and then, belatedly hearing the sarcasm, she started to laugh. "A real gem—that's Todd."

"Obviously your pointer thing there is not the burn-holes-through-walls kind of laser," said Squirrel Girl. This conversation was suddenly super-interesting to her. She had known a "Todd" or two, after all. "But the pointer lasers are still mega annoying. Plus it's prolly not good for eyeballs. But you know what the real problem here is? Spoiler alert: it isn't lasers."

"Then what is it?"

"It's Todd," Squirrel Girl said.

"YES!" agreed Laser Lady.

"I think you need to tell him to back off. Tell him to stop copying you all the time and talking over you and stealing your ideas. That's way more annoying than a laser pointer."

"You're right! Thanks, Squirrel Girl!"

"Aw, that's what Super Heroes are for," said Squirrel Girl.

She put the bicycle back down—which was a relief, because even with proportional squirrel strength her arms had started getting tired. Laser Lady wrapped her cape around her neck like a shawl and pedaled away, dinging her little bike bell.

"*Chkt-cht?*" Tippy-Toe asked, holding up the laser pointer.

"Yeah, good idea—we don't want any other potential villains getting ahold of this," she said, sliding it into a pouch on her utility belt.

Squirrel Girl turned to the Squirrel Scouts, adjusting to make sure her hood was up and all. The hood sported little bear ears—which on a girl with a huge bushy squirrel tail could easily be mistaken for squirrel ears—and was part of her Super Hero disguise.[7]

---

7 TBH I still can't believe they don't recognize me from school, even if I do hide my tail in my pants. They must be like, "Doreen sure looks like Squirrel Girl, but I don't see a squirrel tail, so totes not her, I guess."

"We did it, gang!" Squirrel Girl said, her fist punching the air.

The Squirrel Scouts groaned.

"What?" said Squirrel Girl, her fist coming back down. "Is it constipation? Sudden group constipation? That sounded like a gastrointestinal groan."

The Squirrel Scouts looked at each other and seemed to share a general disappointment. Though from vastly different social groups at Union Junior and Union High, they'd come together to follow Squirrel Girl and fight bad guys. And hadn't that night been just oozing bad-guy fights and Squirrel Girl-ness?

"There was, like, zero punching," said Heidi, the blond leader of the Somebodies.[8]

"Yeah, I like the punching parts," said Antonio, his pale face hidden under a baseball cap.[9] "Remember when we got to punch all those robot drones?"

"And the stomping! Don't forget the stomping!" said his friend Robbie.

"I loved stomping on robots," Lucy Tang said quietly. "It was very satisfying how they crunched under my boot."

"Yeah," said Vin Tang. He was skinny and black-haired, and

---

8 The Somebodies is . . . a popular group, I guess? I don't really get how that works. But Heidi's dad donated a frozen-yogurt machine to the school cafeteria, so for a long time that apparently meant that she and her friends got to decide who mattered? Middle school is confusing.

9 Antonio is basically the leader of the Skunk Club, who used to think making graffiti and tipping over trash cans was fun till I showed them that fighting Super Villains is way more fun.

a full head taller than his sister. "The robot drone battle was the best."

"That was indeed magnificent, forsooth!" said the baron, a brown-skinned kid in a leather breastplate, a feathered cap atop his short Afro.[10] "A tale fit for kings, to be retold long after our scarred hides are hanging on the Wall of Warriors."

"Forsooth," the duchess said sadly.

The Squirrel Scouts walked away, muttering to each other in disappointment.

"When Ana Sofía texted us that we'd be fighting Laser Lady tonight I was all *yeah*, but now . . ."

"But now . . ."

"Yeah, but now . . ."

"Forsooth . . ."

Only Ana Sofía remained. She was wearing so many layers and scarves, Squirrel Girl could only see half of her brown face and her black bangs sticking out from under her hood. The girl did not like being cold.

"So?" she asked.

"At least it wasn't group constipation," Squirrel Girl said.

"Huh? I didn't catch that," Ana Sofía said, pulling her hood back an inch.

---

10 The baron leads the LARPers—Live Action Role Players. They like to pretend they're living in medieval times, I guess? Listen, when you spend most of your life hiding a squirrel tail in the seat of your pants, you don't judge.

Under the clear light of the streetlamp, Squirrel Girl recounted to Ana Sofía the life-changing conversation she'd just had with Laser Lady. Ana Sofía wore hearing aids, but without seeing someone's lips as they spoke, it was nearly impossible for her to parse the sounds and make sense of a conversation. Even then, Squirrel Girl had come to realize, lipreading wasn't a 100 percent accurate sort of thing. Neither of them were fluent in ASL, but they both knew enough that Squirrel Girl often punctuated what she was saying with ASL signs for clarity.[11]

"I think this is a new thing, Ana Sofía!" she said. "Talking criminals out of criming! Why didn't I think of it before? It's so much faster than all the fighting and whacking and punching and gnawing. Seriously, the Avengers should look into the talking thing."

"I'm not sure that would work every time," said Ana Sofía. "You tried to talk the Micro-Manager out of unleashing a droid demolition army on the neighborhood, but he did it anyway."

"Maybe I didn't try hard enough."

Tippy-Toe headed to the park, so the human girls started home, too, texting each other as they walked side by side.

ANA SOFÍA

Did u do your math homework

---

11 I've been studying ASL, but it's a complex language! Even my amazing squirrel powers don't help me learn new languages overnight.

SQUIRREL GIRL

Yep

ANA SOFÍA

Did u

SQUIRREL GIRL

Any second now

Did vin set a time for your date yet?

ANA SOFÍA

I don't want to talk about vin

SQUIRREL GIRL

He luvs u

ANA SOFÍA

stahp

SQUIRREL GIRL

Okay. Love you dude

ANA SOFÍA

I know. Love you too

2

DOREEN

*D*oreen Green, age fourteen, walked into homeroom at Union Junior High School with a loose swagger in her step. She'd talked a criminal out of criming last night (even if it was just Laser Lady), and that gave her some hippity-hoppity, make no mistake. She could almost forget the cramp in her tail, which was stuffed surreptitiously in the seat of her pants.

Besides the large badonk her tail-hiding endeavors granted her, she could pretty much pass for a non-squirrel-powered middle school girl: short red hair, pale freckled skin, round face, front teeth a bit longer than your average teen's. Her powerful thick-thighed legs made it hard to find jeans that fit. Today she wore black-and-white-striped stretchy leggings under an aqua blue flare skirt, and a T-shirt featuring a smiling unicorn wearing braces.

"Hey, Doreen," said Janessa Lopez.

"Hey, Janessa," said Doreen Green.

"Hi, Doreen," said Vin Tang.

"Hi, Vin," said Doreen Green. All chill. Like it was a totally normal thing to be saying hi to *multiple* friends and not just the most amazing thing ever.

Until her family's recent move to New Jersey, she'd never been part of a whole friend group—not a human one, anyway.[12] The Squirrel Scouts didn't know that Doreen was secretly their neighborhood hero Squirrel Girl, of course, but she was still Ana Sofía's friend and a fellow Squirrel Scout.

Doreen was feeling so tip-top, so cartwheelishly magical, she took an apple from her backpack and put it on the teacher's desk.[13]

"Morning, Ms. Schweinbein!"

Ms. Schweinbein glared down at the apple through the glasses perched on her thin nose. Her skin was so pale it was nearly gray, and her hair was in a pencil-thin braid. Her face was smooth yet resigned in a way that made it impossible to tell her age. Twenty? Fifty? While her age wasn't definite, her smell definitely was. Doreen sniffed a couple of times. Yep, always with a

---

12 I left my first squirrel friends back in California. I'LL NEVER FORGET YOU, MONKEY JOE!

13 One of three apples that was part of my lunch, along with a pound of mixed nuts, a sunbutter sandwich, and six granola bars.

very strong odor of animal. Her teacher must have a lot of pets. Doreen's nose wrinkled before she could stop it.

"Excuse me?" said Ms. Schweinbein, glaring at her. "Do you have something to say?"

"Me? Nope. Not at all. Just . . ." She pointed to the apple.

"Are you attempting to bribe me, Doreen?" said Ms. Schweinbein. "Is a piece of fruit the going rate to get a teacher to pretend that your scattered homework is acceptable and that your constant interruptions in class are contributions rather than distractions?"

"No! Not bribe! I just—"

"Well, it won't work," said the teacher, tossing the apple at the garbage can.

Doreen deftly caught it before it went in, and stuffed it back into her bag.

"Geez, why's she always such a downer?" Doreen mumbled, sliding into her desk.

"She's cool to me," said Janessa from the desk to her right.

"Me too," said Vin from the desk to her left.

So it was just Doreen that Ms. Schweinbein despised? What in the heck was up with that?

"Where were you last night?" Janessa whispered.

"Huh?" said Doreen.

"We went out patrolling with *her*," Vin whispered. "Ana Sofía sent a group text about it. You didn't get it?"

"Oh! Yeah! I, uh, couldn't make it," said Doreen.

"Ended up being a *bust* anyway," said Janessa. "It wasn't a *real* villain, and Squirrel Girl just *talked* to her—"

As the late bell rang, the PA system played its familiar five chimes, indicating morning announcements.

"Good morning, Wolverines!" drawled the voice of Heidi, student body president and fellow Squirrel Scout. "Listen up, because we have a legit announcement today after the boring ones. Blah-blah track meet after school, blah-blah Kiwi Club fund-raiser tomorrow. Okay, okay, here's the real scoop: Of course you know about the mall that's going up on the border of Shady Oaks and Listless Pines?[14] Well, the Chester Yard Mall's PR guy sent us a letter, and they're doing a *contest.* When the mall opens in two weeks, there will be an election to vote for the mall's mascot—either a dog or a cat. All the schools in Listless Pines will be campaigning for the dog—"

"BOO! Listless Pines eats garbage!" another voice shouted.

"Shut up, Dennis. Okay, like I was saying. All the schools in Shady Oaks—"

"Including Union Junior. Go Wolverines!"

"SHUT UP, DENNIS! Anyway, we'll be campaigning for the *cat*, and everyone knows cats are way better than dogs. So if the

---

14 Listless Pines is the town right next to Shady Oaks. It got a Burger Frog restaurant before Shady Oaks did, and everyone still seems mad about it.

cat wins the vote for the Chester Yard Mall mascot, then the mall is going to pay for a *pizza* party for our entire school!"

In Doreen's classroom, there was a collective gasp. In middle school, the words "pizza party" invoked reverence. After a moment of respectful silence, the class erupted with ebullient cheers.

"Listen, everybody, we *have* to win," Heidi's voice continued. "No way is Listless Pines going to get *our* pizza party. So, hey, all the school clubs, you *need* to come up with ways to advertise the opening of the mall to the entire community, convince them to come out on mall opening day in two weeks, and vote CAT!"

"GO CATS! GO WOLVERINES!"

"Shut UP, Dennis—" The PA speaker cut off.

The class boiled with excited chatter.

"Cats, huh? I like dogs okay, but if it'll get us a pizza party . . ."

"I can't wait for the new mall! I heard they're going to have a Johnny Blaze Steak Buffet with a full Latverian mustard bar!"

"Listless Pines smells like sewage."

"Oh man, pizza sounds *sooo* good right now. My mom made me drink a kale smoothie for breakfast."

Doreen glanced up anxiously at the teacher, sure she would shush them all with an angry shout. But Ms. Schweinbein just leaned back against her desk, smiling in a satisfied sort of way.

"This is big news indeed!" said Ms. Schweinbein. "Cats and dogs. Which is better? Both, if you ask me, for both are royalty of the greatest kingdom on earth: Kingdom Animalia. But as pizza is at stake, we will naturally join Team Cat. For the rest of the period, split into groups and come up with ways to sway the mascot vote toward the cat." She rubbed her hands together. "How I love a pizza party."

Doreen felt her phone buzz and glanced down. Heidi had texted the Squirrel Scouts group. She saw Janessa and Vin take out their phones as well.

HEIDI

Okay Squirrel Scouts did you hear the news? Are you all psyched?

LUCY

Yeah math class is having a fit you'd think everyone was starving

DENNIS

I'm starving. All I ate today was a candy bar

HEIDI

Stop bragging about your stupid candy bar Dennis

ANA SOFÍA

This is the Squirrel Scout group text for official biz not sure a mall opening qualifies

HEIDI

Totes qualifies. Squirrel Scouts fight bad guys
and now listless pines r da bad guys

VIN

Maybe we should listen to Ana Sofía on this?

ANTONIO

We got the announcement at the high school
too skunk club is mega power in to take down
listless pines

JACKSON

PIZZA PARTY!!!

HEIDI

Cats r best anyway so now we just have to get
everyone in town to go vote for cats and we win

DENNIS

Shouldn't I be on the pro dog side since I'm
a dude?

JANESSA

What are you even talking about Dennis

DENNIS

Dogs are boys and cats are girls that's
just science

JANESSA

WHAT ARE YOU EVEN TALKING ABOUT DENNIS

LANESSA

I for one am loving this, at last something to fight for!

DOREEN

Something to fight for? Isn't justice enough?

LUCY

Haha Doreen ur hysterical

ANA SOFÍA

I didn't realize everyone was so disgruntled

BARON

Ah yesteryear was a time fit for bard tales but of late the bards are silent as we noble warriors do naught but wait and watch

VIN

He means we don't do anything exciting anymore

DUCHESS

Tis true. We long for the adventures we once knew

HEIDI

Yeah no offense to SG I still think she's top drawer but it's just like ever since she cleaned up shady oaks nothing exciting ever happens

JACKSON

PIZZA PARTY!!!

ANTONIO

PIZZA PARTY!!!

The whole conversation was making Doreen feel a bit ill, almost as if the four peanut butter sandwiches she'd had for breakfast hadn't settled well.

"Doreen," said Ms. Schweinbein, suddenly leaning over her desk. "I specifically said to join groups. In class. Not play phone games or google celebrity crushes."

Doreen looked left and right at Vin and Janessa and others also on their phones, who the teacher didn't seem to see. Or care about.

"But they are—" Doreen started.

"What?" said Ms. Schweinbein. "They are what? Hard at work? Not insulting their teacher?"[15]

---

15 So, the first day Ms. Schweinbein came to class I may have made a comment on how she smelled? Not in a rude way, just like *Wow, you smell like a barnyard!* or something. Or maybe she thought I was insulting her one of the times I fell asleep in class? I was just up late fighting crime, is all. I told her she wasn't *that* boring.

Doreen's tail throbbed. Her leg shook, tired of inaction. Everyone not on their phones had already formed groups and were in earnest discussion. She was group-less.

She hopped up and made her way to the back of the class.

"Hey, there!" she said. "I'll join your group."

"A little late for that," said a boy.

Doreen turned to another.

"Hello, fellow middle schoolers. Sorry I'm late. What's our plan for dominating this mysterious mall challenge—?"

"Um, we've already kinda formed our group?" said a girl.

"Nope," came the preemptive denial from a member of the third group.

Doreen sat back at her desk.

Honestly, she thought, *I'd rather face off with a Super Villain or a droid army than a middle school classroom.*

She rubbed her head, feeling exposed without her brown-eared hoodie. Her hand went to her waist for a pick-me-up snack of nuts, but of course she wasn't wearing her utility belt at school. Here she was just Doreen Green, and right now, Doreen Green didn't feel like much of anything at all.

3

ANA SOFÍA

*A*na Sofía walked home from school slowly, her head so full of thoughts it felt almost too heavy for her neck. Something about the mall PR stunt smelled as rotten as Listless Pines on a sweltering hot day.[16]

Ana Sofía couldn't decipher PA announcements, so her teacher had repeated the gist of it for her sake. But still. Classrooms had terrible acoustics plus endless background noise—chairs squeaking against the floor, whispered conversations, creaking desks—and her hearing aid amplified not only the teacher's voice but every squeak, creak, and whisper as well. So whenever she was in class, her teachers wore a small microphone around their neck that transmitted what they said directly to her hearing

---

16 I've been to Listless Pines, and it doesn't really smell bad? Prolly this is just something people from Shady Oaks say? I don't know, I'm new here.

aid. Even with that solution she usually didn't catch everything. Like the name of the mall. What had the teacher called it?

Plus the mall was apparently offering to foot the bill for an enormous pizza party. She did the math:

Student body of Union Junior + Union High =
approx. 3000
$10 per pizza
8 slices in each pizza, 4 per student[17]
Cost of pizza: approximately $15,000

Fifteen thousand! That seemed like a lot of money just for a little PR for a mall everyone was already excited about anyway. And it didn't even include drinks! Though if it did, Ana Sofía hoped there'd be black cherry soda.

Ana Sofía's dad was a construction manager on the mall, and he'd complained that the client was extremely particular about the details. He'd also mentioned that the client insisted on "no overtime!" so the workers got off before dark. According to her dad, that was very unusual.

She took out her phone and browsed the website for the construction company, and from there clicked a link to the mall's homepage.

---

17 *At least* four slices per. Middle school students be hungry.

Chester Yard Mall™
Coming this fall! Bringing apocalyptically
good shopping to the Shady Oaks and
Listless Pines communities!

Chester Yard? That was random. Ana Sofía had lived in Shady Oaks her whole life and had never heard of any person or place called Chester Yard. And that was a weird motto, but whatever.

She scrolled down and for the first time saw the Chester Yard Mall's symbol:

That looked extremely, uncomfortably, confusingly familiar. Take away the exclamation-pointed words, replace the happy face with a skull, and that was . . . that was . . . the Hydra logo, wasn't it?

She texted the link to Doreen.

Does this look odd to you?

Yes why do they have DEALS! twice seems overkill

But it looks like something else right? It's not just me?

They're calling it chester yard mall? Boring. I'd name it something fun like marshMALLow. Or squirrel mall and nut emporium. Or just nut mall but then they'd probably think the stores sold nothing but nuts

Probably

Omigosh can you imagine a mall just for nuts I'm freaking out what a great idea

Are you coming over later?

I'll text you

Doreen hadn't noticed the similarities between the Chester Yard Mall symbol and another, more sinister symbol, so Ana Sofía tried to pluck out those niggling weeds of worry. After all, if an actual secret evil organization was behind the neighborhood mall, why would it make such an obvious allusion to itself with that similar symbol?

When Ana Sofía neared the Arcos Romero family's brick bungalow on Amanat Street, she smelled a faint wisp of sulfur.[18] Then as she reached the door, she felt the rumble of his tremendous voice. Felt it even before her hearing aids crackled with the sound, the vibrations of his deep bass traveling through the earth and up into her sock protectors.[19]

Then there he was in her kitchen—six foot six, blond hair, an empanada in each fist, going on about something while her mother Teresa laughed. Ana Sofía rolled her eyes. Her mom used to only make empanadas for birthdays, but recently, she found the time to do it whenever *he* stopped by, acting all like, *Oh, these delicious meat-filled pockets of goodness? It's no trouble at all, I make them* constantly![20] For the family, she usually baked the empanadas, saying they had less fat, but for the god of thunder, she

---

18 Ana Sofía's last name is Arcos Romero. Isn't that beautiful? It's a Mexican cultural thing for kids to have both their parents' last names and— Wait, she smelled sulfur? Oh, I bet I know what that means!

19 I.e., "boots." She wears boots almost every day solely to keep her socks clean and dry.

20 That's it, I need to go over whenever Thor stops by. I haven't sampled the meat-filled ones, but Teresa also makes sweet empanadas stuffed with apple or pineapple and dusted with sugar. No, *your* mouth is watering.

fried them. The whole house smelled of oil and crisp dough and wondrousness.

"Hola, Mami," said Ana Sofía, leaning in for a cheek kiss.

"Hey, Thor."

"Ana Sofía Arcos Romero!" Thor boomed, turning to face her fully. He finished off his empanadas with a heroic chewing-and-swallowing speed.

"Gracias por la bendición de ser amigo de vuestra casa," he said in heavily accented Spanish. "Vosotros siempre me daís la bienvenida."

To Ana Sofía, Thor's Spanish sounded like Shakespeare's English—with words and verb tenses that seemed formal and old-timey to her, though she knew they were still common in places like Spain. He used uncommon words in both languages, so she was surprised she could follow him. But he also spoke clearly and with so much natural emotion and animation no matter who he was speaking to, she could read his lips more easily than those of just about anyone else she knew.

Teresa said something in Spanish that Ana Sofía didn't totally catch, but no doubt was something like *Es un verdadero encanto, este tipo,* because she was always saying stuff like that. She smiled so huge at the robust Avenger, it made Ana Sofía blush.

Perhaps in past years, Ana Sofía had been the one secretly fangirling over the Norse god hero her family saw on *Super Hero Action TV Live!* news clips, where he was usually punching flying alien beasts and robot sharks and stuff. Not that she had *ever* admitted it out loud, but there was a slight possibility she did sorta, kinda use to daydream about, well, being *buddies* with Thor, like hanging out with him at a carnival, and he'd win her a stuffed frog at the strength game, and she'd introduce him to cotton candy, and they'd go to the face-painting booth and get matching Captain America masks and how they'd laugh and laugh!

But now that he was genuinely a friend of the family, it was Teresa who was all fangirl giggles. Honestly. He wasn't *that* big a deal. Well, he was big—his head nearly touched their ceiling, and he wasn't even wearing his helmet. Just a gray hoodie and jeans today, as if drab clothes could possibly make him inconspicuous. For one thing, there was his war hammer, Mjölnir, sitting there on the linoleum. Kinda hard to blend in with the populace with a giant war hammer. For another, he was so broad and thick and heavy the floor creaked beneath his size-twenty sneakers.

"Whatcha got today?" Ana Sofía asked.

He lifted the hem of his jeans to show her the star-spangled tops of his socks.

"Nice," she said. She slipped off her boots, showing off her purple-and-blue socks knit with a pattern of cat faces.[21]

"Excellent!" said Thor.

---

21 If you're confused, basically Ana Sofía and Thor bonded over their shared admiration of socks. Yes, this really happened. It's canon now.

"Socks," Ana Sofía said with a sigh. "They're hugs for the feet."

"Allow me to sing the praises of socks," said Thor.[22] "Asgard, alas, has no socks.[23] Nor Vanaheim. Therefore praise be to Asgardian goat leather. For it is highly odor absorbent.

"The elves of Alfheim make beautiful socks, but they are far too thin. And tiny! Woe betide any who claim the socks of Alfheim the best in the Nine Realms, for they are useless for naught but to prance upon carpets of grass! Svartalfheim's socks are much like those of Alfheim, except they are evil. Also they only come in purple.

"The socks of Jotunheim serve in terms of size, but what do the Frost Giants care for foot warmth? Nothing, if one is to judge by the quality of their footwear! The socks of Nidavellir are too small and come preloaded with bits of whatever the dwarfish sock-smiths were eating during their labors—primarily yak meat, though oft a well-squashed elderberry.

"Niffleheim's socks are made from the hair of the dead and are known to whisper in a most unsettling manner. And Muspelheim's socks are constantly on fire.

"So you see, Midgard is the only place to go. And the fine knit foot sleeves of Teresa Romero are the best in Midgard."[24]

---

22 Warning: I just read ahead and Thor goes on about the socks of the Nine Realms for like an entire page, so if that doesn't float your boat feel free to skip ahead.

23 FYI: Asgard is where Thor and his folk are from. It's one of the Nine Realms.

24 Midgard is what Thor calls Earth, if you didn't already know, which you probably did because you're so smart.

Ana Sofía was pretty impressed with herself that she'd managed to catch all that he said. But then again, he had made similar sock speeches in the past.

"Oh! That reminds me," said Teresa. "I knit you a new pair. Espérame."

Ana Sofía rolled her eyes again. Thor rubbed his hands together eagerly as Teresa ran off to fetch them.

"Hey, so, Thor," asked Ana Sofía as she picked out an empanada, "what do you know about Hydra?"

"Hydra? Nefarious fools, the lot!" he said. "'Twould do them good to spend a year mucking the stables of Valhalla, by Odin's beard it would. I have heard them claim that like the ancient beasts from whence they stole their name, whenever one cuts off a head of Hydra, two more take its place. And so it would seem! Despite the many labors of my colleagues in the Avengers and S.H.I.E.L.D. to shut down their sordid operations, Hydra still exists, thousands or perhaps millions of humans devoted to their cause of domination and control, ever moving about the planet, always with new branches of their sect concocting evil plans."

Ana Sofía had broken open the empanada and was scooping out the meat filling with a spoon onto a plate. Meat and sauce were unacceptable to the girl whose primary diet consisted of plain crackers and cheese, but she couldn't resist the flaky pastry empanada crust. She handed the plate of saucy meat to Thor like always.

"So what would you say is their main goal?" she asked, taking a bite of the empty empanada shell. It crunched and flaked and tasted of heaven.

He spooned all the meat filling into his mouth and swallowed before answering. "World domination." He waved his hand dismissively, as if their lack of imagination was beneath his notice.

"Do you think they would open up a . . . branch or franchise or whatever . . . of Hydra here in Shady Oaks? And invest in local businesses? Possibly with secret nefarious goals in mind that have nothing to do with quality shopping choices?"

"Nothing is too dastardly for Hydra! Though to be honest, Hydra is no villain fit for Thor Odinson. Too many little people running around in green jumpers. Like ants they seem to me—tiny and yet annoying when they bite. I prefer smacking fiends of more titanic girth with Mjölnir." He gave his hammer a friendly pat. "Like Frost Giants. And leviathans that have come ashore to test out evolution, that sort of thing. Unless Hydra puts on giant robot suits and marches on cities, I leave them to S.H.I.E.L.D. However, I believe the Winter Soldier is well-versed in Hydra's hideous underbelly. Also—"

He stopped, cocking his head in a way Ana Sofía had come to realize meant he was listening to someone talking to him through his tiny hidden earpiece. She touched her own hearing aid with a finger, and a flash of longing brushed through her that she might hear what he heard and answer the calls he got. To be a hero.

"I will come directly. And pity those who stand in the way of mighty Mjölnir!" Thor said to whoever spoke in his earpiece.

He shouldered the hammer, the action almost decapitating a nearby table lamp. Ana Sofía added a mental note to the long list she maintained in her head.

Note: Move lamp before next Thor visit. Shop for more robust style at yard sales.

"Farewell, Ana Sofía Arcos Romero, and many thanks to your generous mother for her empanadas."

"Wait! I found your socks!" Teresa rushed in, handing him a plastic grocery bag full of knitted things.

He took the bag, put a hand on his chest, and partially bowed in thanks. Then, stepping just outside their kitchen door into the backyard, he swung his hammer on its leather strap around and around above his head till lightning fizzled and cracked. With a small *boom* and flash of rainbow colors, he went up and was gone.

The front door burst open.

"Is he here?" said Marco, Ana Sofía's little brother. "I smelled that smell he makes all the way down the street!"

"Aw, pobrecito Marquito," said Teresa. "Tío Thor se acaba de ir. Go wash your hands if you want empanadas."

"Okay, okay," said Marco, and he shuffled off to the bathroom.

Ana Sofía couldn't help a creak of a smile. Tío. *Uncle Thor.*

In Mexican culture, it was common to call adults with close relationships to the family tío and tía even if they weren't officially family, but she'd never seen her family so quickly adopt a tío.

The front door burst open for the second time, and Ana Sofía's father, George, rushed in, looking around wildly. "Is he here? Is Thor here?"

"He's gone, Papi. Sorry," said Ana Sofía.

George banged his fist into his hand. "Every time I miss him! Every single time! I hurried over the second I got your text," he said to Teresa. He slumped into a chair, staring at the slight impression in the linoleum that Thor's hammer had left. "Just once I want to try to lift Mjölnir."

Ana Sofía hadn't quite caught what he'd said, but her mother mimed lifting the heavy hammer, and Ana Sofía put it together.

"Papi . . ." said Ana Sofía, bringing him a plate of empanadas.

"I don't expect to be able to lift it," he said. Then shrugged. "Maybe just scoot it around a little."

"How is the mall coming?" she asked.

"*Mmpf,*" he said with his mouth full. It was nearly impossible to read someone's lips when they were eating. She waited for him to finish. "It will be on time. And before you ask, no, I still don't know if there will be a sock shop."

She hadn't been about to ask about the sock shop—not that she wasn't 100 percent invested in the idea and maybe sometimes prayed for it before bed (actually every night)—but she stopped herself from asking her father the more pressing question.

Hydra? Behind the new mall? It really was ridiculous. Wasn't it?

But maybe her suspicions were dead-on and she should alert Doreen immediately to leap in and save the day. She picked up her cell, intent on texting her that very second. *What if it is Hydra? Squirrel Girl will know what to do.* . . .

No. She put her cell back down, glaring at it as if the phone had insulted her and her family.[25] This whole BFF thing was new for her. She'd had friends in the past, of course, but not like Doreen, not the kind so fierce and true she had no doubt the girl would leap across the Grand Canyon for her. And with past friends (or friendish sorts), Ana Sofía had made the mistake of sharing raw thoughts that were met with mockery. What if she shared her suspicions, and Doreen laughed at her? No, she wouldn't do that, would she? But what if Ana Sofía shared, and Squirrel Girl believed her and took on the mall, but it turned out that Ana Sofía was wrong? She could imagine the look of disappointment in Squirrel Girl's eyes, the diminished trust, the disgust even.

Ana Sofía just couldn't risk being wrong. Best to stay silent. Best to keep these thoughts to herself.

---

25 I'm surprised the phone didn't just melt on the spot, TBH. Ana Sofía's glares are legendary.

4

DOREEN

"**I** remember when all this was just open farmland," Dor Green said, surveying the black asphalt of the parking lot surrounding the new mall.

"You do love your open farmland," said Maureen Green. "Though I don't remember ever coming here since we've been residents of New Jersey."

Doreen's parents looked a lot like her—pale, freckled, human. Maureen had short hair that was once red, now brownish and cut in a mushroom-cap style. Dor's hair was once also possibly red, now gone entirely, except for his coppery orange beard. Neither had a squirrel tail.[26]

"Prairie," said Dor. "Prairie land. The open sky. Yes sir."

---

26 Nobody's perfect.

A crowd had gathered in the lot, and the thrum of antici-pation and electric energy of people waiting zapped through Doreen, too. There'd been plenty of malls back in California, but a *first* mall was kind of special, she supposed. This mall wasn't even open yet. But her mother loved crowds in general and rallies in particular, and had dragged them along to take part in what-ever this pre-opening mall rally thing was.

"Maybe I was here years ago as a boy," Doreen's father was saying. "Maybe I was part of a secret Canadian Special Forces unit stationed in New Jersey before we met."

Doreen's mother laughed. "Ah, yes, the infamous Canadian Boy Commandos."

"You joke," said Dor, "but we could wrestle a musk ox to the ground in under a minute, we Boy Commandos."

"Mean," Doreen said. "A musk ox does not deserve to be wrestled to the ground, even in imaginary dad stories."

Dor grunted. "They were dishonorable musk oxen," he said.

The three of them bounced on their feet and strained their necks, trying to see over the crowd to the temporary stage set up on the asphalt, which was bookended with two enormous speak-ers. Banners stretched above: one on the left read DOGS, one on the right read CATS, and one in the middle read HIP-HIP CHESTER YARD MALL HOORAY. The signs were all the same size and pushed so close together that it seemed to read DOGSHIP-HIP CHESTER YARD MALL HOORAYCATS.

A velvet rope divided the crowd in half, left side dogs, right side cats.

"Are we dogs-hip or hooray-cats?" Doreen's father asked.

"Hooray-cats," Doreen said, leading her parents to the right side. "In olden times, did people use to actually say 'hip-hip hooray'?" Doreen asked her father. "Shout it out all casual and normal, like, *School is canceled. Hip-hip hooray!* or *We got a coupon for twenty-five percent off carpet cleaning. Hip-hip hooray!*"

"Why are you asking me?" he said. "You're smarter than I am."

"It seems like one of those old-person things," Doreen said. "You know, like 'be kind, rewind.'"

"Forty-seven is not old," Dor said.

"It's older than me," Doreen said.

"Me too," her mother said. "I *am*, however, very wise. And can tell you that those words are clearly referencing the ancient art of bad marketing."

"It also borrows from the tradition of Unfortunate Phrases," Dor said. He raised a hand. "And I don't mean that negatively. I am a huge fan of Unfortunate Phrases."

"I'm only in ninth grade," said Doreen. "We haven't studied Unfortunate Phrases yet."

"How is school going, Doreen?" asked her mother. "You haven't said much about it lately."

"Um . . ." It had been going fine. She'd made a best friend.

She'd joined a *group* of friends, even. She no longer hid in bathroom stalls at lunch or anything. But . . . well . . . it was too complicated to put into words. *Ms. Schweinbein . . . the Squirrel Scouts . . . the homework she neglected in order to fight crime . . . that achy, half-herself feeling of hiding in plain sight . . . the ease and freedom of Squirrel Girl buried whenever she had to go back to being Doreen . . .*

"Fine," she said.

"Oh, good," said Maureen.

Her relieved smile convinced Doreen she'd been right not to say any more. Telling her mother the *whole* truth would probably just make her unhappy. Besides, Doreen had a plan! Or sort of a plan. Last night she'd looked up *Steps to Conflict Resolution* online. Talking down Laser Lady had been all instinct. But working through her many Doreen Green problems might take a more academic approach.

Suddenly music erupted from the speakers—a last-century techno beat punctuated with a robotic voice saying "Yo! Yo! Hère we go, dudebro!" A dozen dancers in green leotards marched onto the stage and began flapping their arms in unison. Confetti exploded, and a man in cargo shorts and a Hawaiian shirt leaped onto the stage and "danced" in front of the others. His moves reminded Doreen of her Commander Quiff exercise videos.

"Is that someone I should recognize?" Doreen's father shouted to her over the music.

"Why are you asking me?" Doreen shouted back.

"Because it seems like a young-person thing."

The music paused and the dancers froze in position.

"SHADY OAKS AND LISTLESS PINES!" the man shouted into a microphone. "ARE . . . YOU . . . READY?!"

A few people clapped. A few more let out some weak "yeah"s. Doreen started to feel bad for the guy.

"Because I'm ready," he whispered, the microphone making his whisper super-loud and hissy. Some of the crowd visibly shuddered. It was an uncomfortable experience to be addressed in a painfully loud whisper. Now Doreen felt *really* bad for Mr. Cargo Shorts. And he was trying so hard.

"Yay!" Doreen called out.

A few people looked around to see if there was something else nearby worth cheering for.

"Folks, let me introduce myself," the man said, sounding friendly and normal despite being on a stage with twelve frozen green dancers. "My name is Bryan. That's with a *Y*, and you can call me Bry."

The crowd shuffled, looked away, cleared throats.

"Hi, Bryan!" Doreen yelled.

Bryan waved in Doreen's general direction and continued speaking. "But, hey, you aren't here for me, are you?"

"I probably should have called him *Bry*," Doreen whispered to her mom. "I mean, he just finished saying we should call him that, and then I went and yelled his whole full name."

"It's fine, dear," Maureen said. "I'm sure he was happy to hear it."

Bryan gestured, and the green-leotarded dancers grabbed some big gun-looking things, like they had ripped cannons off a pirate ship.

"Wait, what?" Doreen said. She scampered up onto her father's shoulders. "I need—"

"You're here for FREE STUFF!" Bryan yelled.

The leotarded cannoneers opened fire at the crowd, and dozens of cloth bundles filled the sky. Doreen reached up and grabbed one, careful not to be too phenomenally squirrelly in public.

Doreen's father groaned. "Down, please. I'm not Thor, and you are not six years old anymore."

"Sorry, Pop!" Doreen said, sliding off. "My squirrel-sense was tingling."

"Is that actually a thing?"

"I don't know. It just looked like those dancers had weapons." She unfolded her catch. "But they were just shooting T-shirts." She sniffed one and stuck out her tongue. "Ugh—smelly T-shirts."

"Probably the chemicals they use in manufacturing," said Maureen. "Remember to always wash new clothes before wearing them!"

"Gotcha," said Doreen. She felt a little weird—kinda cotton-brained, a bit tilty. Her chest tightened, the crowd seemed to push in, and she wondered if she was developing sudden and random claustrophobia.

"I got one!" Maureen shouted, unwrapping a yellow T-shirt with the Chester Yard Mall logo on the front and the word CATS printed in large letters on the back.

"What size is it?" Dor asked.

"Too small for you," Maureen said, pulling the shirt on over the blouse she was wearing. "I love this shirt! Nobody touch this shirt—it's mine!"

"Whoa, okay, Mom."

"WE GOTTA FIGURE OUT OUR MALL MASCOT, FOLKS!" Bryan called.

"I thought *that* was their mascot," Dor said, opening up another T-shirt bundle to show the logo on the front. "What is it? A bearded egg?"

The Chester Yard Mall logo featured a smiley face with curly tentacle-like details coming out of the bottom. Ana Sofía had pointed out this logo to her, too, and she took an extra moment to examine it. Yep, definitely an odd choice for a mall logo.

"No one would have a bearded egg as a mascot, Dor," Maureen said. "What even is a bearded egg? This is a happy little octopus."

"We've got it down to two," Bryan was saying. "Cats, represented by the fine people from Shady Oaks, and dogs, championed by the stalwart citizens of Listless Pines."

A few of the high school boys from the dog side began to bark. Doreen felt the Team Cat crowd take a step back as if united in fear. Team Dog barked louder.

"Now, you already know that the schools on the winning side will get a free pizza party—"

Cheers erupted from both sides. Doreen smiled. She wasn't really a mall person, but it was always nice when people got excited about things.

"But I'm about to RAISE! THE! STAKES!"

Someone in the crowd gasped. It wasn't Doreen, but she appreciated the drama of the gasper.

"How far am I raising it? By one hundred dollars! Each!"

More people gasped.

"Those shirts you've got there are your ticket to a one-hundred-dollar gift card good at any shop in the mall!"

The crowd began to mutter and splutter and generally make confused and excited noises. By now everyone had a shirt, but there were a few extras. Small fights broke out, and people shoving and yelling and tugging on the extras.

"*But, Bry,* you say, *what's the catch?*" Bryan continued over his microphone. "Well, folks, the only catch is that you have to be on the winning team. When we have the final vote at the mall opening in two weeks' time, if *cat* wins then people with cat shirts get one-hundred-dollar gift cards."

The dog side of the crowd booed.

"But if *dog* wins, then the people with dog shirts get one-hundred-dollar gift cards!"

One of the kids struggling on the ground for the extra shirts shoved the other one, pulling the shirt from his grip and running off.

"Hey!" Doreen said. "That wasn't nice!"

"Gimme your shirt," a pink-haired girl from the dog side shouted at Doreen. The girl already had her dog shirt on.

"Why?"

A group of people on the cat side started to chant, *"Cats rule! Dogs drool!"*

"Shut up!" the pink-haired girl yelled.

"I didn't say anything!" Doreen said.

"I don't even want your stupid cat shirt," she said. "Dogs are going to win anyway."

People were shouting. Those boys on the dog side were barking again, their tone becoming increasingly wolfish. Doreen's hands squeezed into fists, and she kinda wanted to punch someone. Instead she balled up her shirt and tossed it toward a couple of people who were fighting over one, hoping to break it up— but instead several people swarmed it, elbows out, shoulders shoving.

"There can be only one winning side!" Bryan called from the stage. "To the victors go the spoils!"

"Well, he certainly isn't helping things," Maureen said. The rope between the two sides fell to the ground, whatever had been holding it up knocked over.

"But we've got one more little surprise," Bryan shouted into the microphone, his voice booming over the speakers to drown out the noisy crowd. "You're going to need to convince the rest of the people in your neighborhoods to vote for your side, if you really want to win. And the best way to convince people of something is . . ." He leaned over with a hand cupped to his ear as if waiting for an answer from the crowd.

"Reasoned dialogue!" Doreen called out.

"That's right," Bryan said. "Advertising!"

"I liked your answer better," Doreen's father said.

One of the green-leotarded dancers marched up onto the stage next to Bryan. He was holding a new T-shirt cannon that had been spray-painted yellow and dusted with glitter.

"We have one more shirt," Bryan said. "A *golden* shirt. Ooooooh. Whoever gets this one will be featured in a video on our TuberTV channel! And they will get . . . *free! Ice! Cream!*"

The crowd roared, surging toward the stage. A small boy near the front made a frightened *yip* at the surge and tried to run away but tripped and fell to the ground.

"Oh no," Doreen said.

Maureen unzipped her large purse and showed Doreen— she'd packed the hoodie.

"Go," Maureen said.

The man with the golden gun shot his shirt bullet high over

the crowd, and the people began shoving toward where they thought it would land.

Only it didn't land. Squirrel Girl leaped over the crowd's heads, plucking the bundle from the air and landing fifty feet later on the stage.

"Whoa!" said Bryan.

The crowd still seethed and shoved. But up here out of it, Squirrel Girl's head cleared, and she couldn't smell the muddy, unpleasant odor of those T-shirts anymore. Squirrel Girl leaned over the front of the stage. She swatted people back with her tail, and then grabbed the fallen boy by the back of his shirt. His arms were scratched up, and when she lifted him onto the stage, he just lay down. Squirrel Girl tried to give the crowd her best you-know-better-than-that look, but it didn't work as well on a thousand people as it did on the toddlers she babysat.[27]

"Very heroic!" Bryan said. "Now, young lady, you who retrieved the golden shirt, which animal are you?"

Squirrel Girl intensified her you-know-better-than-that look and twitched her tail.

"Yes, of course," Bryan said. "You are Squirrel Girl. But are you on the dog side or the cat side?"

He tilted the microphone toward her, and Squirrel Girl grabbed it.

---

27 Though between crime-fighting and school, I've had to cut way back on babysitting, which means I am a cashless wonder.

"Thanks, Bryan!" she said. "And you know what, folks? I have to say I'm a little disappointed."

Bryan swiped at the microphone, but Squirrel Girl batted away his hand with her tail.

"I mean, we're all excited," she said. "Free shirts are exciting! And gift cards! And pizza! These are awesome things to get excited about. But you gotta draw the line at shoving your neighbors and trampling people, amirite?"

She leaned over to the boy lying on the stage. "I mean, this kid . . . Hey, buddy, what's your name?"

"Munkel," the boy said, sitting up.

"How do you spell that?"

"*M-U-N-K-E-L*," the boy said.

"Huh," Squirrel Girl said. "Just like it sounds. Kid, you have an awesome name. I have never met a Munkel before, and I am super-happy to meet you."

She handed Munkel the golden shirt and looked at the crowd. "Guys, did you hear that? This kid's name is Munkel. How cool is that?"

Bryan grabbed at the microphone again, and Squirrel Girl jumped out of his reach onto a speaker, and from there to the banner rope just over the second HIP in the HIP-HIP CHESTER YARD MALL HOORAY sign. It swung back and forth beneath her, creaking but not snapping. She smiled. Oh, man, gee whiz, and snap, crackle, and pop, it was good to be Squirrel Girl on a sunny fall

Saturday afternoon, swinging on a banner rope above a crowd that she could help become better citizens and kinder human beings with a few wise words.

"So, Munkel there," she said, "almost got squished by you guys. OVER A SHIRT. I think you know that's not okay. You got carried away. You were excited, I get it. But you know what *always* ruins a day? People getting squished. Like, one hundred percent of the time. So be Team Cat or Team Dog or whatever. You be you. But you know what both cats and dogs don't do? They don't squish people. Or, like, fight over shirts and gift cards and stuff. That's a jerky thing to do. So don't act like a jerk."

Bryan was standing beneath her, his eyebrows lowered in irritation.

"Um . . . Squirrel Girl out," she said, dropping the microphone into Bryan's hands.

"That's it, folks," he said. "Always exciting at Chester Yard Mall events! Enjoy your shirts! We will be in touch."

The crowd broke up as music started to play. Squirrel Girl leaped from the stage and sprinted across the parking lot to the beat of "Here We Go, Dudebro."

One of the dancers shouted to the crowd, "Are you all ready for this?"

And if she had to guess, the answer would be *no*.

No one is ever ready for Squirrel Girl.

5

SHADY OAKS/LISTLESS PINES COMMUNITY FRIENDBOOK GROUP

Yo yo every1ne on sociable medias listen up! Hashtag coming soon! Hashtag Chester Yard Mall™ on Viper Avenue. Join us opening day to vote for the hashtag mall mascot—Groovy Cat vs. LOL Dog—not to mention some "apocalyptically" good deals! ;) ;) ;) ;) trollololololololol

Also free sausages.

Joey
Free sausages! Yeah!
LIKE • COMMENT • UNFOLLOW

Aaliyah
Vote cats! Did you know that petting a cat can lower your blood pressure?
LIKE • COMMENT • UNFOLLOW

> **Nick** So can petting a dog. Plus dogs are friendlier. Vote dogs!

Susie

I attended the rally yesterday. Did anyone else see the t-shirts they were giving away? They had a happy face with tentacles logo that I swear I've seen before.

LIKE · COMMENT · UNFOLLOW

> **John** Um yeah that's because if you replace the happy face with a skull it's the Hydra symbol. Obviously they are poking fun by using a parody of Hydra's logo.

> > **Sandra** Seems in poor taste to me.

> **Hank** Maybe they are the actual Hydra?

> > **John** Um yeah actual Hydra is totally going to open a mall in New Jersey and cleverly hide the horrible truth by barely covering up their symbol with a smile emoji. Way to go, you cracked the case, dipwad.

GreenCowlLver213

What an excellent mall. I will patronize the mall opening day and likely get a great deal on jeans and a corndog.

LIKE · COMMENT · UNFOLLOW

Yolanda

Hydra is evil, do not be fooled run for your lives

LIKE · COMMENT · UNFOLLOW

Nicole

Vote dogs! Dogs' sense of smell is 10,000 x stronger than a human's. They're awesome.

LIKE · COMMENT · UNFOLLOW

Trindy There are millions more pet cats in North America than dogs, so obviously cats are more popular. Plus they're smarter!

Jeremy Fake news! Dogs are actually smarter than cats. #science

Melodie Faker fake news! Cats and dogs are the same smartness. But cats are more self-reliant. Also cuter. Vote cats!

Blane
Free sausages! I am there!

LIKE • COMMENT • UNFOLLOW

Bianca
Weird question: did anyone else feel off yesterday at the rally? Like the smell of the t-shirts made me feel ill and super uncomfortable. And my watch said my heart rate sped way up.

LIKE • COMMENT • UNFOLLOW

Nate The same thing happened to me too! I just had to get out of there.

John Way to go, you're probably hypoglycemic and blaming it on t-shirts. What a wimp.

Sandra
How can the mall use imagery from an Evil Organization as marketing?

LIKE • COMMENT • UNFOLLOW

LaTosha Um I don't think a secret and illegal organization can copyright a logo so basically anyone could use it

Lance Don't be so sensitive! It's clearly a joke! Besides, Hydra has an objectively good logo.

Bruiser And even if it was Hydra, so what? The mall is investing in our community, creating jobs and getting kids engaged!

Joyce Amen! Our county has the highest unemployment rate in the state. We need this mall!

Sandra But what if it really was Hydra? You couldn't be so nonchalant about it then. I mean, they're EVIL

Lance Oh come on, this again? Hydra is just another socio-economic point of view. Everybody's entitled to their own opinion.

Bruiser Plus you can't judge a whole group by what one guy does. The Red Skull was also a man, are you going to condemn all men for what he did?

Sandra *hard eye roll*

Susie Um, no. Hydra's mission statement is World Domination.

Lance Get in line. Every company's mission statement is World Domination.

Susie You make a really good point!

Lance :)

Yvette
Do not trust anything that uses the unpleasant and poorly masked symbol of Hydra

LIKE · COMMENT · UNFOLLOW

GreenCowlLver214

Such exciting times. I will be at the mall on opening day to enjoy the atmosphere of communal capitalism and also to score discounted sweaters.

6

DOREEN

Doreen smelled the nutloaf the moment her dad took it out of the oven. She snapped her math book shut, scurried out of her room, and took the flight of steps down in one leap.

"Dinner—"

"Here!" said Doreen.

". . . time," finished her father.

Maureen came into the kitchen, wafting a plasticky odor of paint.[28] And beneath the paint and nutloaf, a third smell: that weird, dirty smell of the mall T-shirts.

---

28 People commission her to paint tiny plastic elves for them. This week she had a huge order from South Korea for painted elf larvae in addition to her regular elf clients in Oklahoma, so she was working overtime.

"Why do you have a dog shirt, Dor?" asked Maureen.

Dor was wearing the Chester Yard Mall T-shirt, the happy-face-with-tentacles. But it was orange, not yellow like their CATS shirts. And when he turned to get a bowl of cottage cheese with mandarin oranges, they could see DOGS on the back.

"I traded my cat one for this one," said Dor. He sniffed. "I like dogs."

Maureen smoothed the front of her lilac sweatshirt, on which she had embroidered an orange-and-white tabby with enormous kitten eyes.

"We are a cat house, Dor," she said. "You knew that when you married me."

"Well, now, you knew I was a big, big fan of dogs, I'm ninety-nine percent positive."

"I knew you liked dogs," said Maureen. "You've mentioned that. But I *love* cats. They are sweet little balls of floof, and your fondness for dogs is nowhere near the level of my ardent admiration of cats."

"Well, what if it is?"

"Well, what if it ISN'T?"

After a familiar three knocks at the kitchen door, Ana Sofía stepped inside. She smiled, noticed Maureen and Dor facing each other with fists on hips, and then frowned.

"Whoa, everything okay?" asked Ana Sofía.

Maureen turned to face her, a habit now, so Ana Sofía could more easily read her lips. "Doreen's father chose to be Team Dog,

Ana Sofía. I wish I could make up this stuff, I truly do. Then I could be a wealthy soap opera writer."[29]

"A man can love his wife and her extensive embroidered-cat-sweatshirt collection and still believe dogs are the best animal," said Dor. "Scientists have proven this."

"Oh, really?" said Maureen. "Show me one peer-reviewed study that arrived at that conclusion. A single one, Dorian Green!"

"Well, if cats are so gosh-darned great, how come we don't have one?" he asked.

"You *know* why, Dor! You know I'm allergic and must love them from a loving distance!"

"There are hypoallergenic cats, Maureen," he said. "Like pillows. And earrings. The technology exists! I think you just make excuses because you don't love cats *that* much. Not like I love dogs!"

Doreen and Ana Sofía exchanged looks. Ana Sofía put her hand over her mouth.

"Dad," said Doreen, "that T-shirt seriously stinks. You should take it off."

"You haven't washed it yet?" said Maureen. "You know you're supposed to 'Wash Before Wear'!"

"So, um, we're going outside, and I think you should change shirts while we're gone!" Doreen shouted over their chatter, and

---

29 Wouldn't being a writer be the most amazing thing? To have that level of skill with wordage and clever imagination to create awesome books? Writers are the *real* Super Heroes, amirite?

they hurried to the backyard before bursting out laughing.

"No way," said Ana Sofía, climbing up the ladder to the backyard tree house. "I didn't think your parents had fights."

Doreen leaped right up through the window and sat on one of the beanbags. "Sometimes they do," she signed, and then spoke aloud. "It got ugly last year when Mom told Dad she'd never liked *SpongeBob SquarePants*."

"I thought your parents were perfect."

"Whenever the fights come, they're soo funny, and then afterward they get all lovey and make popcorn so we can snuggle on the couch and watch movies. That was a super-random fight, I've gotta admit, but I predict we're only twenty minutes from popcorn. Anyway, what's up?"

"Did you see all the online chatter about the Chester Yard Mall?" asked Ana Sofía, passing Doreen her phone.

Doreen read the comments on the Friendbook post. "Wow, everybody is taking this so seriously! It is weird that the mall is using a logo similar to Hydra's. I guess they're just trying to cash in on their brand."

"Their brand of evil, warfare, and world domination?"

Doreen's tail twitched. "Oh. Yeah. There is that. I guess I'm not completely up on all things Hydra. I know the Micro-Manager was basically being a jerk as an audition to join them."[30]

---

30 That happened in a previous adventure, which I also read and made comments about down here in the footnotes, which is a really weird thing, now that I think about it, I mean, how am I even doing this?

"Yeah, so, they're really bad," said Ana Sofía. "And what if this mall . . . What if it *really is* Hydra?"

Doreen laughed. "That's funny. Hydra building a mall."

Ana Sofía opened her mouth and then closed it without saying anything.

"Wouldn't that be hilarious, though?" said Doreen, still laughing. "Hydra, building a mall! An *EVIL* mall . . ."

But Ana Sofía didn't laugh. She looked down at her feet.

Doreen's laugh faded at the sight. Her instinct was to leap onto the flaking yellow-painted tree-house bench and declare, *Does something trouble you, my friend? Tell me your mind, that we may have no secrets between us. I won't judge you for your thoughts, I will only prize them like star-spangled treasures. Speak out boldly!*

But this whole best-friend business was pretty new for Doreen. Instincts in battle had done well for her so far. She totally stopped that carjacker that one time, not to mention bested a pair of robot parents, and for sure the Micro-Manager business. That had gone A++. So her Squirrel Girl instincts were solid. Her Doreen instincts, on the other paw, were suspect. Even now, being a part of the Squirrel Scouts, she noticed how sometimes she'd say something that seemed perfectly reasonable, but everyone would kinda look at each other out of the corner of their eye. She didn't want to do anything embarrassing that might chase away Ana Sofía, aka One of the Awesomest Human Beings Alive.

But still . . .

"Are you worried about the mall?" Doreen signed.

Ana Sofía shrugged.

"It's okay if you are," said Doreen. "I mean, it's okay if you're not, too. I mean, it's okay whatever is cool I don't know . . ."

"What was that?" asked Ana Sofía.

Doreen had stopped signing and been kinda mumbling, which she knew made it hard for Ana Sofía to understand.

"Never mind," she said. "Sorry."

Ana Sofía looked down again. She took a couple of deep breaths. Was she upset? But what would she be upset about?

"Maybe . . . Maybe it'd be a good idea to text some of those Avengers you have numbers for," said Ana Sofía. "Also Thor said Winter Soldier might know a lot about Hydra."

"Winter Soldier?" Doreen shivered. "I texted him last month for advice when we were battling the Micro-Manager. He's kinda intense."

"Yeah . . ."

"So maybe I'll try some other heroes first?" said Doreen.

From inside, the shouty voices had stopped. And Doreen could smell the popcorn.

She smiled. "Can you stay and watch a movie with us? Mom will probably pick *The Muppets*. We'll definitely turn on the closed-captioning."

7

TEXT MESSAGES

SQUIRREL GIRL

Hey hero friends a question from your friendly neighborhood squirrel girl. How can u tell if a thing is hydra or not

IRON MAN

If it whispers HAIL HYDRA

SPIDER-MAN

Or does one of those evil laughs

SQUIRREL GIRL

Ha! srsly tho

BLACK WIDOW

No group texts pls

SPIDER-MAN

Wait was that an evil ha?

BLACK WIDOW

STOP RESPONDING SPIDER-MAN WE CAN ALL
SEE THIS

IRON MAN

BTW Squirrel Girl I totally knew you'd come ask
for my help again

SQUIRREL GIRL

Oh yeah I'm really trying to include you more
since last time when I accidentally thought you
weren't a hero and all that. I feel so bad! For you!

IRON MAN

So are we pals now?

SQUIRREL GIRL

Um yes? Or advice buddies? Is that a thing?

IRON MAN

Hey why do you have my number saved under
"Facial Hair Thing" on your phone

SQUIRREL GIRL

How can you see what name I used to save your
number?

IRON MAN

I'm a genius

SPIDER-MAN

I call you GUAPO on my phone

IRON MAN

I know

SPIDER-MAN

Which means handsome in spanish

IRON MAN

I KNOW

SQUIRREL GIRL

I just want you to know that I don't think you're ugly or anything

IRON MAN

Um

SQUIRREL GIRL

The facial hair thing is like code in case a bad guy steals my phone so they won't know who you are. Anyway I know some men grow facial hair to hide deep-seated insecurities about themselves but i don't think that's the case 4 u

BLACK WIDOW

OH SNAP

SPIDER-MAN

Secret code sounds like something hydra
would do

BLACK WIDOW

I regret the oh snap. I'm NOT getting pulled into
a group text. Why doesn't my new phone have a
way to block group texts?

IRON MAN

New OS requires you to be friendly

BLACK WIDOW

It REQUIRES you to participate in group texts
which IMO is the greatest evil ever to be
unleashed on earth

SQUIRREL GIRL

Oh man sorry bw

SPIDER-MAN

Don't be sorry you didn't invent group texts. Or
maybe your secret identity did I don't know

I invent some cool things sometimes nbd

IRON MAN

Me too

SQUIRREL GIRL

I didn't invent group text

SPIDER-MAN

Well that's good
You know, because it's evil

SQUIRREL GIRL

Evil like hydra? So . . . any advice there?

BLACK WIDOW

MUTE DELETE BLOCK UNSUBSCRIBE

IRON MAN

Are you trying to tell us something, Widow?

BLACK WIDOW

Only that I'm going to need a new communicator
after this one is smashed by a boot

SQUIRREL GIRL

I'm so sorry to bug you but as I mentioned
before I'm just trying to find out if hydra is in
my neighborhood and also how do you guys get
anything done no offense you just go on tangents
a lot?

SPIDER-MAN

Tangent was my nickname in third grade

IRON MAN

Are you saying you think I should shave?

BLACK WIDOW

Hydra is everywhere. But unless you're 100% sure don't worry about it. Hydra really isn't something you should be taking on

SQUIRREL GIRL

Ok

IRON MAN

Real talk. Hydra is about 3 things. World domination, unsavory memes, and group texting.

SQUIRREL GIRL

Cool! Thanks

SPIDER-MAN

I thought Hydra was about neo-fascism, government infiltration, and global criminal operations

IRON MAN

Those are sub-categories to the other three

BLACK WIDOW

Now smashing my avengers communicator. I will be offgrid until I return to HQ

SPIDER-MAN

You still have a personal phone tho right? For emergencies?

IRON MAN

What's the number, B-dubs?

Widow?

SPIDER-MAN

Dude I think she smashed it for real

IRON MAN

Yeah, she totally smashed it. But back to our conversation, Squirrel Girl. I'm not self-conscious about my looks at all, I'm probably the most humble guy you know. I'm just curious if you were serious about the facial hair?

SQUIRREL GIRL

Wow you were all sooo helpful but I gotta go!

* * *

SQUIRREL GIRL

Hi so hey! This is Squirrel Girl. Remember me? I texted you before for some villain advice?

WINTER SOLDIER

Winter Soldier is go

SQUIRREL GIRL

Yeah about that no need! To go anywhere actually! I just had a question

WINTER SOLDIER

Winter Soldier is go

SQUIRREL GIRL

Got it. So don't freak out but my question is about Hydra

WINTER SOLDIER

I am familiar with Hydra

SQUIRREL GIRL

Yeah that's what Thor said! I just want some nonviolent advice k? Would hydra ever do something weird like open a shopping mall in a suburb

WINTER SOLDIER

In 1946 Hydra infiltrated a small town in Lithuania at night and took the human babies out of their cribs, replacing them with baby goats

SQUIRREL GIRL

What happened to the human babies?

WINTER SOLDIER

They were found in a chicken coop

SQUIRREL GIRL

What happened to the chickens

WINTER SOLDIER

Never ask about the chickens

SQUIRREL GIRL

Ok

WINTER SOLDIER

In 1952 Hydra took over a radio station in Duluth and played the song "I've Got a Gal in Kalamazoo" for seventy hours straight

SQUIRREL GIRL

I know that song!

WINTER SOLDIER

Several people in town went mad

SQUIRREL GIRL

I'm totally humming it right now

WINTER SOLDIER

In 1978 Hydra opened an ice cream stand in Long
Island just so they could serve disturbing flavors
to the public

SQUIRREL GIRL

Disturbing flavors?

WINTER SOLDIER

Motor oil. Bile of convicted murderer. Lizard
tears. Strawberry banana.

SQUIRREL GIRL

Hydra doesn't sound that bad really

WINTER SOLDIER

They believed if they could get people to accept
unacceptable flavors, they could get people to
accept unacceptable government

SQUIRREL GIRL

Were they successful?

WINTER SOLDIER

Often. They have toppled governments, murdered millions, and ruined the second seasons of previously promising sitcoms

SQUIRREL GIRL

They've murdered millions of people???

WINTER SOLDIER

Well probably but I meant millions of bees. During their Cleanse the Air Initiative. Honeybees are vital for a thriving agrarian society. Do not neglect to take a tablespoon of raw honey daily for the health of your lymph nodes

SQUIRREL GIRL

That song is stuck in my head

WINTER SOLDIER

Now more than ever you need a tablespoon of raw honey

SQUIRREL GIRL

You know what winter soldier? I'm really proud of you! You haven't freaked out at all about hydra and gave me top notch advice. Good job buddy!

WINTER SOLDIER

Thank you. Also I am tracing your phone. As soon as I find your location I'll be there to wipe out any suspected Hydra agents within a two-mile radius in a quick and lethal manner, scourging the very earth for any trace of their passage. I will try not to harm bystanders but can't make promises

SQUIRREL GIRL

K powering down my phone now bye!³¹

* * *

IRON MAN

Hey Squirrel Girl you never really said if you were serious about my facial hair seeming to be a way to hide deep-seated insecurities. Because I don't have any btw. Deep-seated insecurities. I'm fine.

That sounded plaintive. Tone can be difficult to read in texts. But I just wanted you to know that I'm serious. Seriously fine. And I like my facial hair and am not needing any outside confirmation of my choices in order to feel good about myself.

Squirrel Girl? Are you there?

---

31 I had to actually remove the battery for the rest of the day just in case. I don't know this Winter Soldier guy, and he prolly means well, but I'm not excited to unleash him on my own neighborhood.

8

TIPPY-TOE

I perched on the shattered stump of a once-mighty oak, the claws of my hind paws flexing against the too-smooth surface. Trees fell, acorns rotted. These were facts of life. But when trees were shaved from the earth by machines, they were left like that stump. Unnaturally smooth.

The humans had cut several trees down to make room for this "mall." It wasn't like there was a true forest here, but Nip Snigglebum and Poppin Pufflegs both lost nests.

The sun had begun to fall, and I watched the human workers pack up their tools, climb into their wheeled metal boxes, and roll home. Humans build machines to cool them off in the day and hide inside buildings to escape the glare of the sun. They even cover their eyes with darkened glass to go outside. Why not just work at night? I was going to have to ask Doreen about this.

A tangy scent of sage wafted on the air, and I knew I was about to be joined by Fuzz Fountain Cortez on this unnerving stump.

"Got another harvest of furless coming," said Cortez, scampering up beside me.

Sure enough, as soon as the last truck of mall builders left, new cars full of humans arrived. The vehicles that left were all different sorts, sizes, and colors, but those that arrived were all midsize gray cars.

It appears some humans did work at night.

Just like the cars, the humans that got out of them looked the same to me. Pale, male, light brown fuzz on their heads. To be honest, unless I could smell them, I had a hard time distinguishing between humans, especially the pale male ones. It irritated me to think that if Thor put on a blue onesie with a star on it, he was Captain America for all I knew. If Hawkeye didn't have his bow, Thor his hammer, and Cap his shield—same guy. I wondered if that was why they had accessories—so squirrels could tell them apart.

Big Sissy Hotlegs leaped onto the stump, towering over both me and Cortez.

"You tell tail from tooth, Tip?" she asked. She wondered if I could tell the difference between the humans.

"Nope," I said.

The three of us headed to the ground, where Chomp Style was sharpening his teeth on a piece of gravel.

2 FUZZY, 2 FURIOUS

"Ma'am," he said to me, nodding.

Our ears twitched at the sound of paw beats on cement. We knew who it was, and that there was nothing to fear, but the instinct to flee from dogs was tough to suppress.

Speedo Strutfuzz galloped up on his terrier mount, Sir Woof. His task was to scout the area for guards.

"Dogless," he said. "No humans, even. Not outside."

I nodded. Getting intel on this nest was going to take more than a stakeout. It was going to take a break-in. After overhearing Doreen and Ana Sofía talk about this monstrosity of a human habitat, I needed to know exactly what we were dealing with. This was squirrel turf. This was *our* scamperland, even if it had been paved over. If evil lurked here, I would know. And I would take care of it. I'm Tippy-Toe, and that's what I do.

And that was why I assembled this group. A break-in of this magnitude required a specialized strike force.

SQUIRREL TEAM SIX

Tippy-Toe

Aliases: Tip, T-Toe, Missus T, The Right Paw of Justice

Rank: Captain

Bipedal Height: 1´0˝

Identifying Features: Pink bow, clever eyes

Special Skills: Genius-level squirrel intellect, languages, paw-to-claw combat

Fuzz Fountain Cortez

Aliases: Bibi Peluchita Furbi Cortez, Furbullet

Rank: Lieutenant

Bipedal Height: 0′10″

Identifying Features: Patched black-and-brown natural camouflage

Special Skills: High-speed pursuit, leaping, tracking

Chomp Style

Aliases: Charles Monroe Styles, The Mouth

Rank: Corporal

Bipedal Height: 0′8″

Identifying Features: Overlarge front teeth, muscular head, short tail

Special Skills: Demolition, infiltration

Speedo Strutfuzz

Aliases: Strutto Speedfuzz, The Centaur

Rank: Sergeant

Bipedal Height: 0′9″

Identifying Features: Extra-long whiskers, missing third claw on left paw

Special Skills: Recon, communication, cavalry

Big Sissy Hotlegs

Aliases: Big Sis, M. Squee Cisneros, Rabbitsbane

Rank: Sergeant

Bipedal Height: 1′5″

Identifying Features: Red-furred paws and legs, large size,
   muscular tail, burn scars on haunches
Special Skills: Paw-to-claw combat, demolition, heavy weapons

Chive Alpha—

"Hold up," I said, looking all around. "Where's Chive Alpha?"

Cortez leaned in. "She shed that name again."

I twitched my tail in frustration. Recently a squirrel named Sour Cream and her children were abducted and nearly roasted alive by a dastardly human villain. Sour Cream's children had collectively been known as "the Chives," but after that ordeal, one of them adopted the moniker Chive Alpha. That didn't last. Every couple of days she changed her name to something else. Currently she was . . . um, which one was it now? *Mudbomb*, maybe.

"Hello?" I said. "Um . . . *Mudbomb*?"

". . . It can destroy the world . . ." she whispered from somewhere nearby.

"Mudbomb—"

". . . It can destroy the world," the whisper came again.

"What can destroy the world?" I asked.

"MUDBOMB can!" she cried, leaping from beneath the dirt at our feet. At some point she had managed to burrow under the earth and remain there without any of us noticing.

That was why I wanted her on Squirrel Team Six.

~~Chive Alpha~~ MUDBOMB

Aliases: The Chive, Hiss the Manslayer, Skyfang the Indomitable, Night
  Weasel, Damocles the Fallen, Doom Claw, Scar Saw, The Terror that
  Scampers, Tooth Lotus, Stig the Stygian Rat

Rank: Private

Bipedal Height: 0´6˝

Identifying Features: Small size, red-black eyes

Special Skills: Infiltration, camouflage, berserker rage

"Sweet skulk, Mudbomb," I said.

She squinched up her nose. "Yeah, maybe I've seasoned out of Mudbomb."

I put a paw on her shoulder and led her away for a chitter session. "Little cousin, the team needs a name to call you. One name. How about you scamp to Chive Alpha till you've set a claw on your exact forever name?"

She chewed a dirt clod off her fur, then nodded. I patted her head.

"Speedo," I said. "You know the plan. Eyes and ears sharp. One bark danger to us, two barks danger to you."

Speedo Strutfuzz saluted, grabbing hold of his mount's neck fur. "Hi-ho, Sir Woof!" he shouted. "Away!"

"Speedo short a few nuts?" Chive Alpha asked as the dog and squirrel galloped away.

"Nope," I said. "Just a squirrel with big dreams. Now let's scamper."

We eyed the cameras and moved in their periphery—slinking under the cars, darting between their gazes, then squeezing tight against the building. Usually a squirrel didn't need to bother. But five squirrels running in formation to a single destination might catch the humans' attention.

We sidled up along the wall of the mall, stopping near the entrance the identical men used.

I twitched my tail at the two cameras mounted above the door.

"How's your mother, Cortez?" I asked.

"Trunk-strong and fluffy," Fuzz Fountain Cortez said. "The haunch fungus is under control now." She tapped various locations on the outer wall of the mall and then scratched a small x on one of the spots.

"I had the fungus once," Chomp Style said, ambling up to the spot Cortez marked. "Terrible thing. Rotted fungus itched more than an ant party in your nethers."

Chomp Style opened his mouth wide and took a head-size bite out of the mall's concrete wall.

"How'd you spook it out?" Cortez asked.

Chomp Style spat out a piece of wall. "Ham," he said.

"Ham?" Big Sissy Hotlegs asked. "You ate ham?"

"'Course not," he said, coughing out rock dust. "Can't stand animal flesh. 'Cept for beetles, but that ain't really the same."

Chomp Style bit again and again till he could scamper into the new hole in the wall. Then he gnawed more, steady this time, like a machine, till he had broken through to the other side. It was a tight head-first squeeze for Big Sis, but Mudbomb—I mean, Chive Alpha—tumbled through no problem.

The inside of the mall was enormous—as big as a park, only no trees and no grass. And no sky. No windows even. It was a big blind cage. I shook my head at the thought that humans chose to dwell in cages.

"So do you rub the ham on your fur?" I asked as we fanned out, sniffing.

"Gross," Chive Alpha whispered.

"No, ma'am," Chomp Style said, brushing dust from his whiskers. "Not exactly, anyway. The hamslime is skin-medicine, not fur-medicine. You gotta treat new fur as it grows, so the old fur's gotta go."

"You shaved your butt," Chive Alpha said.

"Yes, missy, yes, I did."

Fuzz Fountain Cortez's tail rose in a way that meant *I found something interesting,* so we focused our sniffing in her direction.

"Not easy work, fur-shaving," Big Sissy Hotlegs said, moving to a guarded posture behind Cortez, eyes on the shadows. "Rougher still in the rear."

"Wasn't no scamper in the field," Chomp Style said. "Though to chitter true, it was more of a 'scraping' than a shaving."

"GROSS," Chive Alpha said again, scampering up the wall to a single camera mounted high above. "Tell me more."

The camera began to turn toward where Cortez was investigating. I didn't want the wire chewed through, because that would have sent someone to come fix it. But I also didn't want four squirrels on camera. When Chive Alpha reached the camera and opened her mouth, I hissed at her. She tilted her head, looked at me innocently, and pulled a pebble out of her cheek. She stuffed the thing into the hinge of the camera. Its movement halted with a low buzz, and then it turned to scan in the opposite direction.

I gave her a claws-up. She twitched her tail in a shrug.

Cortez took off and we followed. Chive Alpha stayed on the walls, scampering spider-style beside us.

"No way my ma would try Chomp's ham plan," Cortez said, her nose to the floor. "Her cousin was hobbled by meat."

"Straight chitter?" Big Sissy Hotlegs asked from her guard position at the rear.

"Straight as roads and houses," Cortez said. "My nest used to do rounds by a deli where one of the bigger kid-humans flung meat at us."

"Donations?" I asked.

"Target practice," she said. "Kid would acorn-up handfuls and throw them at squirrels and birds."

"Humans are weird," Chive Alpha muttered from her spot on the wall.

Cortez stopped in front of one of the stores, sniffed once, and nodded.

"We didn't bother dodging," Cortez said. "The kid had aim like a mole, and, hey, free meat."

The store was dark inside, a pull-down metal grate protecting it. From other humans, anyway. The spaces between the bars were wider than Big Sissy's skull. Chive Alpha dangled by her rear paws from one of the bars, pulled another pebble from her mouth, and tossed it inside. We listened—tails twitchless, eyes blinkless. No sound returned. So we scampered inside.

"Long story short," Cortez said, "one meat chunk was really a ham bone, and it struck Cousin Jig right on the tail. His balance was never the same after that."

Racks of strange human garments made a labyrinth within the store. Our claws tik-tikked against the floor. A whiff confirmed the floorboards weren't wood but plastic molded to look it. A second sniff brought in another scent—a burning, warning sort of odor, the like I'd never smelled before, not in a human dwelling and not in the wild. Firelike, but not truly fire. Strange.

Cortez sniffed her way to a door against the back wall. Chomp Style looked at me and twitched a whisker in question.

I gave him a "hold on" whisker back as Big Sissy Hotlegs shoved the door with her shoulder. It swung open, and we all darted away just in case there was something behind it ready to pounce. There wasn't. In fact, all that was behind it was an empty closet with a large circle of metal in the floor.

"Trail of human smell stops there," Cortez said, pointing her nose at the disc.

"A door, then," I said.

"Could be a trampoline," Big Sissy Hotlegs said, carefully putting a paw on the disc.

"Why would they store a trampoline in a closet?" Chive Alpha said. "It's a door."

Big Sissy Hotlegs jumped on the disc, only going up about three feet up. "It isn't a trampoline. I think it's a door."

"That's what I said."

"I love trampolines." Big Sissy Hotlegs shook her head at the door in the floor.

Chomp Style scampered around the perimeter of the circle. "No human twigs or knots," he said. He meant switches or buttons.

"How's it open, then?" Cortez asked.

Chomp Style tapped the floor-door with a claw, and then licked it.

"No bark, bone, or stone I bit before," he said.

"Time to change that," I said.

Chomp Style braced his chin on the floor and carefully placed his front teeth against the metal. Then he bit. His head quivered and then . . . *snap!* A shard of Chompy's tooth broke loose, flying off to the side. Chive Alpha snatched it out of the air with her tiny front paw and tossed it back. We've all snapped a front tooth a time or twelve. It'll grow again.

"Husks and pebbles," he said, licking the chipped spot. "Tougher than sewer pipe, this is. It might even be—"

He stopped, but we knew what he was going to say. *Squirrel-proof.* It's not a real thing. It's an idea made up to frighten kits into staying close to the nest.

We stared at this floor-door. This possibly squirrel-proof floor-door.

There was a moment of tense silence, and then Chive Alpha broke it.

"How did you keep the ham on your bum, Chomps?"

Chomp Style tucked the broken shard of tooth into his cheeks. "Underpants," he said.

The five of us turned to look at the ground squirrel.

"Underpants?" he said. "You know, like regular pants, but smaller. And . . . *under.*"

"All squeaks in human-town know what underpants are," Big Sissy Hotlegs said.

"Not me," Chive Alpha said. "I need all the details, from root to leaf."

"Well, see," Chomp Style said, "the humans, they got bums, right?"

I twitched my tail. "She's teasing you. The Chive knows what underpants are."

"Aw, man," Chive Alpha said. "I wanted him to go on about it."

"Focus on the job," I said.

High on the walls were square vents for the mall's air-conditioning system. I flicked my tail.

"Yes, ma'am," Chive Alpha said, scampering up the wall. She nipped a bit of metal off a grate and slipped inside. So kind of humans to create secret passages for squirrels in everything they build.

The rest of us watched the spot where she disappeared and then slowly turned back to look at Chomp Style.

"Underpants are the least of it," Chomp Style said. "A squeak'll do most anything to get rid of the fungus."

Chive Alpha chittered from behind the grate of a different vent than the one she entered. "Like branchwork all inside out! Big hollow tree, vents going everywhere!"

"How about the roots?" I asked, twitching my tail at the "squirrel-proof" door. "The basement?"

"No," Chive Alpha said, scampering down beside us. "Only trunk and branches. No roots. No basement."

We all looked to the door in the floor that was made of something Chomp Style can't bite through.

"Then where does *that* go?" Cortez asked.

"The door isn't always the weakest point," said Chomp Style, bending to the floor around the door.

"Wait," I said. "Cortez, could you take a snuffle?"

She sniffed around the floor, back and forth in a grid pattern.

"Careful, Chomps," she said. "Under the floor here, it smells like a wrong forest fire. Like lightning in an old shoe."

I asked Chomp Style to go real slow, so he peeled a tiny spot layer by layer. In a people house, all we would have found was paint, drywall, cement, wood, and such. But here . . .

A reddish glow peeped through the hole.

"What is that?" I asked.

Cortez sniffed. "It's hotter than fire, and it runs all over beneath this floor."

Fire that didn't burn the building? I sniffed and placed the smell: lasers.[32]

Outside the mall, a dog barked.

"Sir Woof," Chive Alpha said.

In seconds we were out of the empty shop, through the empty mall, and on the other side of the wall-tunnel Chomp Style chewed.

Just as we escaped the parking lot and dove into the safety of the trees, another gray car parked near the others. A man got out, just like all the rest. This one looked around first. Looked hard.

We scampered away in silence. A silence once again broken by Chive Alpha.

"Is no one going to bring up how Chomp Style said—"

"We've put away all further talk about ham and underpants, Alpha," I said. "Hoarded and sealed."

"This is something else."

I sighed. "Go ahead."

---

32 I don't even know how Tippy-Toe is familiar with the smell of lasers, and honestly I'm afraid to ask.

"Chomps chittered about giving sewer pipe the gnaw! 'Tougher than sewer pipe,' he said."

"That I did," Chomp Style said.

"So, how do you know it's tougher than sewer pipe?" Chive Alpha said. "There's got to be some kind of story there."

"There is, but it's as messy as a litter of kits in a chocolate cake."

The five headed on to the neighborhood park, chittering among themselves. I twitched my tail in a quick farewell and veered toward Doreen's. She needed to know about the mystery of the missing basement.

9

SQUIRREL GIRL

"Wait," said Squirrel Girl. "So *is* there a basement or not?"

"Chk-cht-chff."

"The 'squirrel-proof' door goes down?" said Squirrel Girl. "But the ventilation system doesn't?"

"Chit-chikka," said Tippy-Toe.

"Well, you're the expert," said Squirrel Girl. "I personally have never crawled around inside the ventilation system of a building, and so I rely on your vast personal experience. Hmm, I wonder why the builders would do that."

"Cheti-kit."

"I'm not sure I follow. Hot 'not-fire' runs under the floor around the floor-door? Maybe hot water pipes?"

Tippy-Toe sneezed a negating sneeze.

"Huh. Curiouser and curiouser. . . ."

The girl squirrel and the Squirrel Girl were perched in an elm tree on Oak Street. Its leaves had turned golden but not yet fallen, tapping in the breeze with a dry rhythm. The sound was eager, impatient, like fingers rubbing together. The foliage was dense enough in that dark evening to keep them hidden from spying eyes, especially any in, say, the little green house directly in front of them.

"Tippy-Toe, my friend, tell me your thoughts on this creepy little house here."

Tippy-Toe twitched a whisker.

"Yeah, okay, it isn't *so* creepy. But that's her house, Tip. Ms. Schweinbein, the teacher who doesn't like me. There's just something off about her, you know?"

Tippy-Toe lifted her furry nose in the air. It twitched as she sniffed. She flicked her tail in the squirrel equivalent of a shrug.

"I don't know, just an instinct," said Squirrel Girl. "She treats Doreen-me super-weird. Like, why is she always hassling me-slash-her, right? Plus, she transferred randomly in the middle of the term, and *coincidentally* right after Mike Romanger was taken away by S.H.I.E.L.D. to some juvie for young Super Villains. I mean, if the kid I used to eat lunch with turned out to be a Super Villain, *anyone* could be. His parents worked for Hydra, you know. So what if Ms. Schweinbein—"

"*Chek-chitta.*"

"You're right, her house doesn't smell especially evil," said Squirrel Girl. "In fact, it smells like . . . like dogs. And cats. And, I don't know, maybe llamas? What do llamas smell like?"

"*Chkt.*"

"Like an ancient terror ready to shed its skin and devour the world? How do you even—"

Tippy holds up a paw. "*Chk. Cht-chikka.*"

"Oh," Squirrel Girl said. "They smell like *goats.* I misheard. You know, Ms. Schweinbein has a strong animal-y odor about her as well. Isn't that curious?"

A face appeared at the window. Ms. Schweinbein's pale, narrow face, looking out at the night with beady eyes.

Squirrel and girl both froze, still as prey. Squirrel Girl scanned the face in the window for any telltale signs of disguise or perhaps shape-shifting ability. All week in class, Ms. Schweinbein had been on Doreen's tail.[33] And all week, Squirrel Girl had become increasingly convinced that the woman was a Super Villain disguised as an English teacher.

Squirrel Girl wished she'd do something obviously evil super-quick and hopefully in full view. Doreen had told her parents she'd be home in an hour, and she still had to study for that Social Studies quiz.

---

33 That's just a figure of speech. She doesn't know I actually have a tail. I think.

Ms. Schweinbein squinted out at the dark. From behind the cover of leaves, Squirrel Girl squinted right back. Until the teacher snapped the curtains shut.

Squirrel Girl's phone buzzed. Her special, hero-business-only phone that Ana Sofía had given her. She pulled it out of a pocket on her utility belt, hoping as always that maybe it was She-Hulk asking her out for smoothies sometime, which was a thing that hadn't happened recently or actually ever but maybe could happen one day so why not hope for it every single time?

It was a text from Ana Sofía which, while not She-Hulk, was always welcome.

ANA SOFÍA

Check out this link.

The link took Squirrel Girl to a TuberTV video of Bryan from the mall rally. He was wearing a Chester Yard Mall T-shirt and cargo shorts and standing in front of the mall flanked by two teens. They also wore the Chester Yard Mall shirts, the girl in the orange "dog" variety and the boy in the yellow "cat" option.

BRYAN LAZARDO: Hey gang! Bryan Lazardo here, aka your pal Bry, PR guru for Chester Yard Mall. Chester Yard

Mall—where the deals are apocalyptically good! I'm here with two youths of our community who are involved in getting the word out about our mall mascot competition. Alisha is Team Dog, and Connor is Team Cat. Can you tell our viewers why you're—

CONNOR: Cats rule, dogs drool!

BRYAN LAZARDO: Oh my!

ALISHA: Real mature, Connor. You know that cats cause mental illness, right? They're full of parasites that get inside your brain and give you disorders.

CONNOR: That's canine propaganda! Cats are clean. Dogs are dirtier than a sewer.

BRYAN LAZARDO: Hahaha! I love the enthusiasm! I'll give this one-hundred-dollar gift card to whichever of you can convince the other to vote for your candidate.

ALISHA: Cats are predators and they eat people in their sleep ALL THE TIME!

CONNOR: Dogs fart flesh-eating bacteria!

ALISHA: CATS CHEW ON—

CONNOR: DOGS ARE LITERALLY—

As the two kids continued to yell alternative dog and cat facts at each other, Bryan Lazardo kept tilting his head at the camera with a campy can-you-believe-this expression. When the shouting slowed down, he frowned at them both.

BRYAN LAZARDO: Don't go fighting like cats and dogs, now.

He held up the gift card enticingly, and they started yelling at each other all over again.

"I don't know about that dude," said Squirrel Girl. "Seems like he wants people to fight. I'm not one to judge, Tippy-Toe, but I get the feeling I wouldn't necessarily be lifelong buds with Bry."

BRYAN LAZARDO: Before we end this riveting segment, we have one more guest. This young man received the golden T-shirt at our kickoff rally, thereby earning the honor of an appearance on our first video. Come right over here, champ. That's it, where the camera can see you. Well, sport, anything to say?

MUNKEL: Um . . . I'm on Team Squirrel!

BRYAN LAZARD: Ha-ha-ha! You just never know what's going to happen at the Chester Yard Mall! Come to the grand opening in just a few days!

"Aw, did you see that, Tip?" said Squirrel Girl. "That's the boy with the awesome name whose life I miraculously saved one time from a horrible squishing death."

"Chkkt-tat."

"You're right, he does seem like a bright kid."

"Bright" was a thing Doreen's parents always called her, too. *Bright-eyed and bushy-tailed!* And she'd believed them, until middle school.

Squirrel Girl opened up the text message field, her thumbs on her phone, nearly texting to Ana Sofía her suspicions about Ms. Schweinbein. But no. If she kept complaining about how her teacher didn't like her, maybe Ana Sofía would start noticing that Doreen was unlikable and then she wouldn't like her either and that would be catastrophe of the loneliest flavor.

Her phone buzzed with a new text.

ANA SOFÍA

> The skunk club says someone from listless pines spraypainted a challenge on the high school to meet at mall lot tonight and squirrel scouts are headed there now

SQUIRREL GIRL

On it

Squirrel Girl leaped out of the tree, with a wistful backward glance at Ms. Schweinbein's house.

"I'll just have to expose her Super Villain secrets another day," she told Tippy-Toe, who rode on her shoulder.

"*Chek-kit,*" Tippy-Toe said with complete confidence in her BHFF.

The mall was about twenty blocks away. Squirrel Girl hopped from rooftop to rooftop, and as she traveled, squirrels followed. First Tippy-Toe was joined by five other squirrels. And then more came. More squirrels and more squirrels, until a great flowing shape of them followed behind.

When they reached the last house on the block, Squirrel Girl chirped a warning, and the squirrels leaped onto her arms and back, riding as she soared over the street to the next block.

"Look, it's Squirrel Girl!" she heard as she passed. Her tail was out and free; her name was semi-famous. She was Squirrel Girl, and everybody knew it.

Her heart pumped. The Social Studies quiz was forgotten.[34]

At the mall, she spied two groups gathered on the unpainted asphalt that would become the mall's parking lot. In the glow of

---

34 I did remember eventually. The next day in class when the teacher handed out the quiz. I scored 6/10. Oops.

the orange security lights, she could make out one side wearing darker T-shirts than the other. Mall T-shirts. It was Cats vs. Dogs.

And they were howling and hissing at each other.

Also shouting insults and dubious facts about domesticated animals. But the howling and hissing was the most obnoxious part of it.

Squirrel Girl spotted Vin with some other Squirrel Scouts and hopped over to him.

"Squirrel Girl, I'm glad you're here!" Vin said. "They're saying really mean stuff about cats!"

"Okay," said Squirrel Girl. "So, that's not very nice, right?"

"It's not!" said Vin. "We're probably going to have to punch them."

"Wait, what?"

"They're being mean, so they must be villains, so they need to be punched!" Vin said boldly, then seemed to hear himself and had the grace to blush. "Um, I think things are getting out of control."

Squirrel Girl spotted Antonio in front. He wore his dingy white baseball hat low over his eyes, his brown hair straight and shaggy. He took a step toward someone from Team Dog. And he lifted up a baseball bat.

"WHOA!" yelled Squirrel Girl. "Hey now! No weapons, friends. Let's not be hasty—"

A rock whizzed past her, an inch from her head.

"Everyone needs to CALM THE FREAK DOWN!"

No reaction. Probably no one was listening to her. The whole talk-criminals-out-of-criming thing didn't work unless they heard her.

She leaped over their heads and landed in the narrow space between the two groups. The squirrels followed, arranging themselves around her like her own furry shadow. She pulled the bat out of Antonio's hands.

"Hey, I thought you were on our side!" he said.

"I'm on the side of you not getting killed or thrown in jail, Antonio, which means yeah, I'm one hundred percent totally on your side."

But the other Skunk Club members had bats, too. One had a heavy metal chain; someone else held a glass bottle. The LARPers were especially well armed with literal swords and bows with arrows.[35]

They were yelling at the Team Dog group and taking steps forward. She yanked away the glass bottle. Groups of squirrels leaped onto the bats and LARPer swords, their collective weight making the weapons too clumsy to wield, and they were forced to drop them.

"Hey!" the LARPers said.

"Sorry!" said Squirrel Girl. "I still like you! Let's be friends!"

---

35 Dull-edged practice swords. Arrows with rubber tips. But still.

"They're wide open now!" shouted a blond guy on Team Dog. He was gripping a bat. "Let's get them!"

"Um . . . nope," said Squirrel Girl.

As they rushed forward, the squirrel army picked up the fallen weapons and carried them out of the way of the mob. At the same time, Squirrel Girl swiped the Team Dog leader with her tail, knocking him down. She scurried, dodged, and slid around the front line of Team Dog, seizing any tools and weapons as she went and dropping them to waiting squirrels, who quickly carried them off.[36]

The Team Dog leader scrambled to his feet, his eyes blazing. He swung his fist to punch her. Which just seemed rude.

She dodged, grabbed his fist, and pushed up on his arm to vault herself onto his shoulders.

"Now listen up, everyone!" she said, from where she stood atop his shoulders.

The guy punched at her ankles. He jerked around, trying to knock her off. But her balance game, it was good.[37]

"Stop that," she said, swiping his head with her tail. "I'm only going to be here for a minute."

He still lurched around.

"JUST HOLD STILL!" she said.

---

36 Those weapons were never seen again. I think they probably buried them, but I never asked. Sometimes it's better not to be too nosy about squirrel business.

37 Seriously, do not play a balancing game with the girl who has a five-foot squirrel tail.

She rapped him on his ear with one foot. He stopped lurching. "Good boy. Okay, then. So, guys, this is all really silly, isn't it?" The mob stared at her.

"Um," said a girl, "you mean how you're standing on Geoff's shoulders?"

"No, obviously this is a clever solution to the no-one-was-listening-to-me problem. I mean, all this *fighting* is silly!"

"But it's for a hundred-dollar gift card!" someone shouted.

And the group took up the idea, shouting about gift cards, and then started shouting at each other again, their postures aggressive, their domesticated-pets insults fiery. Geoff jolted forward as if to join them. She squeezed Geoff's head between her feet. He squeaked and held still.

"Look, look, I get it!" she said. "Gift cards are, like, one of the best things on the planet, right?"[38]

The crowd nodded.

"But, um, fighting people to get gift cards is so not cool. So, stop it?"

The crowd murmured.

"I mean, stop it!" she said with her fists on her hips, like her mother when she was shouting at the TV news. "Go on home, guys. I'm serious. Squirrel Girl is here and I'm not going to let any of you bash heads or punch faces or whip chains and whatnot."

---

38 I mean, I guess? I wasn't feeling it, but I had to Build on Common Ground and all that.

The crowd seemed to believe she was not going to let them commit idle acts of violence. And she was clearly drawing the line at whatnot. So with no other real reason to be there, they began to disperse. The orange-shirted group headed in one direction, the yellow-shirted ones in another.

"So, can I go, too?" asked Geoff.

"Honestly, Geoff," she said, "you'd think standing on your shoulders for a few minutes was *such* a big deal." She hopped down. "Be good."

"Okaaaay!" he said as he ran off.

And Squirrel Girl found herself alone in the parking lot. She sighed and took out her phone.

SQUIRREL GIRL

I talked them out of fighting! Sort of. They didn't seem 100% convinced

ANA SOFÍA

People are acting extra weird lately right? It's not just me?

SQUIRREL GIRL

No u r not the only one acting extra weird

ANA SOFÍA

Ha ha

SQUIRREL GIRL

Ur right everyone needs to calm the freak down but when I tell them to calm the freak down they don't do it

ANA SOFÍA

Maybe we need a plan b

SQUIRREL GIRL

I thought plan b was when i punch them till they stop criming

ANA SOFÍA

We're gonna need more plans

10

ANA SOFÍA

Everything was completely quiet. Ana Sofía's bed was perfectly cozy. She closed her eyes and waited for the gray wash of exhaustion to roll beneath her, rock her like a boat on water, and then pull her under to float, weightless, in the cola-dark ocean of sleep.

Only that didn't happen. Because of her knotted-up stomach.

Ana Sofía frowned at herself in the dark. She didn't believe in instinct. What some called instinct she figured was actually knowledge and experience that the brain processed superfast. But still . . . something about the Chester Yard Mall just *felt off.* She had to find real, concrete data either to support or refute this nagging feeling, or she wasn't going to get any sleep whatsoever. And sleep was one of her top five favorite things.[39]

---

39 I'm just gonna go ahead and guess: 5) sleep, 4) cheese, 3) me? probably me, 2) socks, 1) her family, so I guess crackers, math, computers, and Thor didn't make the top five. Don't tell Thor.

So she sat up in bed, booted up her laptop, and began to poke around the comments on the Friendbook mall post. There were some new ones she hadn't seen, including:

Jerry

I am gainfully employed by the fine Chester Yard Mall and look forward to sharing with this upstanding community the many hot hot deals on opening day. So many hot hot deals you must be there to see.

LIKE · COMMENT · UNFOLLOW

She tracked the origin of the comment, and that's where things got interesting. It appeared that mall-employee Jerry had been on the "dark net" when he submitted his comment. The dark net was basically a secret internet for nefarious purposes. A breeding ground for villains. She knew this for a fact because when she'd hacked her way into Baddit, a villain forum on the dark net, she'd happened upon this convo:

BADDIT> Battle Tips

KRAVEN

EXCUSE PLEASE I AM LOOKING FOR FORKED BLADE SPEAR WITH SPIKED DORSAL RIDGE

LIKE · COMMENT · UNFOLLOW

LOKI

Alas, cutlery is not sold here. This spot, 'tis for sharing "battle tips," as the title of the chat room so graciously indicates

LIKE · COMMENT · UNFOLLOW

KRAVEN

FORKED BLADE SPEAR WITH SPIKED RIDGE HAS BATTLE TIP. ON THE TIP OF THE SPEAR

LIKE • COMMENT • UNFOLLOW

LOKI

Verily. Though in this case, "tip" means "advice." English can be such a cruel language to new learners, DO NOT AGREE YOU?

LIKE • COMMENT • UNFOLLOW

KRAVEN

I ADVICE YOU NOT TO TAUNT KRAVEN THE HUNTER. FORKED BLADE SPEAR IS VERY IMPORTANT

LIKE • COMMENT • UNFOLLOW

LOKI

I am sure 'tis true in whatever grunting sub-culture you hail from, but here we are looking for tricks. "Top Ten Ways to Stop Iron Man," that sort of thing.

LIKE • COMMENT • UNFOLLOW

KRAVEN

TOP ONE WAY TO STOP IRON MAN IS WITH FORKED BLADE BATTLE SPEAR

WITH SPIKED DORSAL RIDGE

LIKE • COMMENT • UNFOLLOW

Villains apparently felt free to discuss all manner of diabolic skullduggery on their supposedly supersecret Baddit forum. That very morning, Ana Sofía had discovered this:

ULTRON 0.2
Looking for vibranium

LIKE · COMMENT · UNFOLLOW

KLAW
How much?

LIKE · COMMENT · UNFOLLOW

ULTRON 0.2
150 metric tons

LIKE · COMMENT · UNFOLLOW

KLAW
HAHAHAHAHAHA

LIKE · COMMENT · UNFOLLOW

ULTRON 0.2
HA HA HA HA

LIKE · COMMENT · UNFOLLOW

KLAW
Good one

LIKE · COMMENT · UNFOLLOW

ULTRON 0.2
Yes. A good one

LIKE · COMMENT · UNFOLLOW

KLAW
So how much do you really need?

LIKE · COMMENT · UNFOLLOW

ULTRON 0.2

150 metric tons

LIKE · COMMENT · UNFOLLOW

KLAW

. . .

LIKE · COMMENT · UNFOLLOW

ULTRON 0.2

151 would also be okay

LIKE · COMMENT · UNFOLLOW

KLAW

Friend, that much vibranium doesn't even exist

LIKE · COMMENT · UNFOLLOW

ULTRON 0.2

Friend?

LIKE · COMMENT · UNFOLLOW

KLAW

Yeah I can't help you

LIKE · COMMENT · UNFOLLOW

ULTRON 0.2

You are my friend

LIKE · COMMENT · UNFOLLOW

KLAW

This is creepy. I'm out.

LIKE · COMMENT · UNFOLLOW

ULTRON 0.2
Friend?

LIKE · COMMENT · UNFOLLOW

ULTRON 0.2
Friend? Where did you go?

I miss my friend

LIKE · COMMENT · UNFOLLOW

Who was to say if the "Jerry" who had commented on the Friendbook post really was a mall employee. But if he was employed by Chester Yard Mall, *and* he was operating from the dark net . . .

Ana Sofía furiously searched for more info on Chester Yard Mall but found little. Bryan Lazardo, the mall's PR guy, also left a very small electronic fingerprint. All she could dig up on him was a profile on Hooked-In, a website where people randomly shared their work resumes.

Name: Bryan Lazardo

Current job title: VP of Communications at Chester Yard Mall Properties

Previous: Hamilton Yogurts, Dannon Robotics, Americorp

Education: Strucker University

Summary:

Being with Chester Yard Mall feels like being part of something greater than myself. And it is! To be able to contribute to the everlasting growth of mankind by creating MALLS and eliminating HIGH PRICES from the face of the earth is an incredible feeling. If only all CUSTOMERS could see it the way I do they would be spared BAD DEALS when the final reckoning comes. I am always on the lookout for new opportunities to grow within THIS CAPITALIST NATION and will stop at nothing to fulfill the will of MY BOSS and THE MARKET.

Weird, right? Or maybe not. Maybe everyone's Hooked-In profile made them sound like someone disguising their world-domination plans as professional networking. Maybe she was just paranoid ever since the Micro-Manager incident. Maybe she was spoiled for reality and simply imagining villainy and ne'er-do-wells everywhere.

Good thing she hadn't told Doreen that she thought Chester Yard Mall was really Hydra after all. That would have been so embarrassing.

Besides, when Ana Sofía had broached the topic, Doreen had laughed.

She'd *laughed* at her.

Immediately Ana Sofía had felt eight years old again, like the time in third grade she'd been assigned a group project to put on a mini play about nutrition for Parents Night. She'd had a great idea. It was so great, she broke her personal rules about speaking up as little as possible.

"We could all pretend to be Super Heroes! And Punch candy and stuff!"

The other kids had laughed at her idea. Not because it was funny, but because they found her idea laughable. And she'd *known* it was a good one because, come on, *Super Heroes Punching candy*! Instead the group ended up being vegetables standing around and listing off their individual vitamin content.[40]

When someone was mean to Ana Sofía, she wanted to smack them or scream in their faces or slice them to bits with sharp words. But when they laughed at her, she curled up tight inside herself, into a shell she sometimes forgot was there. The hardness of that shell was a comfort, something to lean up against, something solid at her back. But when she curled up inside it, she didn't ever want to come out again.

She'd been partly curled up inside ever since, more or less. Speaking up and sharing ideas generally terrified her, until Doreen Green bulldozed into her life and gave her someone who genuinely seemed interested in her thoughts, someone safe. But then Doreen had laughed at her idea.

And not only that, but when Ana Sofía hadn't understood something Doreen said and asked her to repeat it, Doreen had just spoken that horrible phrase, Ana Sofía's least favorite in the English language: "Never mind." Likewise, in Spanish, she cringed when someone said to her, "no importa." She'd learned that hearing people never-minded each other all the time, and it

---

40 Aw, man, I wish I'd been around then and I could have said, *Ana Sofía, you have the best ideas and let's pretend-Punch candy together forever!*

apparently wasn't a big deal to them. But to Ana Sofía, it was a huge deal. It was turning her off. It was saying, *Making an effort to communicate with you isn't worth my time.* And it hurt. Bad.

Doreen was a sunburst of wonderful and kind, and surely she hadn't *meant* the laugh and the never-minding. But still . . . ugh. Having a best friend was very confusing.[41]

> *Note: Keep unsubstantiated ideas to self. Do not risk Doreen's friendship by confessing too many embarrassing thoughts. When you get comfortable, you get careless, and carelessness leads to lost friendships. And don't tell her when she does something that hurts you. That will just make her even more sure you're not worth the trouble.*

Ana Sofía sat up and turned on her lamp. And there on her side table was the origami unicorn Vin had pressed into superthin leather. Since joining the LARPers, he'd started making things out of leather and gotten pretty good. Had the leather unicorn been a *Whatever, here you go* thing? Or was it a way to say, *Hey, remember all those paper horses I used to fold and leave on your chair in fifth grade? Here's an even cooler one as a way to say I still think you're cool?*

Friendship wasn't the only confusing thing. People were. People in general. The entire population of the planet: confusing.

---

41 It is! For me too! Please don't give up on me, Ana Sofía!

Ana Sofía went downstairs and found her dad at the kitchen table, eating arroz con leche and reading on his phone.

He spoke. She hadn't put her hearing aids back in, but judging by his body language and knowing him, it was probably something like "Can't sleep?" so she replied with a vague "Hmm." She grabbed a box of crackers from a cupboard and sat beside him. This past year, her mom had been working the night shift at the hospital so she could be home for Ana Sofía and Marco after school while their dad was at work. One side effect was that she wasn't around to stop Dad's midnight munching. His belly had started to pooch out beneath his shirt.

"If Mom doesn't switch schedules, you're going to gain a lot of weight, Dad."

He smiled and took a big bite of pudding.

"Sin vergüenza," she said, because it's what her mom would have called him. *Shameless.* "Hey, Dad, what's in the mall's basement?"

"It doesn't have a basement," she thought he said.

"Wait, the mall doesn't have a basement?" she said, double-checking her lip-reading. "Are you sure?"

He nodded and probably said, "I think I would know."

Tippy-Toe had told Doreen there was a basement. But how could one of the construction managers not know about it? Was Tippy-Toe mistaken?

Her phone, plugged in on the counter, lit up. She checked it. It was the Squirrel Scouts texting group.

DENNIS

Did you hear about the dog monster?

HEIDI

What are you talking about Dennis

DENNIS

There's a dog monster in shady oaks for real this is going to be so good for team cat!!!

JACKSON

It's true everybodys talking about it and we sorta saw it running past the circle q

JANESSA

So creepy I swear I heard it sniffing around my house

DUCHESS

Forsooth! A beast worthy of my steel!

BARON

And of my crossbow! We shall make it regret invading our fair barony

ANTONIO

Dibs on dis

VIN

Ana Sofía can you tell squirrel girl about the
dog monster

A dog monster? For real? Maybe they were just as paranoid as she was, imagining villains everywhere, and so obsessed with this stupid mascot competition that they'd seen a large dog and instead thought it was a "dog monster."

She reread the texts, wincing again when she got to Vin's. A while back he'd asked her out and then never followed up on it, so why was he always addressing her in group texts like things were totally normal?

She turned off her phone and left it on the counter when she went upstairs, calling over her shoulder, "Go to bed, Papi, or I'll tell Mom who ate all the arroz con leche."

TIPPY-TOE

*I*n the afternoons, I take naps. Most squirrels do. Why do business in the bright and squinty sun when the light is so much more pleasant at dawn and dusk, when the blue light and the yellow light mix and mellow together and the world is full of cozy shadows? So in the early afternoon, with Doreen still in school, I'd normally be curled up between a pair of friendly branches and snoozing the daylight away.

But a squirrel is not always so lucky. A cloudburst crept up on us like a sneaky weevil, and no fierce sunlight meant no nap. Just a very wet, very early twilight. And for a squirrel, twilight is the time for action.

I scrambled to one of the distant branches of my tree. A leaf heavy with water tipped, and I dodged just in time to avoid a thorough wetting. I scanned the horizon, and I listened.

On one paw, rain cleans everything. And as a squirrel who prefers to smell first and ask questions later, I appreciated the rain-cleaned air. On the other paw, the rain made for a lot of noise. I'm a beast who likes to hear things coming long before they arrive, and the sound of constant rain on branches and leaves and roads and houses is like a young cousin chittering "Hey, hey, hey, hey" in my ear.

I know what you're thinking. *But, Tippy, the human world is noisy. With the cars and machines and constant electric buzzing, how do you cope?*

I tune it out. But I can't tune out nature.

Davey Porkpun, assigned watch for today's daysleep, scampered up beside me.

"Hey, hey, hey, hey," he chittered in my ear, and I flicked a leaf, knocking large drops of water on him.

He shook his head, blinking. "Whoa! Why you tryna drown a squeak in leafspit?"

"Because I'm getting enough pitter-patter stormwise. Don't need the fake-rain chitter-patter on top."

"I don't—" he started.

I held up a paw, and in between peals of thunder, I heard it again. A noise. Subtle, distant. Animal.

"You catch that sound?" I whispered to Davey.

"Mighty thunder, Tip. Maybe that yellow-furred hammer human is about."

"No, *between* the thunder."

I twitched my tail, and three squirrels on below branches took on my tail-command and shot out in different directions to do some recon.

Davey and I sat still, listening. Again, behind the patter of the rain, it came. A howl of some kind. Loud. Angry.

"Well, that's a pig-free rattle, at least," he said. "You know I shuck pigs well—sound, sight, and smell. So straight chitter and trust the squeak. It weren't no pig."

"I . . . I didn't ask if it was a pig."

"Now you got no need to ask," he said, grinning. But the sound, the howl, cut through his chitter. Something was out there. Something big.

"Shiver and twitch," Davey said. "That sounds like a dog."

We have had our differences, dogs and squirrels, but recently we'd reached an understanding with the local canines. I'd thought the days of our having to fear those things were over.

"Find Speedo," I said.

A minute later, Speedo Strutfuzz galloped up on Sir Woof.

"So you caught the chitter?" Speedo asked.

"What chitter?" I said.

"Dog news," he said. "You didn't know?"

"What have they done?"

"Nothing," Speedo said. "Nothing but scurry and huddle. The smell and sound on the air's got all the dogs in town spooked."

"Sir Woof isn't spooked," I said.

"Oh, the Woof is good and spooked," he said, patting the beast. "But he's brave."

I looked the animal in the eyes. There was fear there, but it was under control.

"Something prowls the ground," I said. "It's angry. And it sounds like a dog."

"IT ISN'T A PIG!" shouted Davey, mid-scamper to the branches above.

Speedo opened his mouth.

"Just ignore him," I said.

"May be dog-sound to us," Speedo said. He nodded to his mount. "But it's wrong-sound to the pups."

"Right," I said, sniffing the air. "This is a job for Squirrel Girl."

12

BADDIT FORUM

BADDIT> evil deed bragging

Jerry
It's coming

It's totally coming

It's loose and on its first prowl

All I'm saying is, if you live in Jersey in the Shady Oaks area, don't go outside today

Hee hee hee

Or you'll see IT

The creature I'm talking about

. . .

Doesn't anyone here care about this?

Klaw
Nope no one here cares about this

Jerry
But it's a dog beast! And I made it basically! Don't we brag here? Isn't that a thing?

Klaw
Exactly. This is for *bragging* ie talking about something you've done *after* the fact. You think this is our first rodeo? Come back and brag when your "dog beast" actually terrorizes something and isn't taken down by some caped fool first

---

Jerry
Oh I will. I totally will.

And fyi the dog beast isn't the only one. There is another . . .

LIKE • COMMENT • UNFOLLOW

Klaw
Literally nobody here cares about this

LIKE • COMMENT • UNFOLLOW

Jerry
K fine bye

LIKE • COMMENT • UNFOLLOW

PS my name isn't really Jerry

LIKE • COMMENT • UNFOLLOW

Hee hee hee

LIKE • COMMENT • UNFOLLOW

13

DOREEN

*F*ive minutes to the end of school. And counting.

They were supposed to be working quietly on a Biology worksheet, but Doreen could hear Heidi and Janessa in the row behind her chatting about a weekend party. A party Doreen had not been invited to. Her Doreen Green instinct was to turn around and say, *Hey, guys, is that party you're talking about a Squirrel Scout thing? Because if it is, I'd totally like to come because I'm a Squirrel Scout, too, even though you never technically see me on missions and stuff. . . .*

She got as far as turning around before remembering her Doreen Green instincts weren't the shiniest example of reliability lately. They stopped talking and looked at her. She smiled.

"Um . . ." she said. "So . . . never mind."

She turned back around and adjusted her position in her chair for the fifteenth time that minute. Even if the clock hadn't shown five-minutes-to, the cramp in her tail would have told the time. And the time was almost up.

She glanced around the room to see if anyone noticed the way she kept shifting. But most of the kids were busy scribbling on their papers in an attempt to avoid homework. Three were facedown on their desks. One was snoring.

A familiar furry face peered through her classroom window.

"Tippy!" she blurted before remembering where she was. Which was in class. And now everyone was staring at her. And at the squirrel in the window.

"Ms. Green, you have a question?" Mr. Rodriguez asked.

"No thanks," said Doreen. "I mean, yes, sure, I have loads of questions constantly, but not one for you at this particular moment."

Mr. Rodriguez gave her a thumbs-up, then went back to grading papers.

"So cute," Heidi cooed at Tippy-Toe. "She's just sitting there watching us!"

Tippy-Toe made the ASL sign for "Squirrel Girl" that Ana Sofía had coined—left paw making an *S*, right paw making a *G*, with the *G* swooping off the *S* like a lovely tail. Doreen nodded. It looked like she would not be walking home from school with her BHFF after all. Usually she and Ana Sofía just got each other like milk gets shake, but the past couple of days something felt off. She'd been looking forward to their walk home today to chat and maybe fix whatever was wrong.

"Psst, hey," Heidi said. "That's Tippy-Toe, right? Do you think she's trying to tell us something?"

"Maybe we should be on alert as we leave school today?" said Doreen. "For potential criminal thuggery?"

"Totes," said Heidi, texting on her phone. "I'll let the Scouts know."

Doreen didn't wait to gather with the rest of the Squirrel Scouts. Exactly sixty seconds after the end-of-school bell, Squirrel Girl was tail-out, eared-hoodie-up, and perched with her BSFF in a tree across the street. A crowd of students clotted the front stairs of the school, chatting and laughing, apparently totally fine being themselves and not in a hurry to pull hidden tails out of their pants and start saving the day. On the stoop, she spotted Heidi's blond hair and Ana Sofía's black.

"That was a rough last twenty minutes at school, I tell you what," she said.

"Chkt. Chk-cht-chkka!"

"Right. Sorry. I'm focused. So there's some kind of 'not-dog'? What's a 'not-dog'?" Squirrel Girl asked.

"Chk-kt-chkt."

"Well, by that logic, we're all not-dogs," Squirrel Girl said. "You know, except the actual dogs."

SQUIRREL GIRL

Can't walk home. TT says there's a not-dog around??? Maybe gather the scouts or something

ANA SOFÍA

K

The rain had stopped, and the air smelled as clean and sweet as cut apples. Squirrel Girl took a deep breath. Walking home with Ana Sofía in this weather would have been nice. But being on patrol for not-dogs with her BSFF in rain-cleaned air wasn't too shabby. She took another whiff. And then she smelled it. That weird stinky boy smell from the Chester Yard Mall opening rally, but mixed with feral dog. And . . . motor oil? Maybe? Whatever it was, it had no business intruding on the clean appley air smell.

"I think—" she started, and then nearby, the shattering of glass.

She leaped. She ran. She was Squirrel Girl on the move.

Half a block down, in front of the Boot Scoot & Bootie, was the largest dog she had ever seen, surrounded by a litter of the ugliest puppies in history.

"BARK! BARK! BAR-HAR-HAR-HARK!" the giant brown-furred dog yelled. It didn't bark. It *yelled* "BARK." And then it stood up on its hind legs. It was wearing cargo pants with a hole cut out in the back for its tail.

The dog-man pointed to the shattered glass of the Boot Scoot

& Bootie front window. "GO, MY DOGLINGS! FETCH THE WRETCHED FOOT-COVERS SO THAT WE MAY FEAST!"

The puppies scuttled through the broken window and into the store like the best trained animals in the world. Students from Union Junior began gathering around the spectacle, pointing and whispering, and generally way too close to potential danger for Squirrel Girl's comfort.

"WHO WANTS BROKEN GLASS?" the dog-man shouted to the growing crowd. He picked up some shards from the ground and began throwing them randomly. "YOU DO! AND YOU DO! AND YOU DO!"

People jerked away as glass shattered at their feet and against a nearby car.

"Rude!" shouted Heidi. "He's rude! And a villain, clearly. Get 'em, Squirrel Girl!"

"Yeah, get 'em!" the other Squirrel Scouts shouted.

All at once, Squirrel Girl felt hyped up, nervous, angry, proud, and sick to her stomach.[42]

Tippy-Toe bared her teeth. *"Chkkt!"*

"Don't tear him apart with your lethal squirrel rage yet," Squirrel Girl said as she leaped from roof to roof, Tippy-Toe riding on her shoulder. "I want to try the talking thing first."

She landed on top of the Boot Scoot & Bootie. One of the

---

42 If you haven't felt this recently, you might not be in middle school.

puppies had just dropped a stylish pair of black boots at the dog-man's feet.

"Cute!" Heidi called from the crowd. Squirrel Girl was pretty sure she was talking about the boots, because the puppy-thing was, sad to say, not very cute.

"There are better ways to get new shoes," Squirrel Girl called down.

"BURH?" the dog-man said. He looked up and spotted her. "I AM DOG-LORD," he announced.

"Good," she said. "Names! I AM SQUIRREL GIRL. Nice to meet you."

"KICK HIS TAIL, SQUIRREL GIRL!" Dennis yelled from the crowd below.

She thought she could probably kick his tail if the need arose. She was Squirrel Girl, after all! But she was also fourteen-year-old Doreen Green, and this looked like a legit adult man with possibly awesome dog powers. She scanned the crowd for Ana Sofía, wishing her friend could give her some kind of math info that would tell her if she could, in fact, kick his tail.

Several more puppies charged out of the store and dropped pieces of footwear at Dog-Lord's feet. He picked a loafer off the top of the pile.

"I don't think that's going to fit you," Squirrel Girl said.

"I TAKE A SIZE SIXTEEN," Dog-Lord said. "BUT WEAR-ING SHOES IS FOR THE WEAK!"

He stuffed the shoe into his mouth, bit it in half, and spat out the heel.

"Hey!" Squirrel Girl said. "Those aren't yours! You're going to have to pay for that. And the window."

"DOG-LORD PAYS FOR NOTHING," he said, looming over her. "NOT SHOES, NOT DOG TREATS, NOT AFFORD-ABLE HEALTH CARE."

"Okay, but can you tell your puppy pals to pause the looting for a sec while we talk about your motivations and probably how when you were a dog-kid the other dog-kids were mean to you and caused this dark period in your life?"

"THEY ARE NOT 'PUPPY PALS.' THEY ARE MY DOGLING ARMY!"

One of the doglings, tugging a snow boot in its jaws, got its ear stuck on a shard of glass in the window.

"Oh no!" Squirrel Girl jumped off the roof and rushed toward the puppy just as it pushed free from the glass, leaving its ear behind. Its fake ear. And part of its fake fur. Underneath was metal.

The doglings were little robots in dog suits.

She glanced sidelong at Dog-Lord. "Are you a robot, too?"

"NO! I AM ALL DOG!"

"Ooh, so can you talk to dogs? I can talk to squirrels. We probably have a lot in common!"

"DOGS DO NOT LIKE ME," he said.

"Oh, man, that's kind of sad, especially if dogs are your thing. Is that why you're doing this? Because you're sad?"

"IT IS BECAUSE THEY FEEL THREATENED," Dog-Lord said, sitting back on his haunches. "MY INCREDIBLE DOGLINESS THREATENS THEIR FRAGILE DOGULINITY."

A tinny marimba sound played from the denim fanny pack Dog-Lord wore at his waist. He unzipped it and pulled out a phone, glancing at the screen.

"I NEED TO TAKE THIS," he said, holding up a paw finger to Squirrel Girl.

"Come *on*," Dennis shouted. "Fight already! This is taking way too long, and I'm jonesing for a yogurt."

"What are you even talking about, Dennis?" Janessa said.

Dog-Lord paced slowly, holding the phone to his large doggy ear. "YES," he said to whoever was on the other end.

Squirrel Girl tossed the pile of shoes back into the store. She grabbed at one of the doglings, but its little mouth nipped her finger so hard it drew blood. "Ow," she said. "Bad dog!"

"NO, BOSS," Dog-Lord was saying. "PEOPLE. YES, BOSS. I AM A GOOD BOY. NO MORE TALK. YES, BOSS. I AM DOG, NOT CHATTERBOX. DOG, YES."

Dog-Lord hung up the phone, placing it carefully back into his fanny pack and zipping it shut.

And then without warning, he barreled into Squirrel Girl. She twisted away, but he managed to grab her arm and roll.

Their combined momentum swung her around, and she slammed hard into the sidewalk. Something cracked, and she really hoped it was the concrete and not her skull.

"*Chkt!*" Tippy-Toe declared, and took a bite of the doggish hand that held Squirrel Girl's arm.

"OW!" Dog-Lord yelped, letting go.

"Ow is right," Squirrel Girl said rolling away, relieved to see a significant crack in the sidewalk. "We were having a perfectly good conversation, and you gave me the bum rush!"[43]

Dog-Lord snarled and threw a punch. She was ready this time and caught his fist. Her Doreen Green instincts might be on the fritz, but her Squirrel Girl instincts were a well-oiled machine.

Still holding his fist, she leaped and gave Dog-Lord's arm a yank. He stumbled forward, caught himself, and pushed back, plowing his shoulder into her midsection. She gasped with the impact.

He rushed her again, snarling. Still gasping, she leaped over his head, but in mid-leap he grabbed the toe of her boot with his mouth. She crashed to the pavement, Dog-Lord still clamped onto her foot.

"GRRR," he said, mouth full of boot.

"Look," she said, "points for sticking to the dog theme, but GROSS! You don't know where that shoe has been!"

---

43 That's a thing, right? Like a sneak attack? It's not anything gross, I hope.

He growled again, and his teeth pierced through the leather of her boot.

"Hey!" She yanked her leg away and scampered backward, jumped up ten feet to grab the roof, and, pushing off with her feet, leaped back to the top of the Boot Scoot & Bootie.

"YES!" he crowed. "RUN! FEAR ME! I AM THE ALPHA!"

"Oooh! You know what a good name would be?" Squirrel Girl said, flexing her toes in her boot. They seemed to be okay. "Alpha Dog!"

Dog-Lord tilted his head to the side. "YOU ARE RIGHT. THAT IS A GOOD NAME. BUT I HAVE ALREADY COMMITTED TO THE TITLE DOG-LORD AND THEREFORE YOUR FEEDBACK IS USELESS."

A good hundred students from Union Junior had gathered now. Squirrel Girl would have wanted to observe a half man, half dog, too, especially to peel back his defensive layers and discover what made him tick, but the students were just too relaxed about it. Dennis had somehow managed to get some frozen yogurt and was calmly eating it, like, five feet away. She had to engage this guy in friendly chatter before he hurt someone.

"See, um, you could be Alpha Dog and defend the weak from injustice and stuff, instead of . . . whatever this is. What are you doing here, exactly?"

"I AM BEING A REPRESENTATIVE OF ALL THINGS DOG."

"Huh. This looks a lot like stealing and making a mess," she said. "If you wanted an objective opinion."

Dog-Lord ran into the crowd with that same inhuman speed, grabbed Dennis's frozen yogurt, and held it high. Everyone gasped.

"DOG-LORD TAKES WHAT HE WANTS WHEN HE WANTS!" he shouted.

"That sounds like being a jerk," Squirrel Girl said, leaping toward him.

"SEE ME!" Dog-Lord howled, dropping the yogurt to the ground. "SEE ME DESTROY WHAT YOU LOVE. SEE ME LIFT MY LEG AND—"

"Whoa, gross!" Squirrel Girl said. She grabbed the yogurt, and then, doing a quick side roll, deposited the snack back into Dennis's hands.

"It's perfectly fine—the yogurt part didn't touch the ground," she whispered.

"Th-thanks?" said Dennis.

"I WAS NOT GOING TO PEE. I WAS GOING TO STOMP! STOMPING IS NOT GROSS!"

"Except when you're doing it on yogurt, Mr. Stompy-Pants."

"I AM NOT MR. STOMPY-PANTS! I AM DOG-LORD! WHICH IS A NAME THAT HAS A HYPHEN IN THE MIDDLE. YOU KNOW, LIKE SPIDER HYPHEN MAN!"

He swung his arm at Dennis AND his yogurt. Squirrel Girl

shoved Dennis out of the way and took the blow herself. She flew back with the force of the punch, crashing into a nearby streetlamp. The lamppost cracked, bent, and fell, crashing to the street in a shower of sparks. Her head felt like a drum, her brain still vibrating with the impact.

Dog-Lord ambled over to where she landed. "DOG HYPHEN LORD," he repeated.

"Punch him!" Dennis yelled.

"Demonstrate thy superior breeding all over his heinie!" shouted the baron.

Squirrel Girl hopped up, aching but nothing broken. She held up a hand to the crowd, hoping they would move back.

"BITE!" Dog-Lord shouted, and he clamped his teeth on Squirrel Girl's arm.

"Ow! Hey! Bad dog! Bad dog!"

She slapped his head, but her claws connected, leaving three red scratches down his jaw. He let her go and cradled his face, letting out a soft whine that was the most doglike sound he had made yet.

She knelt down beside him. "Oh, man! I didn't mean to scratch you, sorry. Are you—"

"SNARL!"

He threw a wide punch at Squirrel Girl. She caught it again and jumped back. He was strong, but not, like, Hulk strong. Maybe half a Thor. Or two Captain Americas. Something like that.

"MAD DOG!" he shouted.

He ran at the crowd, grabbed Dennis, and chucked him.

"Aaah!" said Squirrel Girl, leaping up to catch the ninth grader. He slammed into her, and they landed in a bush.

"Whoa, you hurt?" she asked.

Dennis shook his head, his eyes open wide. Semi-frozen yogurt melted off his face.

Someone else went flying through the air. Squirrel Girl leaped as the crowd screamed. Dark hair, brown skin . . . No! She snatched Ana Sofía and hugged her tight, wrapping her tail around the girl's head as they hit the pavement and rolled.

"Oh my gosh, are you okay?" she asked from beneath her friend, her fluffy tail wrapped protectively around her.

Ana Sofía nodded.

"Talking isn't working this time," said Squirrel Girl.

"Maybe you're talking to his man half," said Ana Sofía. "Try talking to his dog half?"

Squirrel Girl was on her feet and running again.

"Oh, no you don't," Squirrel Girl said as she grabbed Dog-Lord's legs and then jumped back, tugging him away from the crowd. "You are being a huge jerk right now. Besides, this is not at all thematically appropriate. When do dogs grab people and throw them?"

He wrenched his body around to snap at her. "GROWL!" he said. "BITE!"

Squirrel Girl dropped him, dodging. He squirmed onto his feet and began hopping around and shouting, "BARK! BARK!"

He got on all fours and charged her, mouth open wide. She put the fingers of one hand together into a kind of duck puppet and jabbed them at Dog-Lord's face. "Tssst!" she hissed. It's what that dog-trainer guy on TV did.

Dog-Lord skidded to a halt, his furry forehead furrowed.

"Burh?"

Squirrel Girl stared him in the eyes. "Focus! Look, I get that you're frustrated. But you can't—"

Dog-Lord shook his head and crouched to jump.

"BARK!"

"Tssst!" Squirrel Girl shoved her hand in front of his face again. The dog trainer always said you had to show the naughty dog who the boss was before they would start to behave.

Dog-Lord froze.

"You are not in charge here," she said.

"OF COURSE NOT. BOSS IS IN CHARGE."

At first she thought he meant her. *That's right, Squirrel Girl is the boss!* But then she remembered the phone call. "Who is your boss, Dog-Lord?"

Dog-Lord glanced at his fanny pack.

"UM," he said. "DOG-LORD. DOG-LORD IS BOSS."

"No," Squirrel Girl said.

"DOG-LORD IS STRONGEST THERE IS, SO DOG-LORD IS BOSS."

"Are you kidding me?! If Hulk was here he would totally smack you for that."

Dog-Lord shrugged. "HULK IS NOT HERE, SO DOG-LORD IS STRONGEST IN THIS PARTICULAR LOCATION."

"Who called you on the phone?"

"TO ME, MY DOGLINGS!" he growled, raising his arms up like the doglings were going to come from the sky or something. Squirrel Girl looked up to check just in case, but there were no sky-dogs.

Something buzzed from inside the depths of the shoe shop. A dog robot crawled into view, made a menacing *beep*, and was tackled by a ball of squirrel fur. Tippy-Toe rolled with the puppy machine, pinning it to the ground. She gave it a sharp bite to the head. It went *beeeep-ph-pah . . .* and collapsed.

"See?" Squirrel Girl said. "Come on. Call off your attack for the sake of the doglings."

"ONE DOGLING IS OF NO CONSEQUENCE," he said. "BECAUSE AS I HAVE SAID, I HAVE AN ARMY."

Dozens more doglings trotted out of the storefront, buzzing angrily.

"Hath the time come to answer our noble lady's call?" asked the baron from the crowd.

"Um, yeah," said Squirrel Girl. "Hey, Squirrel Scouts? Go nuts!"

"Have at thee!" shouted the duchess, whacking a dogling with a broadsword. It may have been dull, but it did the job.

"Gross!" said Heidi, stomping another with her boot.

"You—are—ob—so—lete!" said Janessa, pounding with her backpack.

"FOR FROYO!" shouted Dennis, chasing another and pelting it with the stolen shoes. "Dude, I was SERIOUSLY HUNGRY, TOO!"

Tippy-Toe screeched as she leaped into the fray, followed by waves of furry brown, black, and red rodents in attack mode. The robot dogs gurgled, cracked, and sparked against the squirrel-and-Squirrel-Scout assault.

Dog-Lord growled and howled, trying to get past Squirrel Girl to defend his doglings, but she dodged his punches and leaped about, yanking him back, tripping him up, using speed against his bulk, and randomness against his determined push forward.

Within moments, nothing was left of the dogling army but sparking metal and fake fur. Dog-Lord howled with frustration.

"So," said Squirrel Girl, as she knocked him off his feet again. "Let's talk about your rehabilitation."

"PERHAPS WE SHOULD TALK . . ." Dog-Lord said, "ABOUT POISON SMOKE!"

He reached into the fanny pack, pulled out a small sphere, and threw it at the crowd. When the ball broke, smoke plumed out. Squirrel Girl was separated from the crowd of innocent people by a gray-green Cloud of Doom.

"Wait, what?!" Squirrel Girl backed away and waved her hands at the growing cloud. "This is just wrong! Smoke bombs are *not* a dog thing!"

The people in the crowd were stumbling over each other to get away. Someone, probably Dennis, screamed "RUN!!" and everyone went nuts.[44]

Dog-Lord took off in a two-legged run in the opposite direction.

"Tippy!" Squirrel Girl shouted. "Follow him! I'll find you after I get these people safe!"

She held her breath and rushed into the cloud. The smoke didn't sting her eyes like she was expecting, so she was able to look around. Ana Sofía! She grabbed her first and deposited her on a lawn in the clear air. Another breath and back into the smoke. Several people were curled up on the ground, just lying there, shaking. She grabbed them two at a time, carried them out, took a breath, and dove back in. A breeze ruffled the smoke, and it quickly dissipated, leaving behind a smell more like rank body odor than what Squirrel Girl imagined poison smelled like, so maybe Dog-Lord had been lying about that part. At least it wasn't, like, *lethal* poison, because as far as she could tell, no one had died yet.

"I'M POISONED!" screamed Dennis. He was lying on the

---

44 But, like, in a bad way. Screaming. Shaking. Slapping. Running into each other and bonking heads. That kind of nuts.

school's front grass, rolling around and showing his hands to everyone. They were green. At least the palms were. Parts of the palms.

Squirrel Girl sniffed his hand.

"Dude," she said. "It's grass. Those are grass stains."

He scratched at one hand with a nail, taking off a stripe of green.

"Ohhh," he said.

"You okay?" she asked Ana Sofía.

"Go get him," said Ana Sofía.

"Right!" she shouted, running off in the direction of Tippy-Toe and the fleeing Dog-Lord. "To justice!"

Ten minutes and a brisk run through the park later, justice was served in the form of twenty squirrels surrounding Dog-Lord, now tightly wrapped in wire.

"Where did you find all the wire?" she asked.

Tippy-Toe twitched her tail in a shrug. She'd probably had some buried nearby. Squirrels were prepared.

Squirrel Girl crouched down near the defeated villain. "Okay, lord of friggin' dogs," she said. "Let's talk. Who are you working for?"

"NO ONE," Dog-Lord said.

"Come on," Squirrel Girl said. "Somebody called you. Someone you called 'boss.' Who was that?"

A white van screeched to a halt at the curb, a S.H.I.E.L.D.

logo on the door. A bored-looking white woman in a gray jumpsuit got out, carrying a pole with a loop of rope at the end.

"Hi!" Squirrel Girl said.

"Agent Rozum, Animal Control," she said, walking past Squirrel Girl to the tied-up Dog-Lord.

"Wait, aren't you S.H.I.E.L.D.?" Squirrel Girl asked. "The van says S.H.I.E.L.D."

"Yep, S.H.I.E.L.D.," Agent Rozum said. "Animal-Control Division."

She looped the rope around Dog-Lord's midsection. Or at least it was rope-ish. Tiny bolts of electricity visibly danced down it, and once it was around his body, Dog-Lord stiffened. Only his eyes moved.

"I didn't know S.H.I.E.L.D. had an animal-control division."

"Well, now you do."

Rozum rolled a flat, wheeled disc under Dog-Lord's tail, pushed a button on a remote, and the disc lifted into the air, trolleying him into the back of the van.

"I'm glad you're here," Squirrel Girl said, walking along with the woman. "I'm, like, ninety percent sure there's something going on in Shady Oaks. Like an evil plot or something. He's just part of it."

"Different department," Agent Rozum said. "They're busy, but said Thor called to give us a heads-up about a rampaging dog hybrid."

Ah. Ana Sofía must have alerted Thor, who then called S.H.I.E.L.D.

"Well, you should at least find out who his boss is," Squirrel Girl said. "His boss totally called him on the phone. He has a phone in that weird little pack thingie, so could you give his phone to the right . . . um . . . department?"

Agent Rozum checked the fanny pack. "No phone," she said.

Dog-Lord smiled as the woman shut the van doors, and Squirrel Girl swore she saw little bits of phone still stuck between his sharp canine teeth.

14

TEXT MESSAGES

SQUIRREL GIRL

WHAT IN THE HECK IS GOING ON WITH THIS
DOGMAN THING

ANA SOFÍA

I dunno seems inevitable really. I should've
anticipated it

SQUIRREL GIRL

U should've anticipated a hybrid dog humanoid
villain would attack shady oaks with his robot
dog army?

ANA SOFÍA

Yeah? I mean that's the new normal right?

SQUIRREL GIRL

I miss the good ol days when I was the only super animal powered person in the hood

ANA SOFÍA

So don't think I'm weird but this mall thing is still bugging me

SQUIRREL GIRL

Yeah that whole basement no basement is weird

ANA SOFÍA

Just check out this post and comments

http:/friendbook.usa/shady_listlessGROUP

SHADY OAKS/LISTLESS PINES COMMUNITY FRIENDBOOK GROUP

Yo yo yo yo yo yo take our hashtag mall mascot poll! If hashtag Chester Yard Mall opened today, which would you vote for? LOLolololololololololol ;P

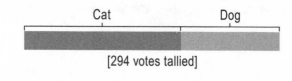

Cat   Dog

[294 votes tallied]

Dennis
Wahoo! Cat is winning!

Kayla

I saw that creepy dog thing. I don't know what that was, but I definitely don't want a dog winning now.

> **Hunter** THIS IS CAT PERSON PROPAGANDA! Come on, sheeples! You think a dog monster just HAPPENED to show up? The Cat people did that! To scare everyone into voting for cat! It's a CAT CONSPIRACY! A CATSPIRACY!

Heidi

The dog beast just proved what we've been saying all along. Dogs are worst! Cats are first!

> **Hunter** Don't be sucked in by their weird cat propaganda!

> > **Pauley** Come on, you really think the Shady Oaks high schoolers or whoever created a genetic dog/human hybrid? What, in their honors science class or something? And then unleashed it on Shady Oaks in an elaborate scheme to scare their own community into hating dogs and voting Cat?

> > **Hunter** Um, YES.

> > **Pauley** Get it? "Unleashed." Because it's a dog? And dogs use leashes?
> > I thought that was pretty good.

> > **Linda** I'm seeing too many people fall for this conspiracy theory. I've had to unfriend five people today already. One of them was my mom.

> > **Wendy** Honestly people will believe ANYTHING.

> > **Pauley** Sometimes the most underappreciated humor is subtle word play.

SQUIRREL GIRL

Looks like Dog-Lord did us a solid. Squirrel scouts will be happy that team cat is pulling ahead

ANA SOFÍA

That's the thing tho. Can't be coincidence that a DOG villain shows up in the middle of mascot election weirdness. Today I found someone named Jerry on the dark net bragging about a dog creature and hinting that there was another. So u probly shld keep eye on listless pines. If a dog thing attacked shady oaks then listless pines might be attacked next

SQUIRREL GIRL

OMGosh u think a cat monster might attack listless pines???

ANA SOFÍA

Honestly I don't know anything anymore

SQUIRREL GIRL

Except all the math EVER

ANA SOFÍA

Yeah except all the math ever

SQUIRREL GIRL

I think I know who maybe would know something about dog lord. Gonna text them

* * *

SQUIRREL GIRL

Hey do you guys know dog lord?

SPIDER-MAN

Is that a name or a title? Like is it a lord of dogs
or a lord that is a dog? I have so many questions

SQUIRREL GIRL

More the second one but I'm guessing that
means you don't know him

ROCKET

At Nova HQ they call Peter the Dog-Lord

SPIDER-MAN

Wait what Peter who I don't know any Peter

ROCKET

Peter Quill! He calls himself Star-Lord but
nobody else does

SPIDER-MAN

Right of course

ROCKET

On Arcturus they call him Hog-Lord

ROCKET

Centaurians skip the "Lord" bit and just call him
something that translates to "meat-in-waiting"

GROOT

I AM GROOT

ROCKET

This IS me being nice, Groot! You want I should
tell her what *I* call him?

SQUIRREL GIRL

Back to Dog-Lord I thought maybe he might be
related to Star-Lord or something?

SPIDER-MAN

Same last name

SQUIRREL GIRL

Exactly! Or I thought spiderman would have run
into him before cuz u have all those animal villains
which is a weird thing I wanted to ask u about

SPIDER-MAN

Yes good question why do animal villains seek
out the Spider-Man? I have three theories

ROCKET

Not the theories again, make it stop. What's
Dog-Lord look like?

SQUIRREL GIRL

Half human half dog all menace

ROCKET

Could be a Corguan. About seven feet tall,
whines a lot?

SQUIRREL GIRL

Bit shorter. whining sounds right tho

ROCKET

Constantly talks about how his fur is better than
your fur even though his is oily and smells like
old cheese?

SQUIRREL GIRL

Um no. He did have an army of little puppy
robots, that seems alieny

ROCKET

Nope, dealbreaker. Corguans hate any robot
smaller than them. Creeps em out.

SQUIRREL GIRL

Darn it! He did talk sort of like a human tho. Or
like he used to be human

SPIDER-MAN

Cool! Like a werewolf?

SQUIRREL GIRL

More like a weredog

SPIDER-MAN

Maybe he was bit by a radioactive dog!

ROCKET

Yeah no that would straight up kill you.
And the dog

SPIDER-MAN

But it happens all the time! SG, you were bit by a
radioactive squirrel, right?

SQUIRREL GIRL

No

SPIDER-MAN

Genetically engineered squirrel?

SQUIRREL GIRL

Nope. Born this way

ROCKET

I was bit by a radioactive raccoon

SPIDER-MAN

There! See? It happens!

ROCKET

Whoops sorry voice textualizer got that wrong. I was bit by a radioactive BADOON

SPIDER-MAN

A radioactive baboon?

ROCKET

No, flarknard, BADOON. Lizardy guys from the planet Moord.

SPIDER-MAN

Do you have badoon powers now

ROCKET

No but I guess we're all pretty clear how you got spider powers

SPIDER-MAN

. . .

It was a radioactive spider

SQUIRREL GIRL

My friend told me that online someone was bragging about dog lord and hinted there might be another evil animal person wandering around soon, probably cat

ROCKET

There are way more earth people with tails than I
was led to believe

SPIDER-MAN

I have more to say on my animal villains so
whenever you're ready for that

SQUIRREL GIRL

Not now I've gotta go to school thanks for your
help I guess!

SPIDER-MAN

Hey I have experience with cat people too if you
need help

Does your cat person have a domino mask?

And a form-fitting black suit?

ROCKET

Squirrel Girl's gone

SPIDER-MAN

Does she have soft white hair

And a coy smile

ROCKET

Stop this is just sad

15

DOREEN

"**S**ome educators believe that there are three types of learners," Ms. Schweinbein said. "Auditory—those who best process spoken information . . ."

Meh, thought Doreen.

". . . visual—those who best process pictures, diagrams, the written word, etc. . . ."

Meh, thought Doreen.

". . . and kinesthetic learners—those who learn best by doing, by participation."

"Oh! That's me for sure!" said Doreen, feeling very kinesthetic-y.

Ms. Schweinbein rolled her eyes at the outburst. She began to pace at the head of the class, back and forth, back and forth, her sneakers squeaking on the linoleum. Watching other people pace made Doreen's legs feel all antsy and envious. But Ms. Schweinbein didn't pace as an invitation for, say, fourteen-year-old students to hop up and join her in a fun and uniting joint-pacing extravaganza, as Doreen had learned firsthand a couple of weeks ago. Since that incident, Ms. Schweinbein had posted signs around the room:

STAY IN YOUR DESK

NO FIDGETING

WIGGLING IS INAPPROPRIATE HUMAN BEHAVIOR

"In an attempt to reach you kinesthetic learners," Ms. Schweinbein continued, "I will be taking suggestions for our next essay's theme."

She stopped, surveying the students as if she expected them to do something. Doreen fidgeted. Just a little.

"Suggestions," Ms. Schweinbein repeated. "From you. The students. You get to participate in the decision-making process. I thought that would elicit something of a positive response."

Shoulders in the class relaxed.

"Awesome," whispered Vin.

"Yes, Vin," the teacher said. "It is awesome."

Doreen's hand shot up even before she knew what she might say. Ms. Schweinbein glanced at her, and then Janessa raised her hand. She called on Janessa.

"How about justice?" Janessa asked.

Doreen liked that idea, but was still a little peeved the teacher ignored her. She kept her hand up.

Ms. Schweinbein called on Maurice next.

"Maybe grass? Or, like, landscaping in general?" Maurice said.

"Good," the teacher said, writing GRASS ETC beneath JUSTICE on the chalkboard. She then called on Kisha. And then Henry. And then Megan.

YOGURT

VIDEO GAMES

TEETH

"How about you, Dougie? You always have good ideas," Ms. Schweinbein said.

Dougie hadn't even been raising his hand. Only Doreen had been raising her hand. The whole time. Now she dropped it. There was no point.

"Um, maybe, um . . . gum," Dougie said. "And all the stuff that is called gum, and was once gum, and things that might one day be gum again."

Ms. Schweinbein wrote THE JOURNEY OF GUM. "Very thought-provoking. Thank you, Dougie. I'll consider your suggestions and tell you which I've selected tomorrow."

Doreen's hand shot back up. Ms. Schweinbein sighed as she sat at her desk.

"Class will be over in ten more minutes, Ms. Green," she said. "You can go to the restroom then."

"But I—" Doreen began.

"Everyone open your books to page one forty-two," Ms. Schweinbein said, speaking over Doreen. "Review the questions there. They might just be on a quiz tomorrow."

Doreen lowered her hand.

Squirrels, she thought. *And computers. And dinosaurs living at the center of the earth. And fashion-forward Super Villains. That's what I would have said.*

As soon as the lunch bell rang, Doreen ran normal-human-speed to Ana Sofía's locker. She signed, "My teacher hates me. Really. She really hates me."

"Sorry," signed Ana Sofía. "If she hates you, she's wrong."

Doreen paced now. A growly/angry kind of pacing, like a wild squirrel in a zoo cage.[45] She paced till words built up so high in her she felt like she'd swallowed an Eiffel Tower of words, and the top was poking out, and she just had to speak. She stopped pacing so Ana Sofía could see her lips clearly.

"Ms. Schweinbein said a third of the grade is in-class participation, but then she doesn't let me participate. You know what that is? It's injustice, that's what. It's straight-up, friggin' injustice."

---

45 That is, if they had squirrels at the zoo. Which they don't. Which is good, 'cause, yay freedom! But also a little *huh?* Don't think squirrels are good enough for your precious zoos, do you? Well, that's your loss, buddy boy!

"It is," Ana Sofía agreed. "That's not fair. You're trying your best, and she's not even giving you a chance."

Doreen stood up straighter. "Yeah! You're right! And I fight injustice things all the time, so I should definitely get on this, pronto! Or *someone* should." She signed, "Squirrel Girl."

"I know this whole situation stinks, but Squirrel Girl can't just go fight a teacher," said Ana Sofía.

Doreen shrugged. She could if Ms. Schweinbein was a villain . . . which maybe she was. . . .

"Speaking of participation," said Ana Sofía, and she fiddled nervously with the cord on her backpack, "sometimes I don't participate on purpose. I mean, after a few times of people making fun of your suggestions, and even *laughing* at you, it can get easier to just keep them to yourself."

"That's true," said Doreen, though she had never reached the limit on that particular point.

"So . . ." said Ana Sofía, "I *really* don't like it when people laugh at me. Or, you know, dismiss me with, like, a 'never mind' or whatever."

Doreen nodded. Ana Sofía looked at her. There seemed to be something she wanted Doreen to say, but Doreen was stumped.

"Dude," Doreen said in an I'm-all-in-agreement kind of way.

That didn't quite seem to do it, though. Ana Sofía was still looking at her in that waiting/hopeful way. Doreen's forehead started to prickle with sweat.

This was probably one of those really, really super-important moments in a friendship when she needed to say just the right thing. Doreen's mind was blank. She swallowed.

"Yeah," she said, her voice dry, "that's really rude when people laugh at things we say when we're just trying to be helpful and all, so we should join forces and just stop that stuff, right?"

Ana Sofía shrugged and walked away.

Oh no! Had she failed? Had she not said just the right thing? And did that mean that Ana Sofía might not want to be her BHFF anymore? Sometimes keeping friends felt like putting together a nuclear warhead, and if you breathed wrong or hammered too hard or touched the wrong wires together, it would just explode on you in a huge and deadly and unfixable way. And after, when you were looking at the black crater at your feet, you still weren't sure if it exploded because of the breathing or the hammering or the wiring, so you didn't know what *not* to do next time.

Doreen didn't want to wait for next time.

She ran after Ana Sofía, who had joined the Squirrel Scouts at their long cafeteria table. She wanted to say something to Ana Sofía, even if it wasn't exactly the right thing, but Heidi was talking.

". . . and it was *ah-mazing* to fight robots again, right? Even weird little dog robots?"

"Weird robot dogs!" said Jackson. He lifted up his hand as if waiting for a high five. When no one immediately obliged, even though she was nowhere near him, Doreen rushed forward, hand out and ready to save the day! Or at least the moment! Or just the high five! But with her tail tucked in, her balance was always off, and she bumped into the table, knocked against Bianca, who said "Ow!", and Dennis, who said "Watch it!", and tumbled onto the floor.

When she stood up, everyone was staring at her.

"Oopsie whoopsie!" she said, imitating Penny, an adorably clumsy kid on the TV show *Penny for Your Thoughts*, but no one seemed to get she was trying to make a joke. Not a smile was cracked. She glanced at Ana Sofía to see if her trip and failed joke had made her rethink their best-friendship, but she couldn't catch her eye.

"I just think we need to make it clear to Squirrel Girl," said Heidi, "that we want to be in on that kind of action more."

"Or," said Doreen, "we could text her when there's a problem and then let her take care of it since she wouldn't want any of us to get hurt!"

"What are you even talking about, Doreen?" said Janessa. "We never get hurt."

"Well, you almost did," said Doreen. "With Dog-Lord, I mean."

"You weren't even there, Doreen," Lanessa said. "You didn't show up."

Doreen shrugged. "That's what I heard, is all. . . ."

The conversation continued, but for perhaps the first time in her life, Doreen had indeed reached the point where participation hurt too much. Way easier to sit in silence, eat her three leftover nutloaf sandwiches, and replay in her mind every stupid thing she'd ever said.

16

SQUIRREL GIRL

Doreen had sooo much homework it wasn't even funny. An hour of online math, three chapters of history textbook, and an essay for Ms. Schweinbein's class called "Why Animals Are Better than People." She hadn't remembered that suggestion coming from a student, and even though Doreen was completely open to exploring the topic, she honestly didn't know why she bothered to try. She was destined for a C-, the only grade Ms. Schweinbein ever gave her.

Doreen had homework all right, but Squirrel Girl was out on patrol in Listless Pines.[46]

---

46 Listen, if you have the option of choosing when you become a Super Hero, maybe wait till after middle school? Gets complicated, is all I'm saying. But do NOT tell my parents I said so, they are already pro-waiting-for-adulthood-to-fully-embrace-Super-Herodom, which just isn't an option for me, thanks.

"Tip, I swear, she just straight-up hates Doreen-me," said Squirrel Girl, as she leaped from one roof to another.

"CHKKT!" said Tippy-Toe.

Squirrel Girl snorted. "Ouch, that sounds painful. Thanks, but you don't need to do that."

Tippy-Toe sneezed in a way that meant she was ready at a moment's notice to exact severe squirrelly vengeance on this teacher, but in the meantime would respect her friend's desire for a peaceful resolution.

"I mean, if we find evidence that Ms. Schweinbein is a super-powerful villain plotting to rain terror on Shady Oaks, and only a girl and her squirrel can stop her, then the squirrel gloves are off, obvs."

Squirrel Girl leaped from a housetop to the windowsill of a two-story building and then climbed to the roof. A commercial center of Listless Pines lay before her. Frankly, it looked a lot like Shady Oaks. Streets, houses, businesses. A canal of gray water slithered alongside a street. She sniffed, but the air was no more stinky or pleasant than Shady Oaks. And yet the Squirrel Scouts insisted this area was enemy territory. She wondered what she was missing.

"Ana Sofía said to keep an eye out around Listless Pines," said Squirrel Girl. "Online someone was threatening a second attack in this area. I don't know what we're looking for exactly, but I suspect—"

Several people came running out of a nearby Shop-N-Pop, a chain grocery store where you could get your groceries *and* make custom bottles of soda, with flavors like Honey Kiwi, Blue Grapefruit Delirium, and When Frankincense Met Myrrh. Also, the people were screaming.

"Chetti-kit?" said Tippy-Toe.

"Yeah," said Squirrel Girl, "whatever they're running from is probably what we're looking for. Hey, will you round up some squirrel friends and I'll go inside and check it out?"

She jumped off the building and landed on the roof of a parked car. Which suddenly wasn't parked anymore.

"Sorry!" said Squirrel Girl, leaping off the car as it screeched out of the parking lot, nearly colliding with another car that was leaving in an equally screechy manner.

Squirrel Girl dodged screeching cars and fleeing customers till by the time she got inside the grocery store, nobody was there but one man in a Shop-N-Pop apron, holding a phone to his ear.

"I don't know what it is!" he whispered into the phone. "Some kind of animal girl with a tail!"

"Squirrel," said Squirrel Girl. "It's a squirrel tail."

"What? Oh, not you." He pointed into the store with a shaky hand.

At first she didn't see anything, except that the store was a mess. Shopping carts abandoned mid-trip, food items scattered all over the floor. Then a flicker. A shadow in Aisle 8: Pet Supplies.

"What is it?" Squirrel Girl whispered.

"She calls herself Mistress Meow." He gulped. "The county police say they can't be here for twenty to thirty minutes. Since the Dog-Lord thing resolved without their attention, they've downgraded hybrid human-animal apparitions from 'urgent' to 'check-out-able.'"

Squirrel Girl took out her phone.

SQUIRREL GIRL

> Can you tell thor to tell shield to send their animal control peeps to the shopnpop for a cat monster thing?

ANA SOFÍA

> I guess this is a normal text that I get in my life now

ANA SOFÍA

> Should I alert the squirrel scouts too?

SQUIRREL GIRL

> I guess?

Squirrel Girl hesitated before clicking Send. At first the Squirrel Scouts were a win-win: a group of friends for Doreen, a group of supporters for Squirrel Girl. But were they friends really? Doreen wasn't 100 percent clear on that point. And Squirrel Girl wasn't 100 percent clear on what they wanted from her. In fact, just thinking about them made her feel hyped up, nervous, angry, proud, and sick to her stomach. That particular emotion combo was becoming more and more familiar.

From the depths of the store came a low-throated growl. The employee took a step closer to Squirrel Girl.

"Why don't you wait outside?" she said. "Could be dangerous."

The guy shook his head. "I was promoted to store manager yesterday. And I took a sacred Shop-N-Pop oath to look after this store. I am its captain, and a captain goes down with the ship!"

A *thump*, a sound of breaking glass, and a soft *hiss*.

He gulped. He looked at Squirrel Girl with pleading eyes, his forehead sparkly with sweat.

"What's your name, Mr. Store Manager?"

"Herb," he said.

"Great name," she said. "A-plus, for real. Never met a Herb before and I always wanted to.[47] So, have you tried talking to her? I find that reasoned dialogue can solve, like, eighty-two percent of interpersonal conflicts."

"No?" he said, as if afraid she'd get mad at him.

Squirrel Girl sighed. He was, like, thirty years old. She was fourteen, for nuts' sake. People were way too willing to just trust anybody with authority, in her experience, whether that person got their authority from a uniform or from super powers.[48]

---

47 Once I thought I did, but it turned out his name was "Herp," which sounds, like, totally the same at first.

48 Or from an objectively magnificent tail. Tails are the new uniforms.

"Don't worry, Herb," she said. "I'm really good at this stuff."

Squirrel Girl stalked down Aisle 8, hopping over spilled dog food, tiny brown nuggets still rolling as if recently disturbed.

"Hello?" said Squirrel Girl.

A flicker. Something moving above. Squirrel Girl leaped on top of the shelving. Nothing. Nothing except for packs of dry angel-hair pasta, crackling beneath her boots. She landed in Aisle 7: Pasta, Pasta Sauce, Pickles.

And there, at the end of the aisle, lying atop the dairy case, was a . . . a . . . um . . . woman? Or cat? Or both? She had gray fur over her arms and legs, which were visible beneath her short-sleeved blouse and cut-off jeans shorts. Her head fur was longer, rising up in a kind of fauxhawk and tumbling down her back. Her face was mostly human, with pinkish pale skin and a thin nose, though her cheeks had long whiskers.

"Meow," she said.[49]

"You must be Mistress Meow. I'm Squirrel Girl. I see we both prefer gendered, animal-centric monikers. We probably have lots of other stuff in common. Like a fondness for tails, and small furry creatures, and interesting smells, and . . . *justice?*" she added hopefully.

"Meow," said Mistress Meow.

Then she reached out a lazy paw and swatted a display of

---

49 She didn't meow. She said "Meow." There's a difference, so I just wanted to make sure we're clear.

Heavenly Gravy, knocking it flat over. The glass bottles shattered against the concrete floor.

"Geez, dude! That's not cool!" said Squirrel Girl. Splatters of gravy had splashed over her tail.[50] She shook it, and some drops of gravy landed on Mistress Meow.

"Come, now," Mistress Meow said in a slow, low voice, "don't be like that. You're making a mess."

"*I'm* making a mess?"

"Yes, just look at that gravy everywhere! First you came up to me so rudely, startling me, and making me knock it over—"

"I . . . I . . ." Squirrel Girl took a deep breath and tried again with the Steps to Conflict Resolution by establishing some common ground. "So, you're a cat-person human, huh? That must be interesting. And challenging! I know for me it's not always easy to fit into the human world *or* the squirrel world, let alone both! Maybe you feel the same?"[51]

Mistress Meow stood up slowly and, balancing on the edge of the dairy case, began to pace its length. "Yes, I can see why humans would be suspicious of you. And squirrels . . . well, you know how *they* are. . . ."

"Huh," said Squirrel Girl, not quite sure if she was being insulted. Or if squirrels were being insulted. Or both.

---

50 Whoever said gravy makes everything better was obviously not talking about beautiful, fluffy squirrel tails, which don't need anything to make them better, thanks.
51 That was some solid Establishing Common Ground, if you ask me. It should've worked like a charm! I used I-messages and everything!

"I hate to be direct," said Mistress Meow, "but your conversation is dull and is getting in the way of my shopping."[52]

She leaped onto the display case of Aisle 6: Rice, Soup, Ethnic Food. The end display of microwavable goulash crashed to the floor.

"Wait!" said Squirrel Girl, hurrying after her. "I haven't had a chance to Listen First, Talk Second! Or Agree upon Common Goals! Also, FYI, a life of crime doesn't pay!"

Mistress Meow had leaped to Aisle 4: Paper Products, and was ripping open packages of toilet paper with her claws.

"Stop that! You're making a huge mess. Have some animal girl pride, will you?"[53]

"Fine, whatever," said Mistress Meow. She sauntered down Aisle 4. Her tail swished back and forth, knocking off boxes of aluminum wrap and sandwich bags.

"Hey!" said Squirrel Girl. "Mistress Meow! You can't just come into a grocery store and make a mess like this."

The lady cat just kept walking, seemingly unaware that her tail was leaving a trail of destruction. Squirrel Girl followed her to the soda station at the back of the store. Rows of syrups in huge tanks dazzled with a rainbow of colors, labeled with flavors like Vanilla Explosion, Berry Jamboree, and Licorice Dreams. The occasional bubble rose up, emitting a low, slow *gulp*.

"Mistress Meow? Um, excuse me? Did you hear what I said?"

---

52 Now I was 95 percent sure I was being insulted.
53 Not exactly one of the Steps to Conflict Resolution, but I was getting irritated.

Mistress Meow looked lazily over her shoulder and blinked her green eyes.

"You're still here? Wow, I wish *I* had sooo few responsibilities that I could waste hours just following people around grocery stores. How nice that must be."

"Actually, I have a ton of—" Squirrel Girl was about to say *homework*, but she didn't have homework—that was Doreen! And best to keep that part of her life secret. "—um, a ton of respect. For cats. They're so . . . furry. And tailed. And just because sometimes they climb up trees and then can't get down again doesn't mean I would ever make fun of them."[54]

Mistress Meow sharpened her claws on a wall of the soda station, cutting right through to the tanks of soda stored behind it. Plain soda shot out in white fizzy streams.

"Look what you made me do! All your blabbering is so distracting."

"I'm sorry," Squirrel Girl said automatically. "Wait . . . what are you even talking about? I didn't make you do anything, but I'm going to. I don't like getting all Super-Hero-demanding, but you need to leave this store right now!"

Mistress Meow blinked. She put out a paw, holding it behind a twenty-five-gallon tank of Egg Salad Syrup.

"Don't—" Squirrel Girl started. "Ew, gross, egg salad–flavored

---

54 Okay, this is a straight-up lie. The squirrels and I think cats stuck in trees are hi-lar-i-ous and were just laughing about it this morning TBH.

soda syrup? But still, don't. Don't you do it. I mean it, Mistress Meow!"

Mistress Meow held her gaze. Her paw twitched. The syrup tipped over, gushing yellow-green liquid all over the floor.

"Oh dear," said Mistress Meow. "I bet now you wished you'd left me alone. How will you ever explain this mess to Herb?"

"That's it!" said Squirrel Girl. "No more chatting. Let's go nuts!"

She leaped, claws out.

Mistress Meow dropped to the floor, her arms out in front, her elongated body stretching.

Squirrel Girl passed over her head, landed against the wall feetfirst, then pushed off and pivoted, coming to a stop in battle stance, arm cocked and ready for punching time!

Mistress Meow yawned, her mouth open wide to reveal a row of sharp teeth. She curled up on the painted concrete floor, just out of reach of the pool of syrup and soda. She closed her eyes.

"Hey," said Squirrel Girl. "What are you doing? You can't nap in here."

The tip of Mistress Meow's tail flicked in annoyance. She rolled over, eyes still closed.

Squirrel Girl stood over her. Fists ready. Claws ready. Boots well prepared to stomp out injustice. And her opponent appeared to fall asleep.

17

TEXT MESSAGES

ANA SOFÍA

Hey I just got a text from Squirrel Girl.
She's battling a cat person monster thing?
I guess?

THOR

Epic! A massive, fearsome feline rage beast is fit
opponent for any hero!

ANA SOFÍA

I think it's more like a regular lady with fur and a
tail? And catlike enhanced abilities? Can you tell
someone at S.H.I.E.L.D. to come pick her up like
they did with Dog-Lord?

THOR

Verily

I am told S.H.I.E.L.D.'s Animal Control Unit is currently engaged chasing a cabal of hyper-intelligent crocodiles in the Manhattan sewers. Doth your friend need immediate assistance?

ANA SOFÍA

She says the cat lady is being super annoying but won't fight just curls up and naps

THOR

Fearsome rage beasts are appropriate foes for the son of Odin. For villains of the annoying variety one might send a textual inquiry to Spider-Man.

ANA SOFÍA

Ok. I don't have his number

THOR

Ah, cats. In Asgard, the mighty Freya travels in a chariot borne by two cats of epic girth

ANA SOFÍA

Wow! How does she get cats to pull her chariot?

THOR

She is mighty! Also she does not go many places.

ANA SOFÍA

I see

THOR

In the halls of Valhalla, cats are trained to bring spice milk in pewter mugs to the mightiest warriors

ANA SOFÍA

Really?

THOR

Most certainly! However, they do not excel at this practice.

ANA SOFÍA

Not great at it?

THOR

So much spilled spice milk. So many scratched-up warriors.

ANA SOFÍA

Cats are hard to train

THOR

They are distractible, tis true. Perhaps thy heroic friend might try to distract her feminine feline with a well-placed ball of yarn or catnip-stuffed mouse toy

ANA SOFÍA

Sure and I'll let you know if we encounter something mightier, like a Thor cat

THOR

Indeed! If there were such a creature as Cat Thor 'twould be the mightiest pet of all.

18

SQUIRREL GIRL

*M*istress Meow was napping in the produce section, curled up on top of a display of oranges. This was her third nap in fifteen minutes.

"C'mon, man," said Squirrel Girl, poking her with a zucchini. "I promised Herb I'd clear you out."

She could see the store manager standing there valiantly by the front doors, his underarms dark with sweat. Poor Herb. She was not going to let him go down with the ship! Or let the ship go down! Or let this cat beastie destroy this market where she had never before shopped but might consider it now as the soda flavors were really interesting!

She renewed her hold on the zucchini. *Poke. Poke.* It was surprisingly hard to engage in battle with a villain when they were catnapping.

Her phone buzzed. Finally, Ana Sofía was answering her desperate texts!

> Shield busy. Thor says cats are super distractible and to try a cat toy or something

Hmm. Distract her? As she put her phone back into a utility-belt pouch, she remembered an item stowed away in another pouch. Laser Lady's laser pointer.

"Hey! Kitty!" Squirrel Girl pointed the dot of red light at an orange near Mistress Meow's head. "Kitty, what's that? What's that?"

Mistress Meow's eyes opened to narrow slits. She sniffed. She twitched. Her eyes widened.

Squirrel Girl pointed the laser at the floor.

Mistress Meow tensed all over. Her gaze locked onto the wiggling dot of light. She pounced.

But the dot of light danced out of the way, moving through the produce section.

"What's that, huh?" said Squirrel Girl, moving down an aisle. "Get it! Get it!"

"Mrooow!" said Mistress Meow. On all fours she chased after the light, pouncing but always missing, until she jumped right through the doors of the Shop-N-Pop. In the bright sunlight, the red dot disappeared.

"Aha! I got you outside!" said Squirrel Girl, standing between the villain and the market. "Victory!"

Mistress Meow hissed. And then she pounced.

"Aah!" said Squirrel Girl as two hundred pounds of intellectually advanced cat flesh landed on her. Cat claws struck at her face, and Squirrel Girl only managed to roll in time to keep her eyeballs intact. She kicked her off and scrambled to her feet.

"Dang, Mistress Meow, I have not seen this side of you."

Mistress Meow pounced again, but several dozen squirrels jumped onto her back mid-leap.

"Chktti!" said the one with the pink bow, and at the same time all the squirrels bit down.

Mistress Meow screeched and rolled onto her back, trying to dislodge the squirrels.

"Get off, vermin! Get off!"

"Ha!" Squirrel Girl laughed. "I told you I could defeat you! And then you said, 'You and what army?' Well, I think I just answered your question!"

"I never said that!" said Mistress Meow, rolling on her back as squirrels jumped out of her way.

"You didn't?" said Squirrel Girl. "Dang it! I was just thinking about how if you said 'You and what army,' then I would know just what to respond, but you're right, you never did, and now I wasted the perfect comeback."

She moved in on the attack, and Mistress Meow countered—claws swiping and tail lashing, powerful kicks and agile leaps. But with an army of squirrels at her side, Squirrel Girl was easily pressing her advantage.

So Mistress Meow turned and ran.

"Stop!" said Squirrel Girl, chasing her. "I think I'm supposed to turn you over to the authorities or something! The county police will be here in twenty minutes or less! Probably!"

Mistress Meow ran, but Squirrel Girl was faster.[55] She was almost to the open street when a van screeched to a halt right in her path. Mistress Meow leaped onto its roof. Antonio of the Skunk Club jumped out of the front seat. The sliding doors opened to let out a bunch of other Squirrel Scouts, spilling them out right under Mistress Meow's nose. They were in their Team Cat shirts and sounded like they were in mid-argument.

"I told you to drive faster, Antonio!"

"I got us here, didn't I?"

"Yo, this the right place?"

"Yeah, is that the right cat person?"

---

55 Yes, cats are often faster than squirrels, but it's all about proportions, my friend. Proportionally, I am, like, fifty times the weight of a squirrel, while she was twenty times the weight of a cat, so I might run fifty times faster than a squirrel while she only runs twenty times the speed of a cat . . . and I think that's how it works.

"Squirrel Girl started without us! Typical."

"Here we come to save the—" Dennis started. Mistress Meow grabbed him and held him fast, her claws out and poised right above his jugular.[56]

"Whoa, easy now," said Squirrel Girl. She glanced at the assembled Scouts and was relieved Ana Sofía wasn't among them.

"Please, I have so much to live for!" said Dennis.

"Such as?" asked Mistress Meow.

"Um . . . I just meant in general." Dennis whimpered. "I didn't know there was going to be a quiz!"

The sound of an electronic drum beat rang out. Mistress Meow stuck one claw into the phone hanging on her belt and lifted it to her ear.

"Hello, boss. . . . Probably. . . . Well, I didn't know you meant *now*. . . . Fine, whatever."

Squirrel Girl sprang, her eyes zeroed in on that phone, but Mistress Meow yanked it out of her reach. Squirrel Girl somersaulted to a stop.

"Dang it, I really want to know who you were talking to!"

"Boss says to make havoc," said Mistress Meow, "and I'm *such* a *good* kitty."

She picked up Dennis and threw him.

"Not—" Dennis started.

---

56 Good grief, why is it always Dennis?

"—again!" Squirrel Girl finished. She jumped, catching him in the air, and landed hard.

"Such a good little pet," said Mistress Meow. "Here, fetch this, too!" She threw a silver ball that had a very familiar glint.

Squirrel Girl started to jump for it, but Heidi shoved her.

"Stop stealing all the hero spotlight!" she said, catching it instead.

Immediately brown gas leaked out of dozens of tiny holes in the ball. Squirrel Girl grabbed Heidi and leaped free of the smoke cloud. When she went back for the rest, instead of trying to escape, they were throwing punches. At each other. Sure, sometimes the Squirrel Scouts had fought among the group—but never with their fists. Why was everyone so crazy lately?

"Stop it!" said Squirrel Girl. "Calm the freak down!"

From outside the cloud, she fanned at the smoke with her fluffy tail, joined by dozens of other squirrels, all their tail winds directed at the smoke. It broke apart and blew away.

"Stop fighting, guys, I'm serious!" said Squirrel Girl. "Or I won't bring you next time, got it?"

"Fine, *Mom*," said Janessa.

Squirrel Girl rolled her eyes. She was about to go full mom on them when she heard a car screech followed by a crash.

Mistress Meow was in the middle of the street, waving her tail sassily at a crash involving three cars. She leaped from car roof to car roof, scratching them with her claws, hissing and laughing.

"This is not acceptable behavior!" Squirrel Girl called. She

chased her from car to car, and though she was the faster run-
ner, Mistress Meow was agile and unpredictable, always one car
ahead. Now ten cars were stopped, scratched up and dented, their
drivers madly calling on cell phones or filming the scene.

Squirrel Girl finally caught up and knocked Mistress Meow
off a car. Another car turned the corner and swerved to miss
them, slamming its brakes. It went over the edge of the street,
and stopped inches from falling into the slope down to the canal
that ran parallel to the road.

"That was close!" said Squirrel Girl.

The driver, a white-haired dark-skinned woman, was looking back and forth between Squirrel Girl and Mistress Meow, her
hands gripping the steering wheel.

"Now, come with me," said Squirrel Girl with as much
Super-Hero-y authority as she could muster.

"What was that?" said Mistress Meow. "I can't hear you over
all the traffic. Let me get this out of the way."

With enhanced feline strength, Mistress Meow gave the back
end of the car a shove, pushing the front wheels over the edge
into the canal. The car began to tilt. The driver inside screamed.

Squirrel Girl scurried around to the front of the car. She dug
her heels into the downward slope and pushed against the front
bumper. Her feet were sliding, the car coming after her, about to
push them both into the deep water.

"Look what you made me do!" Mistress Meow shouted from
the street.

Tippy-Toe landed on the car's hood. *"Chek-itit,"* she said, suggesting that they chase Mistress Meow up a tree, where she would surely be trapped for life.

"Stop—*hee-hee*—stop, Tip! Don't make me laugh right now! This car is superheavy. Though if there's a tree high enough, that's not a bad idea. But if not, can you guys go after Mistress Meow and maybe pin her down with your collective squirrel weight till the cops get here?"

Tippy-Toe sneezed in a way that meant it would be absolutely no trouble whatsoever for her team of squirrel heroes to stop a cat-human hybrid, and with a flick of her tail she was off.

From halfway down the canal slope, Squirrel Girl could hear all sorts of things happening on the street: meowing, chittering, glass breaking, cars slamming into each other, honking. But mostly the driver lady still screaming. Then she started pounding on her car horn, as if a hundred decibels of honking in her face was going to help Squirrel Girl push a two-ton car any faster.

"Don't worry!" said Squirrel Girl through gritted teeth. "I . . . will . . . save . . . the . . . DAY!"

With a great heave, she pushed the car back up to flat level. She brushed off her hands. And looked around at the chaos.

No Mistress Meow, but traffic was completely stopped by at least twenty damaged cars.

"Um, hey, everybody, sorry about the crashing!" said Squirrel Girl. "I guess I couldn't actually save everyone. But did you see how I saved that one car from the canal? No? Nobody?"

Under the clatter of horns and rattle of broken cars, she heard some rapid-fire chittering. Following the sound, she ran down a couple of blocks and found Mistress Meow facedown on a sidewalk. Or at least, she assumed that was Mistress Meow thrashing around beneath a furry, twitching pile made up of hundreds of squirrels.

"Squirrel pile!" she said. "Oh man, I so want to jump in right now, but I'm afraid I'd squish some adorable tails. Tippy, any wire?"

The pink-bowed squirrel atop the pile shrugged with her tail. They hadn't buried any handy wire or twine nearby. Squirrel Girl suspected the cat-lady could just claw through it anyway. What she needed was—

A white van pulled up. With a S.H.I.E.L.D. logo.

"Agent Rozum!" said Squirrel Girl. "You made it!"

The agent had her nifty pole-and-rope device again, and she stood on the curb and surveyed the squirrel pile with the same bored expression. "Thor said you have another?"

"Yep," said Squirrel Girl. "So does this happen a lot, then? Super-powered cat and dog people?"

The agent shrugged. "Classified."

Squirrel Girl pointed down. "You have some hyper-intelligent-crocodile slime on your boot."

The agent looked at her shrewdly, and wiped her boot on the grass.

"So what's the plan?" asked Squirrel Girl. "Want to put your floating-disc technology under the whole squirrel pile and take them in the van, or— No, better, I'll tell the squirrels to move, and you just be ready to collar her with that thing. Ready, squirrels? Jump off!"

The squirrels leaped, popping off in all directions, and instantly Mistress Meow was in the air, too, claws out, leaping right at Squirrel Girl.

The rope caught her in midair and she fell hard, right onto the disc. Her muscles temporarily paralyzed, she couldn't even hiss as the van doors closed.

"Man, I wouldn't mind one of those pole things," said Squirrel Girl.

"Not for civilian use," said Agent Rozum. She locked up the back of the van and climbed in the front, calling over her shoulder, "This is the first lady cat person in jeans shorts I've seen, FYI. Kinda weird, though in this job, that word loses all meaning." And she drove off.

"Huh," said Squirrel Girl. "That is a thing that just happened."

She looked back at the hundreds of squirrels.

"I could be on the bottom . . ." she said.

"Chktt," they said.

Squirrel Girl dropped onto the pavement, shouting "Squirrel pile!" just before hundreds of pounds of squirrels briefly buried her in furry goodness.

She was still laughing when she started the run back toward home. That C- paper on why animals are better than people wasn't going to write itself.

Wasn't it interesting, she thought as she leaped from lamppost to lamppost, how Ms. Schweinbein assigned a paper on animals being better than people the very week two animal-people attacked the neighborhood?

"Huh," said Squirrel Girl, as she ran down the sidewalk a little faster than the cars in the street.

"Hey, Squirrel Girl!" people called out. She waved, too deep in thought to reply.

And hadn't she noticed that the teacher's house smelled like cats and dogs just before Dog-Lord and Mistress Meow showed up to hassle Squirrel Girl?

"Huh," said Squirrel Girl, as she leaped from one street corner to another.

Also, just the other day in class, Ms. Schweinbein had mentioned "animal-human hybrids" with a wistful tone and a gleam in her eye, punctuated with a slow and villainous "hee-hee-hee" laugh.

"Aha!" said Squirrel Girl as she pivoted to run along the ridge of a roof.

She was no longer headed toward home and homework. That would have to wait. Again. She had a potentially villainous teacher to face.

19

SQUIRREL GIRL

A delivery van pulled away from Ms. Schweinbein's home just as Squirrel Girl arrived. Ms. Schweinbein was dragging several large boxes from her porch into the house.

Several large, suspicious boxes. And they seemed even more suspicious when Ms. Schweinbein looked around suspiciously before shutting the door.

Tippy-Toe climbed up the trunk of the tree in two leaps, landed on a branch in front of Squirrel Girl, and stared at her, inches from her face. With two claws she pointed to her own black, blinkless eyes.

"Yes, I see you, Tip," said Squirrel Girl.

"Chkt-chuk," Tippy-Toe said.

"Yes, I can see the rage in your black, blinkless eyes, Tip. And I thank you for being on my side. But before we attack, we should try the talking thing with Ms. Schweinbein, too . . . I guess."

Tippy-Toe twitched her tail and let out a stream of chittering that roughly translated to *If any more of those weevil-brained dog-men or cat-ladies are in there I am going to personally bite off every one of their toes.*

"Whoa! Dial it back a little, Tip," Squirrel Girl said. "I know you're upset at having your territory invaded by villainous animal-humans, but I don't think things are so bad that we need to start eating people."

"*Chkka.*"

"*Or* biting off body parts. Same difference."

Squirrel Girl and girl squirrel stared at the house.

"Maybe I could just go knock," Squirrel Girl said. "That worked before."

Tippy-Toe sniffed. The last time Squirrel Girl had just knocked on the door of someone she thought was a bad guy, evil robot people had answered. That unexpected encounter had ended in a big fight involving crashing trees, totaled cars, and terrified neighbors.

"Okay, so maybe that last time wasn't *ideal*," she said. "But we did end up stopping the bad guys."

"*Chukka.*"

"Let's just go take a closer look."

Tippy-Toe and Squirrel Girl tipped on their toes across the street and to Ms. Schweinbein's house. Something in the basement squealed. Squirrel Girl peeked into a window well. The basement windows had been covered over with newspaper.

"She's definitely hiding something," Squirrel Girl whispered.

Ms. Schweinbein's neighbors switched on their porch light, bathing Squirrel Girl in a yellow glow. She scampered to the roof just as a woman opened the porch door and came out carrying a full garbage bag.

A voice from inside the neighbor's house said, "How's the stench house tonight?"

The neighbor woman groaned, looked at Schweinbein's house, and shook her head.

"Still smells like a zoo," she replied, "but at least the wind isn't blowing our way."

The neighbor went back inside and shut the door. The outside light turned off.

"Ugh," Squirrel Girl whispered. "I hate sneaking around. I'm the good guy. I'm not supposed to sneak."

Tippy-Toe sniffed again and twitched her tail.

"You are so one of the good guys, Tippy," she said. "You just do your thing, and if people don't notice you, that's on them for being supremely unobservant of the great furry ones."

Tippy-Toe scampered to the chimney, held up a paw, and motioned Squirrel Girl closer. Squirrel Girl knelt to listen. From the chimney came a muffled voice, full of echoes but still very familiar: Ms. Schweinbein.

". . . this is better than the cage, though, isn't it? . . . Yes, I know you want to go outside, but it isn't time. . . . They wouldn't understand. . . . They don't want you here. . . . Only I love you. . . . Let's see what's in your formulation today. . . . Ah, a meat day. . . . Ugh . . . I wish they would tell me who the meat was from before I feed it to you. . . ."

Besides Ms. Schweinbein's voice, other unsettling noises leaked out of the pipe. Chewing and smacking sounds. Like living things eating. Or being eaten.

"Omigosh!" Squirrel Girl said. "That is so messed up! We have to stop her!"

She slid down the roof and landed on the front steps, already knocking forcefully (but politely) on the door before she'd even landed. She crouched in battle stance. "Get ready, Tippy."

Tippy-Toe ran her claws through her head fur, making it stand up in a ridge like a Mohawk. Claws out. Face fierce. Pink bow tied like a dream.

There was an angry grunt from the other side of the door, and then it cracked open an inch. The equally angry eye of her teacher stared out of that crack, and then grew wide in surprise.

Squirrel Girl was just about to pounce the door open when it swung wide. Her teacher took tiny little hops like a toddler who needs to go to the bathroom, wringing her hands and smiling more than seemed possible for that face.

"Oh, oh, oh," said Ms. Schweinbein.

Squirrel Girl relaxed her battle stance. "Um, are you okay?"

"You . . . you . . . you . . ." she said, still hopping.

Squirrel Girl looked to Tippy-Toe, who shrugged.

"You're Squirrel Girl!" the woman shouted, and then began to squeal like a teapot.

The neighbors' porch light came on again.

"Hey, yes, yes I am," Squirrel Girl said. "Do you mind if I come in?"

"Please!" Ms. Schweinbein said, taking those tiny steps backward now. "Come in, come in!"

Squirrel Girl darted inside while scoping out her surroundings for any sign of a trap. The living room was small, furnished with a single table, lamp, and recliner. It all looked *normal*.

Except for the smell. Now that she was inside, the smell of animal was so strong, her eyes watered.

"Your tail is ah-*mazing*," Ms. Schweinbein said.

"Um . . . thank you."

"How did you know? How did you know to come here?"

"Well . . . I . . ."

"Did you get my letter? You must have gotten my letter! I sent it care of the Shady Oaks Neighborhood Council, but I never thought you'd actually get it!"

"Wait. Are you—"

"Hannah Schweinbein! I AM YOUR BIGGEST FAN!"

"Oh, wow," Squirrel Girl said. Tippy-Toe made a coughing noise that was her attempt to disguise squirrel laughter.

Ms. Schweinbein ran into the next room and came back with what looked a brown tea cozy with doll eyes glued on it. The woman thrust it at Squirrel Girl.

"It's *you*," she said. "In crochet form! I made it!"

Squirrel Girl reached for the little effigy, but Ms. Schweinbein pulled it back.

"It's mine, though," she said, clutching the doll to her chest.

"It's pretty cool," Squirrel Girl said, all her attention on her surroundings for any sign of what was really going on here. The idea that Ms. Schweinbein was both a superfan of Squirrel Girl and a super-not-fan of Doreen Green was super-weird. There had to be hidden cameras or something. Was there a show that pulled pranks on Super Heroes?

Ms. Schweinbein was talking. ". . . so when I saw you online with the squirrels and the hero stuff and the tail and the leaping I thought, she loves animals just like I do and thinks doing good is good and is also so nice and cool, I thought I just had to come to Shady Oaks, and when I did, I saw you for real! I moved here you know, just recently, and I saw you out leaping through the trees, like, a few weeks ago and I wanted to call out a greeting or a 'Hey there, good job' or something, but I was too shy and . . ."

While she spoke, a blur of something moved in Squirrel Girl's periphery. It'd been pale, fast, and low to the ground, tiny steps clicking against the tile. Squirrel Girl inched down the hall toward where it'd gone, Ms. Schweinbein following behind without a pause in her monologue. Squirrel Girl peeked into a room.

There was a chicken. An actual, real chicken. It raised an orange foot and froze, looking at Squirrel girl with one wide yellow eye as if it was surprised to be discovered.

"Chicken," Squirrel Girl said.

"Oh, I know you're friendly," said Ms. Schweinbein, "and I shouldn't have been scared to talk to you but—"

"No," Squirrel Girl said, pointing at the bird. "*Chicken.* There is a chicken in your house."

Ms. Schweinbein spun around.

"Mrs. Bubs!" Ms. Schweinbein cried, rushing to the bird. "Upstairs is not for chickens! How did you get out?"

The woman bundled up the animal and hurried down a stairway.

"I'll be right ba-ack," she sang out. "Just a se-cond. . . ."

When Ms. Schweinbein opened a door at the base of the stairs, the animal smell wasn't just strong. It was robust. It was undeniable. It was superhuman. Downstairs, underground, the air was thick with dirt, water, grass, manure, and fur.

Also something began to bleat.

Ms. Schweinbein jogged back up the stairs, out of breath and smiling. She shrugged. "Chickens! What are you going to do?"

"Ms. Schweinbein—" Squirrel Girl said.

"Call me Hannah," Ms. Schweinbein said.

"Okay, uh, Hannah," Squirrel Girl said. "Don't take this the wrong way, but do you have some kind of experimental animal lab in the basement?"

Ms. Schweinbein's expression clouded, and her eyes shifted down. "Um," she said. "It . . . um . . . it isn't a lab exactly."

She looked like a little girl who had sneaked a frog home in her pocket. Squirrel Girl took a deep breath. She was suddenly the adult here, and her teacher was being naughty.

"I'm going down," Squirrel Girl said.

"Okay," Ms. Schweinbein squeaked.

Squirrel Girl jumped. Ms. Schweinbein followed. Not jumping, though.

The basement floor was covered in dirt. It had to be pretty deep, because one corner was growing alfalfa or something. There was a big plastic trough of water in the center and sun lamps in every corner. Mounted to the ceiling, a large fan slowly turned. And there were animals. A dog, a goat, two pigs, and a handful of chickens in cages. Mrs. Bubs peered out through the chicken wire.

"So it's kind of a farm," Ms. Schweinbein said.

"This is SO cool," Squirrel Girl said, crouching to pet the goat.

Ms. Schweinbein brightened. "I'm so glad you think so! I knew we both love animals!"

"I didn't even know you could do this in basements," Squirrel Girl said. "Why don't more people do this in basements?"

"Well," Ms. Schweinbein said, "it's not exactly . . . you know, legal."

"That's not good, then."

"I know. But I love them so much. And I need them. They keep me sane. You don't know how terrible my day job is."

"Look, Hannah, this is normally the kind of thing that I stop," Squirrel Girl said.

"Animal farms?"

"No. Criming. Law breaking."

Ms. Schweinbein sniffed. Her eyes glistened.

"But the thing is," Squirrel Girl said, "I think you can figure this out on your own."

"I can?"

"Yes," Squirrel Girl said. "But you are going to have to do something. Move them, move you, I don't know. You just can't keep a barnyard in a basement, can you?"

Ms. Schweinbein shrugged. "I guess not," she said.

A brief but loud sound of flatulence echoed against the basement's cement walls. Ms. Schweinbein sighed. "That was the goat. She has gas, poor dear."

Squirrel Girl put her hands on her hips. It was a little difficult to feel heroic around farting farm animals, but she was doing her best. "I will let you care for your flatulent goat, then, Hannah. For I have evildoers to root out of hiding!"

Squirrel Girl was up the basement stairs and almost out of

the house before Ms. Schweinbein came chasing after her. "Wait! I've got an idea for you."

Squirrel Girl paused, her hand on the doorknob. She did, in fact, have evildoers to root out of hiding. But Doreen Green knew how it felt to raise your hand and hope and hope that your teacher would call on you so you could share your idea. The fair thing would be to ignore Hannah as Hannah had ignored Doreen. But that would not be the *heroic* thing.

Squirrel Girl took her hand off the door handle. "Tell me," she said.

Ms. Schweinbein grinned. "Are you hunting Dog-Lord and Mistress Meow?"

"Well . . . yeah, sorta," said Squirrel Girl. "Do you know anything about that?"

"Human-animal hybrids?" The teacher's eyes still glistened, but no longer from sadness. "That's the dream. I subscribe to *Hybrid Lover* magazine, so I know that A.I.M. used to experiment with hybrids, but they're out of that game now. Whoever created them, that's no mom-and-pop operation. That's big-time." She shrugged. "Um, that's all I've got, I guess. Sorry. I just really wanted to help you!"

She stared at Squirrel Girl so adoringly, stars seemed to twinkle in her eyes.

"Hannah, I've got to say, you're not what I expected," said Squirrel Girl. "And you know what? I bet there are people around you—say, at your workplace, for instance, wherever that might be—who are not what you expect either. Maybe be nice to them? Like, super-nice? For me?"

Ms. Schweinbein nodded, but she was still so starry-eyed, Squirrel Girl wasn't sure how much of that had soaked in.

She waved as she bounded away, feeling just a tad grumpy. This Doreen Green problem was just something else that Squirrel Girl couldn't fix with a quick punch. She sighed.

And then she laughed.

"Chickens in the basement," she said.

Tippy-Toe had climbed onto her shoulder as she raced across rooftops.

"Chek-tita," said Tippy-Toe.

"What's that? You're wondering what other basements hide?"

The squirrel sneezed in a way that meant, *Yes indeed, ma'am, I sure am.*

20

E-MAIL

TO: [Undisclosed Recipients]

DATE: Today

SUBJECT: RE: The Creatures that Stalk Our Halls

Please disregard the previous e-mail below. Mistress Meow and Dog-Lord will no longer be among us due to some extremely aggravating heroing. Related note: I am in a bad mood so don't talk to me today.

xoxo,

BOSS

TO: [Undisclosed Recipients]

DATE: Friday

SUBJECT: The Creatures that Stalk Our Halls

If you see the canine or the feline hybrid in our secret base, don't shoot at them with your plasma guns! Give them a hug! If you do try to shoot them, you might end up our next mauling victim. HAH! "MALL"-ING? That's crazy what with the mall and all, right? ;)

But, Boss! you ask, How can we tell the difference between people in our base that need to be shot and those that shouldn't be shot? These genetic monstrosities aren't in uniform!

Yes indeed! You just keep on shooting people out of uniform! BUT . . . and this is a big BUT (HA! big butt . . .), FUR IS NOW A UNIFORM! Isn't that incredible? Natural fur, that is. Don't be skinning your neighbor's pets for comfortable new slacks! Because we'll shoot you!

Yes, I know that Larry in Tanks and Siphoning appears to be covered in "natural fur," but actually he's just really hairy. When I say "natural," I mean "genetically merged with animal DNA." So sorry, Larry, no free pass for you! Everyone, if Larry's ever out of uniform, feel free to shoot him! Same goes for if he betrays us! (Hi, Larry! Don't betray us!)

A note about food. We all love food! And the food in our cafeteria is the best food! BUT! (Another BIG BUT!) Unless you are me or Barry, our beastly compatriots outrank you. They get first choice at the buffet line. If you push in front of them or take their food, they WILL bite you. Like, probably a lot of times! You might die! I'm okay if they eat you, frankly! So be smart!

BOSS OUT! 👍

P.S. I have reconsidered. If you see the hybrids in the base, DON'T try to give them a hug. Don't give anyone a hug. We are a 100 percent hug-free workplace.

This e-mail message may contain confidential material. If you are not an intended recipient, please delete this file from your computer, then throw your computer into the ocean, then row yourself as far away as you can.

21

SHADY OAKS/LISTLESS PINES COMMUNITY FRIENDBOOK GROUP

Yo yo yo slick with sociable medias!!!!! The hashtag Chester Yard Mall™ grand opening is just two days away! ;D ;D ;D ;D Lol get rekt m8. Join us this Saturday at high noon when we open our doors for the first time. 👍👍👍👍👍👍👍👍👍👍👍 What groovy shocking surprises AND HASHTAG GREAT GROOVY DEALS await inside??? YO!!!!

Every1ne remember: opening day is also hashtag election day! Take our meme-a-tubular poll. Which far out animal do you think should be our hashtag mall mascot? ;P

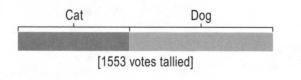

[1553 votes tallied]

Frankie
Some creepy cat thing scratched up my car! I never liked cats before, but now I hate them!

LIKE • COMMENT • UNFOLLOW

Beau Yeah well cats probably hate you too!

Frankie Jump in the lake, jerkwad!

Beau Same to you, gorseface!

Frankie Um

Beau I meant horseface

Erin I saw that cat beast on the news! Creeeeeepy.

William It's dog propaganda! No way some cat monster randomly appears days before the mascot election. They're trying to scare you away from voting!

Earl I'm on Team Dog and I know lots of people on Team Dog and I promise you none of us made a cat monster in order to sway your vote. Vote dog because dogs RULE!

Cyndee No it was Team Cat that made the cat beast! My brother-in-law's best friend is friends with a cop and he said that Team Cat is tricking everyone into thinking Team Dog did it so that people will sympathize with Team Cat.

Penny Well I'm on Team Cat and that's all lies! You are a lying liar and so is your brother-in-law's best friend's cop friend!

Cyndee Team Cat thinks police are liars! You saw! Dogs are the team of law and order!

Matthew
Someone spray-painted dog faces all over our house!

LIKE • COMMENT • UNFOLLOW

Carson Someone painted cat FECES all over OUR house!

> **Penny** Oh yeah? How can you tell it was cat feces and not dog feces?

>> **Carson** They painted a big arrow pointing at it with the words "These are cat feces"

>>> **Penny** Wow. I mean, I guess you've gotta admire the forethought.

Sasha
Listless Pines punks drive their noisy trucks through our neighborhood and shout awful stuff at people. Awful!

LIKE · COMMENT · UNFOLLOW

Inna
Am I the only one who thinks this mall might actually be Hydra?

LIKE · COMMENT · UNFOLLOW

> **Cyndee** You're probably on Team Cat and just trying to scare everyone so they'll stay away and won't vote. And you know what? That's even eviler than Hydra. You disgust me. Vote Dog!

Greencowllvro818
A fine shopping mall is the hallmark of a civilized society. I eagerly anticipate many peaceful shopping experiences in the climate-controlled, windowless splendor. Might there even be a fountain of crystal waters? I am hoping with great cause!

LIKE · COMMENT · UNFOLLOW

Jake
Cats are literally spawned from the devil!
LIKE · COMMENT · UNFOLLOW

> **Penny** Dogs are literally demons in fur disguises!

Gladys
This is my last warning. Chester Yard Mall is Hydra for real. I'm telling you do NOT go to that opening day or it will be your last.
LIKE · COMMENT · UNFOLLOW

> **Inna** Okay never mind, I don't want to sound like Gladys the Nutjob. I'm sure Chester Yard Mall isn't really Hydra. Also, go Team Cat!

Ana Sofía shut her computer and pressed her palms to her tired eyes. Too much screen reading. Not enough evidence finding. And so much nastiness! After a few hours online, Ana Sofía was a hop, skip, and a jump from giving up on humanity entirely and locking herself in the attic Emily Dickinson–style—but with the internet. She could totally do Dickinson as long as she had a laptop with a high-speed connection.

But even offline, the tension kept building. At school that day, by seventh period the teachers had given up and let the students talk through class: about Mistress Meow and Dog-Lord, the contest, and the polling that showed Team Cat was behind. Even the weather seemed to be held tight in the grip of anticipation. No wind, no sun, gray clouds solid as a Vibranium shield, each day holding its breath and waiting, waiting for something to happen. The stillness raised goose bumps on her arms.

Her phone buzzed.

DOREEN

> Hey just watched 3 squirrels imitate how humans dance and OMGosh 🐿 😊 Can hardly breathe. K anyway ur the awesomest Doreen out

Humanity in general might be a lost cause for all she knew, but Doreen Green was not. She was someone worth fighting for. If only Ana Sofía could be certain about this stupid mall. Chester Yard Mall. Again, that name seemed so strange to her.

On a whim, she opened her laptop back up and went to a site that decoded anagrams. She typed:

CHESTER YARD MALL

And got dozens of variations.

THERMALLY SACRED

HYDRATES ARM CELL

ALCHEMY LARD REST

Ugh. Useless. She was about to shut her laptop again when her eye caught one word.

SECRET

Her skin danced with goose bumps. A word pair. She took out a pencil and paper and began to play with the remaining letters. If she left off "Mall" and just rearranged "Chester Yard" she got:

SECRET HARDY

Wait! Rearrange "hardy" into "hydra."
Chester Yard Mall = Secret Hydra Mall.
"What the crap!" Ana Sofía said aloud, jumping to her feet. "Secret Hydra Mall? ¡No lo puedo creer!"
They were barely even trying to hide. They were toying with everyone, as confident as bullies, as careless as big huge jerks.
Ana Sofía pulled on her battle socks—the thick gray merino wool ones with reinforced heel and toe. She wasn't going to be able to solve this mystery entirely from a laptop. It was time to go into the field and kick up some dust.

22

TIPPY-TOE

I gathered the team. Word had been getting around the squirrel community that we couldn't get into the basement of a human building. If we had a mind to enter, nothing should keep out squirrels. Nothing. I heard Pattersnip's daughter Miggy-Moo ask her mother what would happen if she got locked in a squirrel-proof house. Pattersnip told her there was no such thing as "squirrel-proof," but Miggy wasn't convinced. I didn't think Pattersnip was either.

The family depends on me to keep it safe. Knock me out with goose down if I fail them.

And so it was that Squirrel Team Six was lined up along the border of the empty lot facing the Chester Yard Mall parking lot. We took a moment, posing with tails lifted to the breeze, as if heroic music were playing in the background, like in those war movies I sometimes watch at Doreen's. I don't mind a little drama, when there's opportunity.

I caught wind of a discarded gumdrop on the pavement nearby, but I didn't even dive for it. I was *that* committed to holding the pose.

"They sapped over Chomp Style's gnaw-spot already," said Fuzz Fountain Cortez, eyeing the freshly cemented spot in the wall where we made our entrance the last time.

Chomp Style grunted, and we all knew he meant it would be no trouble to make another one.

"What is it, boy? What is it?" Speedo Strutfuzz said. Sir Woof was pawing the ground, whining, wagging his tail. Speedo acted like this was language, and maybe it was.

"Sir Woof smells someone," said Speedo. "A human nearby. Weed-lurking."

I twitched my tail at the team, and we spread out, Speedo and Sir Woof taking point. The weeds were so high I could barely jump to their tips. Once I could fully smell the human, my tail twitched in recognition.

"Ana Sofía?" Cortez asked.

Nestled between two trees with a blanket over her shoulders and head, Ana Sofía sat on the ground, tapping keys on her computer.

I poked my head up over the back of the computer screen.

"Hey," I said.

"Eee!" she squeaked. I waved.

"Tippy!" she said. "You totally freaked me out!"

"Sorry," I said, doing my best to make a sign in the hand language she and Doreen use. It reminded me of Tailspeak, which is also a silent language, unlike Chitterspeak. But like all humans minus one, Ana Sofía can't understand Chitterspeak. Or Tailspeak. "What are you doing here?"

"Yeah, I got the 'sorry,' but the rest I'm going to have to guess is a question about why I'm hiding out here with a computer?"

I nodded.

"Well, see," she said, "this is just close enough to tap the mall's administrative Wi-Fi. If I can log onto that locally, I might be able to grant myself access to whatever databases or systems they're using and get definite proof on how this mall is evil. Except the only thing even on their system is, like, stupid HVAC and property-management tools."

She pointed to the screen of her computer. I scampered onto her shoulder to get a look.

"That's a map of the mall," she said. "But what are you all doing here? I mean, beyond, you know, just being in nature like squirrels do. Is Doreen with you?"

The lines of the map showed what the mall might look like if it had no roof and you were flying over it. I felt dizzy trying to get oriented. Squirrel maps aren't so flat and bird's-eye dependent. And they use smell more than sight. But eventually I located where on the map the room with the floor-door probably sat. I tapped a claw on the spot.

"That's the Victor's Secret store," Ana Sofía said.

I tapped again, right on the spot in the back room of the store where the floor-door was.

"What is—" She started pecking at the keys. "Is that—"

I waited. She typed and new things appeared and disappeared on the screen.

"There's a door in there," she said. "In the floor. And it has way more security than any other door. You want to get in?"

I nodded.

She tapped and swiped at her computer. "I think . . . ugh . . . Just a second . . . Nope. I thought I could open it for you from here, but it won't let me."

I hopped down from the computer. I had hoped finding Ana Sofía here would provide us with a safer way to get in than Squirrel Team Six's Covert Move Gamma: Wrecking and Entering, but it looked like the door was "human-proof," too.

"Wait!" Ana Sofía said, her screen flashing. "Someone is going in the door now! Maybe I can—"

She typed so fast, it sounded like a dozen squirrels scampering across glass.

"Mudwhistles!" she said, balling her hands into fists. "I thought I had it, but the best I could do was redefine the closing parameters to one-point-seven-seven meters instead of one-point-eight."

I twitched a whisker in confusion.

"I can't open or close it," she said. "All I could do was make the door think it's all the way closed when it isn't. They might not even notice, the gap is so small. Just a crack."

I laughed, and I think Ana Sofía recognized the way my tail moved as something we do when we're happy.

"Oh," she said. "Is that good?"

I patted a bit of the sock that covered her calf and gave her a claws-up.

"A crack is all we need," I said.

True to her word, when we broke back into the mall and arrived at the floor-door, it was open. Or open enough, anyway. It was a tight fit for Big Sissy Hotlegs, but she's used to scamper holes made for more petite squeaks.

A narrow set of stairs led down from the floor-door to a hall-way lined with human-size lockers. At the end of the hall, an archway opened into a darkness my squirrel eyes couldn't pierce.

A draft blew in through high wall vents. I glanced at Chive Alpha, who had already seen it. I nodded, and the little squirrel scampered up the wall like a spider. Or a squirrel. A spider-squirrel.[57] In a moment, she was through the metal grating and into the ductwork.

Chomp Style started biting locks off lockers, and Big Sissy Hotlegs popped the doors open.

"Nice weather for a break-in," said Fuzz Fountain Cortez.

---

57 Seriously, have you seen little squirrels in action? I swear gravity doesn't apply to them.

"Like a cool autumn night atop a full hoard," I said.

As Cortez, Chomps, and Sissy tossed the contents of the lockers, I scampered past to the dark end of the hallway. Narrow beams of light crisscrossed in the threshold. Lasers? Like the ones in the floor? I picked up a fallen scrap of paper and tossed it through. Nothing happened. No burning or alarms or anything. Carefully, I put my paw through.

"ORGANISM DETECTED," a robotic voice declared from a speaker on the wall.

I looked back at my team, who had frozen in their tasks and stared at me, wide-eyed.

"WORKER UNKNOWN," the voice continued. "STATE YOUR SECURITY-AUTHORIZED NAME."

Something mechanical within the walls made a clunking noise, and a panel slid open. A weapon-looking thing extended through the hole.

"PROVIDE YOUR SECURITY-AUTHORIZED NAME WITHIN FIVE SECONDS OR BE DESTROYED," the voice commanded.

My teeth clenched. I do not take kindly to threats of destruction.

"My name is Tippy-Toe," I said. I scampered up the wall to perch on the barrels. "And my authorization is JUSTICE!"

I bit through the housing at the base of the barrel and tore it from the wall.

"'CHK-CHKKA-CHT' IS NOT A SECURITY-AUTHORIZED NAME," the voice continued. "YOU WILL NOW BE DESTROYED."

Three more panels opened, revealing new weapons. I zigged and zagged out of there as beams of burning light erupted around me. My team was already waiting for me at the top of the stairs, their mouths full of stuff they grabbed before they ran. Cortez glanced up at a vent, and I knew she was telling me that Chive Alpha was still in there.

A ball of fire bursted from inside a vent.

"HOT HOT HOT HOT," Chive Alpha shouted as she ran past us and through the gap in the door. Cortez and I followed, locker-room lasers firing at our tails with a *fzzzzzz fzzzzz*.

We fled Victor's Secret and darted through the mall. Men's voices were shouting. We didn't turn to look.

We scurried so fast through the passage Chomp Style made in the mall wall that our faces were in the bums of the squirrels in front. Like we practiced, we scattered in the parking lot, no straight line to follow, each of us disappearing into adjoining lots.

We met up again at Ana Sofía's camp. Chive Alpha was steaming in a puddle, and she sighed.

"I hope she's okay," Ana Sofía said. "She didn't seem to want my help."

"Chive Alpha?" I asked. "You okay?"

"Peaches and nuts," she said. "But that thingie burned off

some of my bum fur. If Chomp Style has any spare underpants, I'll take them."

"Earned your ham-pants today, I think," said Big Sissy Hotlegs through a full mouth, her cheeks stuffed round.

"Maybe I'll change my name to Little Sissy Hotbum," said Chive Alpha.

"NO!" we all said.

Not that it wasn't a right decent squirrel name, but we couldn't take another change. I patted her tiny head. She moaned, but her tail flicked a smile. The rest of the team emptied the loot from their cheeks, piling it up at Ana Sofía's feet. She sorted through it, seemingly unconcerned by squirrel spit. Doreen chose her BHFF wisely.

"Ooh," she said. "This looks incriminating. And this—wow, Tippy. No smoking gun, but enough that I think I'm ready to tell Squirrel Girl that we've officially got ourselves a Hydra problem."

WHAT SQUIRREL TEAM SIX STOLE:

- tin of Red Skull–brand brand chewing tobacco
- pamphlet titled *Obedience & Hatred: The Foundations of Success*
- two sticks of Barnyard Chicken–flavor chewing gum
- a burned sock
- Food Heap Cafe rewards card, two punches remaining

- one signed photograph of a donkey or small horse named Fig
- a dead beetle (possibly was already in Chomp Style's cheeks before the raid)
- a receipt for twenty-five pounds of lard and a cowboy hat
- cheddar-flavored mouthwash (travel size)
- one "No Evil" kit containing noseplug, earplugs, and a mouthplug (eyeplugs missing)
- gardenia seeds
- Serpent-B-Gone–brand snake repellent
- a piece of blueberry waffle (also possibly previously in Chomp Style's cheeks)
- one baggie of Chafe Master–brand rubber-suit powder
- and a flyer for a suspicious party

D-DAY VICTORY BASH!

In the Chester Yard Mall
Secret Basement Lair
12 Midnight after D-day

We've worked hard toward opening day (shout-out to the basement construction crew for keeping it on the DL!), and now it's time to PARTAY with your bros!! The midnight after we successfully launch Hate Initiative Beta, come let loose. Karaoke! Darts! Bobbing for apples! Death poetry! Belching contest! Torture tips! Plus . . . a special musical performance by Garry's pop band, Your Racist Uncle!

UNLIMITED TACO BAR!
Whenever you eat one taco,
TWO MORE TACOS
TAKE ITS PLACE!

23

ANA SOFÍA

ANA SOFÍA

> I'm in the tree house

Ana Sofía turned on the tree house lantern to shove away the heavy, ominous feeling of that night, a night she now was certain lurked with Hydra agents. She sat on the weather-worn boards with her back to the thin wall and waited. And tried to ignore the buzzing in her belly and that generally sick feeling that assured her she should just run away from any social encounter and wouldn't it be nicer to not have any friends whatsoever and move into that sequestered attic she'd been dreaming about?

Yes, she believed Hydra was right in her own neighborhood. And yes, she was more worried about having a conversation with a friend.

She even started to get up, but Tippy-Toe chose just that

moment to hop onto her lap. A squirrel was so much lighter than a dog or a cat, but she felt that familiar comfort of a pet—a small, fuzzy, warm, alive thing that chooses to be near you. It felt like an honor. She lightly petted her back, the fur tickling her fingertips. Tippy-Toe's five squirrel friends from the mall break-in gathered around, too. One of them set to arranging their treasures on the tree house floor, the flyer in the center.

It didn't take long. Within moments of receiving the text, Doreen leaped out of her second-story bedroom window and hopped across her backyard lawn and up through the tree house window.

"Hey—oh, hi, everybody! Wow, is this a party?" she said.

Or at least, Ana Sofía thought that was what she said. Doreen had signed some of the words. Ana Sofía adjusted the tree house's battery-powered lantern to more fully hit Doreen's face.

"Doreen," said Ana Sofía, steeling her nerves, "I think the new mall really is being built by the real Hydra, and my reasons are—"

"Oh no!" said Doreen. "And you said that Hydra is the evilest of evil. That means we've got to stop them like A-SAP!"

"Wait, say that again?" Ana Sofía said in case she'd misunderstood.

Doreen repeated herself.

"So you believe me?" said Ana Sofía.

"Of course I do!" said Doreen. "If you say it's Hydra, then it must be Hydra. Oh wait, I interrupted you, didn't I? Sorry! I think I'm always doing stuff like that. Interrupting. Being difficult. Crap, sorry. You probably wanted to show me how you figured it out, and I really do want to know."

"Oh! Okay." Ana Sofía had imagined it might take some convincing. She'd prepared herself for the chance of laughter. She hadn't once run through in her mind what to do if Doreen just believed her outright. But she presented her discovery of the anagram as well as the evidence the squirrels found in the mall basement and her reasons why each item pointed to Hydra.

"So . . . that's what I think." Ana Sofía paused.

"You're the awesomest detective friend I ever had," said Doreen, signing, her expression glowing, her signs big and empathic and full of emotion.

Ana Sofía blushed. "I guess."

"So why does Hydra want to build a mall anyway?" asked Doreen. "Like, what is their evil plan?"

"Honestly I have no idea," said Ana Sofía. "I guess we should tell the Avengers and they should come take care of it, right? Now that this is legit evil mastermind-y Hydra?"

"Yes. Totally. I'll do that."

Ana Sofía nodded. They were both quiet for a time. The squirrels seemed to communicate with each other and then began gathering up the evidence to store in whatever way squirrels do.

"So here's a funny thing," Doreen said when the squirrels were gone. "I thought my English teacher was a Super Villain, but turns out she's just easily annoyed with me."

"Schweinbein?" said Ana Sofía. "Yeah, I looked into her

when she transferred mid-semester and figured out she came here because she's a huge Squirrel Girl fan."

"I should have told you my weird suspicions! It would have saved me so much time!"

"Me too," said Ana Sofía, and then, though she hadn't once pre-run through this conversation in her head, she dared to say, "But you laughed at me."

"I did?"

Ana Sofía nodded. "I told you I thought maybe the mall really was Hydra and you laughed. That's a thing for me. I really, really don't like it when people laugh at me."

"Dude, I'm so sorry. For real. I don't even remember. I probably thought you were kidding. But clearly you were right."

"It's okay. Also, when I didn't understand you and you said 'Never mind'—I know you didn't mean it like a big deal, but just thought you should know, that's a thing that . . . *hurts* me. It's like you're saying that repeating something I wasn't able to hear the first time isn't worth the trouble. That because I'm deaf, *I'm* not worth the trouble."

"Oh, wow. I am so, so sorry."

"It's okay." She gulped. This was getting way too reveal-y for her personal comfort, and she smiled like it was nothing. "I'm just weird about some things, I guess."

"No, that's *not* a weird thing, that makes total sense."

Ana Sofía's smile felt more real. It wasn't nothing. It *was* a big deal to her. What a relief that her friend took it seriously.

"And anyway . . ." Doreen held up her flattened hand. "Hello! I'm weird about so many things!"

Ana Sofía lifted her hand and allowed a high five, even though the concept of high fives was one of those things she was weird about. "From now on we talk, okay? Me too. Even though conversations like this are strangely super-hard for me. Even if our thoughts are embarrassing."

"*Especially* if they're embarrassing!" Doreen laughed. "Oh, sorry, I'm not laughing at you."

"I know," said Ana Sofía. "There's a huge difference."

Suddenly Ana Sofía felt so tired. Sometimes it happened like that, *snap*, and she'd hit the bottom of her ability to keep trying. Reading lips, examining expressions, working so much harder than a hearing person to try to communicate and understand. The miraculous thing was, Doreen seemed to notice immediately.

She took out her phone.

DOREEN

I'll walk you home k?

Ana Sofía nodded, and they texted each other as they walked.

ANA SOFÍA

So that flyer. I think the victory party is supposed to be celebrating the success of whatever hydra is planning to do in shady oaks

DOREEN

Their victory party plan is a little premature imho

ANA SOFÍA

Right. But I think d-day is mall opening day. And that's the day after tomorrow

DOREEN

I'm really hoping d stands for donuts. Or dinosaurs. Oh man why don't I get to regularly fight dinosaurs? Or ride them at least? Moon Girl gets all the fun

ANA SOFÍA

All the PR pushing to get people there opening day I think hydra has something big planned

DOREEN

And bad. I'm guessing it's bad

ANA SOFÍA

Since it's hydra that would be a logical assumption

Also I found a thread on a baddit forum of supposed mall employees and one literally said "saturday is d-day and it's gonna be bad"

DOREEN

Don't worry I'll tell the avengers

So we promised to share embarrassing thoughts.
You got any?

Escorted through the dark neighborhood by a squad of furry rodents, they shared embarrassing thoughts all the way to Ana Sofía's house.[58]

---

58 Her embarrassing thoughts included daydreams she used to have about being friends with Thor, and mine were mostly about engaging in epic battles with Thor-size acorn weevils.

24

TEXT MESSAGES

SQUIRREL GIRL

Hey Avenger pals! So my best human and squirrel friends believe it really is real Hydra for real setting up a mall for bad guy reasons. Can some of you come and, you know, avenger them out of my neighborhood?

IRON MAN

Sorry can't help now. I'm in space fighting Thanos.

BLACK WIDOW

I'd love to help. But I'm also in space. Fighting Thanos.

CAPTAIN MARVEL

Literally in space rn fighting Thanos

SPIDER-MAN

So am I! I'm totally in outer space! Like the actual real outer space that's not on earth but in the sky with the stars not even kidding!

Also fighting Thanos too. Not just sightseeing. Contributing like a team member

Making real legit contributions so probably officially an Avenger now or something

ROCKET

You know how you sound, right? Like, you can hear yourself after you hit send and are capable of feeling shame?

SPIDER-MAN

. . .

yes

ROCKET

Also I'm in space fighting Thanos

GROOT

I AM GROOT.

ROCKET

Yeah, Groot, she knows you're in space fighting Thanos too, where else would you be?

GROOT

I AM GROOT.

ROCKET

Solid point, I stand corrected.

WINTER SOLDIER

I'm actually pretty free this week if anyone needs help clearing out a Hydra cell. Or you know traveling to space to fight Thanos.

SQUIRREL GIRL

Oh dang winter soldier i didn't mean to bother you with this group text never mind pretend you never saw this ha ha

THOR

Were I not at this moment in the black nether battling the foul monster Thanos I would fly to thy side!

SPIDER-MAN

I just don't want you to think I'm only tagging along or anything. Because I'm actually physically fighting Thanos. Like right now. Or any second now.

ROCKET

Please stop. You're making me laugh so much it's getting hard to fight Thanos

SPIDER-MAN

Is it possible to delete texts once they're sent

GROOT

I AM GROOT.

ROCKET

Yeah, time travel is your only option, and time travel ALWAYS works out great for everyone, so good luck with that

IRON MAN

Wow, Squirrel Girl, here you are again asking for my help! I guess we must really be "advice buddies" as you said. Maybe even "pards"!

SQUIRREL GIRL

For sure! I want to be there for you iron man whenever you need a friend. Sometimes I feel so sad when I think about you and how hard it must be to be just the guy in a robot suit when like captain marvel is around and just soooo powerful?

CAPTAIN MARVEL

Dying

IRON MAN

I appreciate the friendship offer, Squirrel Girl, but I think I've been unclear. I see our relationship as the wise and powerful battle-scarred soldier mentoring the novice fighter

SQUIRREL GIRL

You are the sweetest! I have seen a few battles tbh but I don't think you need to call yourself a novice. Black widow says you really are a real hero and I believe in you too!

CAPTAIN MARVEL

This is my favorite conversation ever

BLACK WIDOW

Agreed. Rethinking my anti-group text policy

SPIDER-MAN

Dude Tony I so know how you feel right now

IRON MAN

I believe you, and yet I find little comfort in that

CAPTAIN AMERICA

Everyone off this delightful group text. Time to focus on fighting Thanos in space

SPIDER-MAN

Aye aye Cap

SQUIRREL GIRL

K luck in space fighting Thanos! No prob I'll take
care of hydra!

WINTER SOLDIER

So I remain available

SQUIRREL GIRL

Um yeah?

WINTER SOLDIER

I stand ready, willing, able, and actually quite
eager to permanently dispose of any Hydra
agents in your vicinity and anyone else that
might get in the way of my awesome metal arm
of justice

SQUIRREL GIRL

It's probably not hydra after all thanks k bye!

25

LIZARD BRAIN

*T*he Grand High Sub-Lieutenant of Hydra operations in Greater Shady Oaks and Lesser Union County first heard the phrase "lizard brain" from his oma.

He had come home early from kindergarten one day because everyone in his class, including the teacher, had gotten "sick." Everyone except him.

"Vhat kind of sick vas it, boy?" his oma had asked. She had an accent where she pronounced *w* like *v*. He liked it.

"The kind when everybody stabs each other with crayons and screams. That kind," he said.

"Ah," she said, as if she had seen it before. "Ze lizard brain."

At first he had thought "lizard brain" was the name of a sickness, like mad cow disease or bird flu—something rare and terrible and animal-adjacent. But after a riot in his play group, repeated lunch tray fights in the cafeteria at school, and countless days when the kids with desks near his curled up and shivered, he realized "lizard brain" was something *everyone* had: a core part of themselves that needed to either fight or run away. And occasionally, just being near him brought that out of people.

"You are special," his oma told him the day he returned home after being expelled from middle school. His lab partner had nearly burned down the building, and he had also been blamed as a co-conspirator, though all he'd done was watch and laugh. Life and the unfairness of it![59]

"Because of the lizard brain stuff?" he said. He had not been fully convinced of his special-ness. It was entertaining to watch people try to hurt each other, but he was only ever a spectator, strangely invisible to the people during their brief primal bouts in his presence.

"I haf made you some-zing," his grandmother said, handing him a bundle.

He unfolded a leather jumpsuit, stitched together from the hides of reptilian animals.

"It is a BEAST suit. A BATTLE suit," she said.

"For me?"

"For ze Lizard Brain," she said. "For ze man you vill become."

Many years later, the Grand High Sub-Lieutenant of Hydra operations in Greater Shady Oaks and Lesser Union County wiped away the condensation building up on the inside of his

---

59 Uh, going out on a limb here and saying if your lab partner tries to burn down the school and you just watch and laugh, then, yeah, that's a problem.

shower stall. He had finally become that man his oma had seen. The Lizard Brain. And he demanded all who served him recognize that fact.

This was no ordinary shower. It was the Hydra Slough-Catcher 2000, designed to collect what was special about him, the very thing that made people lose their minds—his *musk*. Tubes snaked away from the drain of the shower and carried the nectar of his musk into giant titanium storage tanks.[60] And from those tanks his minions synthesized the gas that would allow him to share his Very Special Aroma with a larger audience. And it would all begin with the upcoming mall massacre.

Hydra had made it possible, of course. Sweet, sweet Hydra. They had been the ones to identify the special pheromone he exuded that short-circuited people's brains. They had taken him in as a teenager, trained him to control when and how much musk he secreted.

When people breathed in his musk, their higher brain functions shut down. Their threat response amplified. People became primal. Raw. Reduced to the basic survival instincts that lizards possess in their tiny ancient brains. When under his power, people would either run away screaming or tear each other apart. His odor was power. His sweat was like gold. That is, if gold was a thing that made people go bonkers and try to kill each other.

---

60 So his musk is, like, BO or his sweat or body oils or something. Can I just say, GROSS.

Which, he supposed, it was.

He chuckled at his own thoughts. He was a funny guy, and he enjoyed a good laugh.

Someone tapped on the glass.

He wiped away the fog from the shower again. Regular Shallow Sub-Lieutenant Barry peered back. Barry wasn't his real name. These names were all assigned at the beginning of field duty. Barry glanced down at Lizard Brain's only article of clothing—black swim briefs—and then quickly away. Lizard Brain had had them modeled after Namor the Sub-Mariner's tighty shorts. He felt certain they looked quite fetching.

"What's up, Barry, my man?"

"The scientists say the rate of musk retrieval is nearing zero, Grand High Sub-Lieutenant, sir."

Lizard Brain smiled patiently. "Try that again, Barry."

Barry took a deep breath. "The mad scientists say you've showered long enough, er, Lizard Brain, sir."

Yes. That was who he was. Who he had become. The honor bestowed upon him by his grandmother so many years ago. The mantle he had finally taken up.

Also, for practical purposes, "Lizard Brain" was much simpler than, say, "Grand High Sub-Lieutenant of Hydra operations in Lesser Union County."

"Oh, you know how the mad scientists are," said Lizard Brain, pushing open the stall door. He liked buddying up to the lesser agents, complaining about management and such. He was certain it made them more devoted to him.

"Mad, sir?" Barry asked. He held out a plush green robe—a little too quickly for Lizard Brain's liking. Almost as if he wanted to cover up the sight of his fetching Namor shorts.

"Yes!" Lizard Brain said, slapping Barry on the back. "Mad!"

"Er . . . they also say it will take longer to distill the gas if the musk-to-water ratio goes beyond one to one thousand."

"I'm sure they do," Lizard Brain said. He had no idea what that meant. He was not the mad scientist of the organization. He was the power. The architect. The brain. The Lizard Brain.

Lizard Brain quizzed Barry about different aspects of the Hate Initiative as they descended from the shower spire. When Barry got something wrong, Lizard Brain bopped him on the nose. It was funny! He wasn't uptight and stuffy, like *some* in this organization. He was a *fun* boss. Weirdly, Barry didn't laugh. No sense of humor, probably. A sense of humor was genetic, Lizard Brain was certain.

In the bunker's command center/dressing room, Lizard Brain shed the robe. He glanced longingly at the patchwork leather suit that hung on a nearby peg. Oma's battle suit. He reached for his dress uniform instead.

Soon it would be time for the battle suit. Soon.

Not until he was fully dressed did Lizard Brain realize he'd forgotten to take off his wet Namor shorts. Barry glanced down at the wetness already seeping through the seat of his pants.

"Warm in here, isn't it, Barry?" said Lizard Brain. Maybe he wanted wet pants. Maybe he liked how they felt. Maybe they were an efficient cooling system.

A screen on the opposite wall flickered to life, resolving into the face of his immediate supervisor. Barry, in the process of retrieving the bathrobe, dove to the floor to get out of camera range. He was frightened of the Grand High Sub-Supervisor for Special Projects. Lizard Brain didn't understand it. The supervisor was a lovely gal, a real go-getter.

"REPORT!" the Grand High Sub-Supervisor bellowed from the screen.

Lizard Brain smiled. "All is going according to plan, Madam Supervisor." He always said those exact words to superior officers, no matter the context. It was one of the first things they taught in the academy—a civility, like saying "Fine, thanks" after someone asks you how you are, even if you're ecstatic or miserable or currently being bitten all over by rabid red ants.[61]

"You have stored sufficient musk to blanket the entire mall?"

"Yes, Madam Supervisor," he said. "Everything we are collecting now is extra. Gravy, you might say."[62]

She raised an eyebrow. "It will be enough to saturate the entire premises?"

"Yes indeedy! We experimented with other delivery systems first. The mad scientists managed to create a stable version of the

---

61 Wait, people are supposed to say "Fine, thanks" all the time? Seems boring, not to mention uninformative, especially if you are being attacked by rabid red ants.
62 *Musk gravy*. I just gagged a little.

musk that could be coated onto objects, like our mall T-shirts. But the effects are minimized, merely irritating those who wear them and making them slightly more violent than normal. To get the whole effect, people need to be saturated with the musk in a closed environment."

"We shall see," she said. "And the resistance?"

"Resistance, madam?"

"The squirrel creature," she said. "As I understand it, her presence was one of the reasons you requested this post."

"Oh yes, the Squirrel Girl," he said. "You know, I studied genetic hybridization in the academy before moving to management. Humanimals are something of a hobby. Dog-Lord and Mistress Meow were a fun find in the old A.I.M. storage facility, not necessary to the plan per se, but definitely adding some pizzazz!"

Since the hybrids he'd been able to get were a cat and dog, he'd chosen those two animals for the mall mascot race. How serendipitous, he realized after, the symmetry of the two beasts, a symbol of constant battle. If he was successful, Shady Oaks and Listless Pines would indeed be fighting like cats and dogs.

"But the squirrel hero defeated them," she said.

"*Pfff.* She did exactly what I wanted her to do—engage them in a destructive, public battle that would make a lot of people angry and stir up fear and hate."

"Toward dogs and cats?"

"Well, yes, and by extension, toward their supporters. These two neighborhoods already disliked each other. It's not difficult to tip that over the line into hatred."

"And does the Squirrel Girl herself present a threat?"

Lizard Brain stifled a laugh. "No, madam. I'm pretty much an expert in animal hybridization; I can say the only combination less threatening than a 'squirrel girl' would be something like a 'mouse baby.'"[63]

"Very well, then," she said. "In two days' time I will be expecting the national news to be using words like 'catastrophe,' 'tragedy,' and 'horror' to describe the opening of your mall."

"Don't worry, I've got it covered," Lizard Brain said.

The Grand High Sub-Supervisor nodded curtly and ended the transmission. Lizard Brain reached to turn off the screen when he noticed a small text message in the lower corner, blinking red.

MMV20

you are so screwed

Lizard Brain narrowed his eyes. Someone named "MMV20" had been hacking texts to his computer from the moment of his transfer to Shady Oaks. At first he'd worried that S.H.I.E.L.D. or some other silly hero initiative had infiltrated the network, but tech support confirmed all traffic was internal to Hydra.

---

63 OMGosh I know he's evil, but that's just rude! Also Mouse Baby sounds amazing!

"MMV20" was likely some bored kid at the academy trolling for fun. Or Barry. Probably Barry.

LIZARDBRAIN

No you are the one who is screwed

MMV20

oh man thats the best you got almost feel sorry for you

LIZARDBRAIN

You haven't even seen my best it is amazing

MMV20

listen i want to see you toasted but for the sake of the organization you need to stop

LIZARDBRAIN

Haters going to hate

MMV20

go dark. pull out. open up shop anywhere else just NOT SHADY OAKS

LIZARDBRAIN

Payers going to pay

And by payer I mean me. I am a payer that is going to pay the piper!

MMV20

> you are hopeless. squirrel girl is going to straight
> up destroy you[64]

The connection dropped. Lizard Brain pushed the keyboard away, feeling grumpier than he usually permitted himself. He checked his pockets and discovered a single Mento. Strawberry— his least favorite. He threw the Mento at the screen.

"Up yours, Em Em Vee Twenty, whoever you are," he said. "No squirrel can destroy me. No girl can destroy me. And definitely no squirrel girl. FOR I AM LIZARD BRAIN! AND I AM MONSTROUS!"

Barry cleared his throat, standing in the doorway. Lizard Brain spun around, a new smile pasted to his face.

"Sorry to disturb you, sir," Barry said. "But your Hot Pockets are ready."

Lizard Brain's fake smile widened into a gleeful grin. Demusking always made him hungry. And how he loved a good Hot Pocket.

---

64 Holy cow, I think I know who this is. A Super Villain I defeated in a previous adventure who somehow escaped S.H.I.E.L.D. custody. Aw, it's really sweet of him if you think about it! I hope he's doing well studying villainy in the Hydra Academy! Sort of.

26

DOREEN

The avengers really can't come?

SQUIRREL GIRL

They're all in space. Fighting Thanos

ANA SOFÍA

D-day is tomorrow

SQUIRREL GIRL

Yeah and no avengers to save the day. Dude what should we do?

ANA SOFÍA

I don't know. ur squirrel girl

SQUIRREL GIRL

Yes I am. I am squirrel girl. i am the hero that says not today evildoers. Not in my neighborhood. You may have terrifying evil plans for tomorrow morning but too bad so sad not gonna happen cuz i will stop you tonight!

so there!

ANA SOFÍA

YES!!!

Tho for real I don't think hydra is something either of us can just take on

SQUIRREL GIRL

But space. Thanos.

ANA SOFÍA

This is hydra

SQUIRREL GIRL

I know

ANA SOFÍA

I'm not sure we can just fight hydra

SQUIRREL GIRL

I know

But what else can we do?

ANA SOFÍA

Fight hydra I guess. Should I contact the squirrel scouts

SQUIRREL GIRL

No

ANA SOFÍA

This is hydra

SQUIRREL GIRL

Yeah this is hydra. They're not ready for hydra

ANA SOFÍA

We're not ready for hydra

SQUIRREL GIRL

Omgosh we're so not ready for hydra but we're so doing this anyway you are the best ever

ANA SOFÍA

I'll ask my dad if I can meet you at the mall

SQUIRREL GIRL

Yeah. I'm nervous. But I'll meet you at the mall in 20. If I can get permission

ANA SOFÍA

Me too. If I can get permission

Doreen slipped her secret secure Squirrel Girl phone into her skirt pocket and walked into the kitchen. Or moseyed, really. Strolled. Meandered. Sooo casual and calm, nothing whatsoever squirrelly about her at all.[65]

"So, hey there, parental units," Doreen said, still über-casual. "Whatcha doing?"

Dor and Maureen were putting together a puzzle of a kitten and a puppy playing together in a box of yarn.

"Why? What's going on?" asked Maureen.

"Hmm? What?" said Doreen. "Nothing. A puzzle, huh? Well, it's not squirrels, but still pretty cute."

Maureen's eyes narrowed. Dor's mouth twitched.

"In all my years, Maureen," he said, "I never thought our daughter would start to lie to us."

"I know, Dor, I know," said Maureen. "To us, of all parents! After all, we're so understanding. And reasonable."

"And adorable," said Dor.

Doreen plopped down into a chair, elbows on the table and her chin on her hands. She had been planning to lie but hadn't even gotten that far yet. Dang it all, she was terrible at this.

"So Tippy-Toe and Ana Sofía figured out that an evil organization is behind the mall and they're planning on doing something awful on opening day, so someone should probably go stop them."

---

65 Except for my huge fluffy beautiful squirrel tail. And superstrong front teeth. And proportional squirrel abilities. And fluency in Chitterspeak.

"Tonight?" asked Maureen.

"Well, yeah," said Doreen. "I mean, it's not a school night."

"What evil organization?" asked Dor.

"Hmmda," Doreen mumbled.

"What was that, angel?" asked Maureen.

"Hydra," Doreen whispered.

Maureen jumped to her feet. "Hydra? Am I to understand that you are asking permission to go out after bedtime to single-handedly fight the most destructive, heartless, hateful, bigoted, sinister world-spanning organization in human history?"

"It's just one tiny branch of Hydra, not like all of it ever," Doreen said. "It's not *that* late, and it's not even a school night.[66] *And* I'm not trying to defeat them alone. Go ahead, ask me, 'You and what army?'"

"She'll say 'My squirrel army,'" Dor whispered.

"Yes, I guessed," said Maureen. She sighed.

"Dang it, when am I going to get to use that line?" said Doreen.

"You're fourteen—" her father started.

"And so I'm too young to take on Hydra even if I do have the proportional strength, speed, and agility of a squirrel?"

Her parents nodded.

"Yeah, you're probably right," said Doreen. "But there's no one else. Like, everyone is literally in space fighting Thanos. And

---

66 Looks like I mentioned the not-a-school-night thing twice. I was feeling desperate.

they didn't ask me to go to space to fight Thanos because, you know, I'm only fourteen, and I'm only Squirrel Girl. . . ."

"Hey now," said her father, "you're not *only* Squirrel Girl. You've never been *only* Squirrel Girl. You're also Doreen Allene Green, and that's someone to be proud of!"

Doreen nodded, and she tried to just let it go, but what he'd said made her chest feel all squeezed and her chin all quivered and her legs all noodle-loose, and she sat down hard in a chair.

"I don't know," she said.

"Know what? What don't you know?"

Now Doreen's nose felt all sniffled. "Lately, it's easier to be Squirrel Girl than to be . . . Doreen Allene Green." And then she sniffed some more, and her eyes felt hot. She took a breath, and the promise she'd made Ana Sofía about talking stuff out made the words inside all hot and liquidy and they just poured out of her.

"School's not going so great with all the homework and no time to do it with all the Super Heroing, and there's a teacher that's always annoyed with me even though she's the one with a secret and illegal barnyard in her basement, and I am part of a group of friends who love Squirrel Girl but kinda overlook Doreen, and Ana Sofía is awesome of course, but it seemed like she was pulling back lately from our friendship and I think I super hurt her feelings without even realizing it by never-minding her, so how do I know how to not, like, permanently damage a best-friendship when I do bad stuff without even realizing, and I think we worked that out, but you know me with friends that don't last unless they're small and furry and, I don't know, like, I feel better and do better when I've got my tail out and I'm talking criminals out of criming or, you know, punching them, and I don't feel fourteen then, I only feel fourteen when I'm Doreen and Doreen doesn't know what in the heck she's doing!"[67]

She cried some. And she felt her parents put their hands on her shoulders, on her head.

"Can I tell you a secret?" Maureen said. "We don't know what we're doing either."

"Well, *yeah*," said Doreen.

They laughed, and Dor cut into the butter pecan cake he'd baked earlier without knowing how much they'd need it now.

"You know you're doing great, right?" said her father, his mouth full of cake. "You know nobody knows what they're doing and we're all just figuring out how to be us as we go along."

"So it's okay that I have no idea how to defeat Hydra so I should just go jump in and figure it out as I go?"

Her parents sighed again.

"Too soon?" said Doreen.

"We worry," said Maureen. "There's no parenting manual for this, no *How to Be a Good Parent to a Super Hero in Twelve Easy Steps*—"

"Ooh, maybe I should write that," said Dor.

It was Doreen's turn to sigh. "There's no *How to Be a Super*

---

67 Look, I'm not complaining, but being fourteen is hard, yo.

Hero When You're Fourteen either. But there's no one else. Someone once said with great power comes great accessibility—no wait, that doesn't sound right. Trust me, it was a good phrase and, like, really inspiring. Anyway, I've got to try. Being Squirrel Girl is the only thing that really makes sense right now. And what if I did nothing and people got hurt tomorrow or even died?"

Her parents exchanged looks. That was a good sign. All this practice talking criminals out of criming had increased her persuasive conversation skills in everyday life!

"I'll be careful, okay?" said Doreen.

"Middle school years are weird," said Maureen. "I was terrified anyone would notice me, and yet I wore a tiger-ears headband every day for, like, a year."

"I formed a rock band," said Dor. "None of us knew how to play our instruments. We didn't realize that until we were onstage in the school talent show."

"But it gets better," said Maureen. "Please be careful and come home safe so that you can see that it does get better."

They hugged. They ate cake.[68]

And then Doreen Green put on the hoodie with the little ears. She laced up her sneakers. She fluffed out her tail. And she ran.

---

68 Hugging + cake is how my family solves 90 percent of our problems. Also popcorn + movies. And sometimes games of crokinole. It's a Canada thing.

27

ANA SOFÍA

*T*here were no security guards at the mall. That was the first thing. The parking lot was empty. The lights were off. The GRAND OPENING banner hung from two ropes over the front doors, twisting in the wind and slapping against the concrete front with an eerie *whump whump*. But if this was a brand-new mall full of merchandise, why weren't there any guards?

Because they're not worried about break-ins, Ana Sofía thought. *Maybe because there is no merchandise, and it's all a hoax. Or maybe because they have other forms of security.*

She hid behind a bush on the empty lot next door and waited for Squirrel Girl to find her. Somehow, she always found her—by smell, she presumed. Ana Sofía was lucky to have made it there at all. Gracias a Dios her mom was working tonight. Her mom held pretty tightly to Mexican cultural norms about curfews and protecting daughters. Before Doreen, Ana Sofía had rarely been permitted to even go to a friend's house. Her dad on the other hand was second-generation Mexican American and was generally more lax. She knew her mom just wanted to protect her, and she generally preferred staying in and playing on her laptop anyway, but the maternal protectiveness was really inconvenient when she was needed to take down a Hydra cell operating out of the local mall.

Guilt gnawed her. She hadn't lied to her dad about her plans, but she had been vague about needing to "meet up with Doreen for a project." She really, really had to try to not get killed or she'd be in so much trouble.

Ana Sofía felt the ground vibrate behind her. She whipped around. Squirrel Girl had just jumped down from a tree and now stood there, fists on hips, outlined in silver moonlight. In bushes and trees behind her, the leaves trembled.

"So you think you can take down Hydra, huh?" Ana Sofía said. "You and what army?"

"This one," Squirrel Girl signed. The shivers in the shadows leaned forward, dozens of blinkless squirrel eyes reflecting back the city lights. Then more and more, a hundred, two hundred, the tree's boughs bending beneath the weight of them, the night's shadows ragged with their shapes, the breeze carried by their breath.

Squirrel Girl doubled over, laughing quietly and saying

something, most likely thanking Ana Sofía for setting up the awesome line. And then she hugged her. Hugs were not Ana Sofía's favorite thing, but Squirrel Girl was in her top five, so she didn't *hate* it.

"You're welcome," she said.

And then without a word they set off across the dark parking lot. Two girls, two hundred squirrels. Tippy-Toe was there, of course, her pink bow a slash of gray-purple in the night. She loped off in front, the five other squirrels from last night surrounding her, running in sync. The rest of the squirrels followed en masse, flowing behind them like a great black fuzzy river.

The mall doors were locked, of course. Squirrel Girl pulled on one. Then she pulled harder. And then it was open, dead bolts curved like bendy straws.

It was moments like these when Ana Sofía remembered that, whoa, her best friend Doreen was a legit Super Hero. She smiled at her and signed, "Good job, Squirrel Girl."

Squirrel Girl made the signs for "shy" and "embarrassed," but her posture was straight, her eyes sparkling, and she looked ready to tear down the mall by hand.

They entered the giant cube of a building, the dark rodent bodies surging around their feet.

It smelled like a mall. A smell Ana Sofía couldn't place exactly—not just paint and wood and electricity, but some other unique odor. Maybe malls sprayed bottles of Genuine Mall Scent so they could all smell the same.

Note: Malls are eerie after hours. Avoid entering dark, empty malls in the future.

It looked like a typical mall. The dim emergency lights cast dull orange shadows over the center court, the still water fountain, the escalator frozen in the moment. The storefronts were closed, the names on their signs familiar—sort of: Off Topic, Clot Dog on a Stick, Trick-fil-A . . .

Something was not quite right.

"This place isn't . . . quite right," Ana Sofía said. She hoped she said it softly, but whispering wasn't her strongest skill. Anyway, it was hard to sneak into a place quietly after you've torn the steel doors off their hinges.

The squirrels took the lead, and soon they were at *that* door. The impossible door. The hack-proof door. The squirrel-proof door. The solid some-kind-of-rare-and-impossible-metal door.

But an unopenable door was not The End, not in Ana Sofía's mind. It was a problem. And problems have solutions.

"I have an idea . . ." Ana Sofía said, signing. She swallowed. She frowned. She wished she could take back the words.

"I'm not going to laugh," Squirrel Girl signed back. "I promise."

"Okay," she said aloud. "Well . . . you seem to have the *proportional* abilities of a squirrel, right? I did some research. By some metrics the jaw muscle is the strongest muscle in the human body. Our bites can create two hundred pounds per square inch of pressure. Well, squirrel bites are capable of *seven thousand* pounds per square inch." From the corner of her eye, she saw two squirrels high-five. "So . . . if squirrels can bite with seven thousand pounds of force, what would your *proportional* biting strength be?"

Squirrel Girl closed her eyes, as if calculating in her head. Her eyes popped open. "Wait, are you telling me to chew through this door?"

Ana Sofía felt her face go hot with embarrassment, but she said, "Squirrel Girl, I am telling you to chew through this door."

Squirrel Girl seemed to need a moment to take this in. Then she whispered a word. Ana Sofía thought it was probably "Awesome."

Squirrel Girl put her hands against the door, she opened her mouth, and . . . what happened next was unlike anything Ana Sofía had witnessed before. There was gnawing. There was chomping. There was nibbling. There was even climbing, as she maneuvered around to get the right angles. And by the time Squirrel Girl stood back up, there was a hole about two feet in diameter in the center of the door. And flecks of metal on her lips.

"That was hard-core," Ana Sofía said.

Squirrel Girl wiped the metal off her mouth. And smiled.

"Squirrel power!" she said in ASL.

"Oh, dude, you broke a tooth!" Ana Sofía pointed to one of Squirrel Girl's front teeth, which was broken off halfway to its root at a ragged angle.

"That's okay, they grow back. Also, high five that I got you saying 'dude.'"

Ana Sofía high-fived very reluctantly, but Squirrel Girl had just chewed through several inches of solid metal, so a little indulgent social celebration wasn't unthinkable.

Squirrels poured through the chewed-through hole. Squirrel Girl went next, her hips, thighs, and tail area barely squeezing through.

Ana Sofía paused before the hole. Behind her was the cavernous, dark mall. Her hearing aids buzzed, picking up indistinct sounds. Had Dog-Lord and Mistress Meow escaped S.H.I.E.L.D.'s pound and come back? Was it Hydra guards? Other things? She peered back into the dark, and it seemed to move. She peered through the hole Squirrel Girl had chewed open, which led into the underground lair of the most evilest organization on the planet.

See previous note about avoiding dark, empty malls. Add new note: best practice is always to stay with Squirrel Girl.

She took a deep breath. And she dropped through the hole.

There were narrow stairs, and then a narrow hallway lined with lockers. It even smelled like a middle school locker room. Squirrel Girl and the squirrels sniffed and scowled, no doubt in agreement.

"Tippy says there's some kind of scanning machine down there at the end of the hall, and it shoots lasers if it doesn't recognize you," Squirrel Girl said. "So that's probably the entrance to the rest of the underground base."

"Right," Ana Sofía said. She sat on the floor and pulled the laptop out of her backpack. She took a deep breath, typed and tapped and began to worm her way past security using the path she'd created last night. Eventually a field prompt came up, a way to insert names into the database of those people with approved access.

"This is the tricky part," said Ana Sofía. "I need to input a name for everyone as we pass through the scanner so the system believes we're authorized and doesn't set off an intruder alert."

"I love that you know how to do that and maybe can you teach me how you do it sometime when we're not actively breaking into a Hydra secret base?"

Ana Sofía gave her a thumbs-up.

"I can type in the names if you want since I know everyone," said Squirrel Girl.

Ana Sofía took a deep breath and handed over her laptop. Her precious laptop that she had earned by doing a year's worth of chores for the extended family. Her laptop was not just a toy or a tool, it was often her primary means of interacting with the world. Handing it over felt like tipping backward in a trust fall, and her heart beat painfully, but she did it.

Squirrel Girl smiled. "Thank you," she said, as if she understood what it cost Ana Sofía to trust her with it. And honestly, that helped.

As the squirrels scurried over the threshold one by one, Squirrel Girl lightning-speed typed their names into the hacked database of Hydra workers. The robot voice of the scanner announced them as they passed through.

"Tippy-Toe," said the scanner. "Fuzz Fountain Cortez, Curd Spiderwhey, Cartwheel Kate, Elbow Hides-in-Fur, Stink Pampershield, Chet the Mound King, Lorraine Cuddlywink Cink, Timp Weaselrider, Stephan the Mud-Monger, Maxwell von Snort, Samich the Uneatable, Gary Branch-Walker, Handsome JJ, Marieke the Unblinking, Titus Glittersnoot, Sniffle Sidepockets, Teeter Furflint, Totter Furflint, Vegan Podburglar, Cellophane Sally, Pete Flipperpaws, The Innsmouth Creeper, Prince Ramon the Sub-Earther, Imperious Tex, Davey Porkpun, Dewey Decimate aka the Librarian, Platypus Kate, Bartleby the Scamperer, Calendar Earl, Kurt Poundofguts, Tablecarver Tito, Chomp Style, Millicent the Uncouth, Emo Pat, Shawn Swingsinger, Toot Trainskimmer, Squirm the Exceptionally Comfortable, Mighty Micah Fuzzfist, Thistledown Kistleback aka the Sizzler, Zoë Twig-Hunter, Violet 'Spectrum's End' Nutsworn, Peggy Eggsbane, Polymorph Patty Who Was Once a Gerbil, Rebel Tablescraps, Indistinguishable Ben, Distinguishable Ben, Amy Danderbags, Joggy McSweatscourge, Tail-Pinned Pudu, DG Leaps, BATRA the Unforgiving, Jessica Harmfist, Sir Reggie Fuzzface, Spencer the Brave, Babs the Bubble Witch, Little Sissy Hotlegs, Big Sissy Hotlegs, El Fantástico, Campbell the Unsoup, Rich Reeders, Stu Swarm, Stony Germ, Grinbumm,

Roxie the Rock Proxy, Ms. Gnomer, Edfur Cullen, Jacob Blackfuzz, Abbot Shamescuttle, Hotcap Hugglebum, Alexander Hamsandwich, Pardon Menot, Rictus the Screamer, Parking Strip Sue, Bedbug Ballyhoo, Startlekins the Unwieldy, Gary Gardenguard, Meep the Misunderstood, Lady Sportswear, Dirk Stircrazy, Jamie Grizzlechops, Dawn of the Bread, Lefty Girl, Not-That-Stark, Skylar the Twitchy, Skylar the Twitchier, Chive Alpha, Liberty Mel, The Muttering Scallop, Wiggy Nubknees, Puck Tenclaws, Gore Soupstain, Alias the Under-Toad, Pillbox Matt, Speedo Strutfuzz, The Last Empress of Pillbugs, Gordon Soondead, Gordon-Still-in-Waiting, Kit Hulu, Star Spawn of Kit Hulu, Hashbrown the Unspeakable, Diggen Fishlips, Horsebelly Hat, Gayle Bagley, Illum I. Naughty, Spot Welder, KURGAN, Purrmaster Nottacat, Pip Elf-Eater, Keebler the Unbound, Twitch Perfect, Moxie Spectacular, Plexiglass Jones, Fiddler Three, Stinky Boots, Mr. Lumpkins the Grave, Standard M. Lee, Catsy Walker: Halecat, Trespassers William, Silver Streak, Captain Tennille, Ryan of the North, Erica: Son of Hender, Precious Bagginses, Ellen Shuffleclaw, Lana 'the Librarian' Shelfstalker, Shannon Pursepaw, Gnome Chompsky, The Laundry Ghost, Humdinger Nelson, Nancy Grew, Bear Bodkin, Danger Mouse, Jessica O. Berrybits, Henry Manbug, Josephine Cream-Hoarder, Oliver Nutton, Kristen Shawl-Skulker, She Who Must Not Be Named, Thing One, Thing Two-and-a-Half, Gwynn Rummy the Card Shark, Fitzwalnuts Darcy, Michael S. Hat, Woodness

Gracious, Flip Furstinger, Kip Furslinger, Pip Fursinger, Melon Brawl Betty, Slicktongue Tablescrap, Tillie Badmeal, Tasha 'the Haunch' Middlesbury, Gordie Gizzardfist, David S. Pumpkins, Humpty Skysword, Big Nod Jellyheart, Pam the Wig Ninja, Carlito Sway, Buddy the Branch Wizard, Keratin Bouquet, Wet William: Formerly Known as M.O.I.S.T., Slim Slickery Suit-Muppet, Table Chaw, The Marble Nugget, Glasstooth Wildebeest, Fuzzhopper Frogskin, Stepback Eyeneedler, Timothy Muffin-Crouch, Captain Ice Weasel, Unidentifiable Blur Junior, Shaka Wall-Faller, Orange Scream Machine, Westminster Wally, Chudslayer Rex, Marty 'the Elephant Among Us' Walnut, Six-Pack Miffy, Five-Pound Baggins, Stimpy Ape-Soul, Savannah Gnarl-Paw, Gravy Chickenskin, Cube-Gleam Kennedy, Creaky Speakeasy, Melanie Neverblink, Herbert Mustard: Crawlspace Commissar, Stevie Stippleback, Fabrizio Furslough, Electric Cashew-aloo, Judy Plume, Ana Sofía, Squirrel Girl."

Once through the scanner, they nestled together in a narrow entryway, barely space for two humans and a couple hundred squirrels. Tippy-Toe volunteered to venture first into the unknown. After a few seconds she poked her head back to chitter at Squirrel Girl.

"She says when we go in," Squirrel Girl said, signing, "be careful and stay close to the wall."

Ana Sofía put her laptop into her backpack and didn't hesitate this time to follow Squirrel Girl. Partly just to escape the locker room smell, but also because if her mother could see her, after Teresa Romero exploded with anger that her daughter would put herself in this situation, she most definitely would advise her to stick close to the girl with squirrel powers.

Ana Sofía passed through the dark, narrow passage and through an arched doorway toward a rush of fan-driven air. She clung to the wall as instructed and was immediately glad for it. They were in a circular room about forty feet in diameter, standing on a narrow ledge. Except for that ledge that wrapped around the wall, there was no floor. She held fast to a knob on the wall and leaned a little, looking down. It was a legit Star Wars kind of shaft—metal and plastic walls, blinking electronics, going down, down maybe a hundred feet.

There were no stairs. There did not appear to be a ladder.

"So, about those proportional squirrel abilities?" said Ana Sofía. Her voice felt trembly in her throat. "Did you know squirrels can fall twenty feet and be fine? Well, if a squirrel is one foot long and takes a twenty-foot fall no problem, and you're about five feet long, then proportionally you should be able to fall one hundred—"

Beneath her hand, something clunked within the walls, and Ana Sofía got no further in her analysis of squirrel super powers. Apparently they'd been detected. Robotic arms shot out of the wall at ankle height and began sweeping along the ledge. Squirrel Girl had walked around the ledge to the other side of the shaft. When the sweepers hit her feet, she leaped up, clinging with her claws in the wall.

Squirrels, too, leaped out of the way, popping up around Ana Sofía like popping corn. Ana Sofía jumped over the sweeping metal arm, but no sooner had she landed back on the ledge than a second arm shoved against her ankles.

She fell. Fell into the chasm, face-first, staring at the dark gray spot where she would no doubt go splat in a few seconds.

She fell and fell. In the two and a half seconds it took to fall a hundred or so feet, her adrenaline-spiked brain went through every stage of grief about her upcoming death:

1. denial (*No way I am seriously falling into this random chasm!*)
2. anger (*Stupid Hydra, I'm going to tear them apart!*)
3. bargaining (*I promise I'll never lie to my parents again if somehow this isn't happening.*)
4. depression (*Cruuuuuuud. . . .*)
5. and finally, acceptance (*Um . . .*)

Never mind; she didn't quite make it to acceptance. She pivoted back to anger, a space of comfort and familiarity for her, and when one is falling to their death, one really yearns for some comfort and familiarity. Ana Sofía Arcos Romero was royally cheesed off to be dying at age fourteen before she did all the amazing things she was sure she'd do, and in *such* a *stupid* way.

Stupid Hydra. If she wasn't about to die, she would totally make them pay.

28

SQUIRREL GIRL

*L*eap before you look. That was Squirrel Girl's motto.[69]

So she leaped. And then she looked. She was falling down a smooth metal shaft, about forty feet wide. One hundred feet down? Maybe it was. It sure looked like more. Did she really have *all* the proportional abilities of a squirrel? Could she take the impact? Welp, too late to stop now.

She dove, arms forward, hands in prayer position, head and tail tucked in to be sleek, aerodynamic. Ana Sofía had fallen a half second before her, but she flailed as she fell, and Squirrel Girl was able to catch up. She grabbed Ana Sofía's long black hair and pulled her into a tight hug. Now she fluffed up her tail, hoping to slow their speed.

---

69 At some point, logic says that will prove to be a faulty motto, but it hasn't failed me yet!

This was a daring rescue for a hero without flying ability. So much talk about flying squirrels! But they'd been born with awesome skin flaps connecting wrists to ankles so they could glide. Where were *her* awesome skin flaps?[70]

As the floor came rushing in, just a couple of seconds after she'd leaped, her adrenaline-zapped brain thought of a million things at once. Had she finished her history homework? Wasn't that essay due on Monday? How did Ms. Schweinbein feed all those animals on a teacher's salary? The second season of *That's So Speedball!* really wasn't as good as the first, and the subplot about his cat, Hairball, didn't really go anywhere. And even if she could take the jolt of landing, could Ana Sofía?

So in midair, she tossed Ana Sofía up. Squirrel Girl landed on her feet, her knees bending, her head whiplashing back, her every bone vibrating, her tail out straight to balance her jarring touchdown. A millisecond later, Ana Sofía came at her. Squirrel Girl caught her, letting her arms dip with the weight to ease her impact. Then she set her friend on her feet.

"Whoa," said Ana Sofía. Her eyes looked wobbly in her face.

"Yeah," said Squirrel Girl. Or more squeaked. Her voice seemed to be having trouble. Probably because she'd spent the past several seconds screaming.

The bottoms of her feet were hot, her spine felt compacted,

---

70 I totally have skin flap envy. But on second thought, skin flaps are probably not a feature that would make middle school any easier?

the landing kind of squishing her all together. Honestly she wouldn't be surprised if she was a couple of inches shorter than she had been. She lifted up one leg, shaking it out. Then the other. Lifted her arms and stretched.

"I'm sorry, miss," said a voice in the darkness. "You must have mistaken our high-security underground lair for a yoga studio."

A man stepped forward into the light of the shaft. He was wearing full body armor with a helmet, all pea green, the chest emblazoned with a yellow Hydra emblem—not the smiley face of the mall, the real one with the tentacled skull. And he was holding a glowing blue weapon that Squirrel Girl figured must have been a plasma gun because that's the sort of thing guys like that preferred to tote around.

Behind him, a dozen more people stepped up. They were all men. All pale-skinned, and all wearing green shirts with yellow belts and yellow suspenderlike stripes to form big *H*s on their torsos.[71] Their eyes and scalps were covered with cowls that were also green, and to be honest it wasn't a great color for them. As a fellow pasty-skinned person, Squirrel Girl knew that certain shades of white skin couldn't be paired with green or it just made them look sallow and sickly.[72]

"Aha, so you detected our clever break-in!" said Squirrel Girl.

---

71 Yes, we get it, you're Hydra! The huge *H* is overkill, guys.
72 I know what you're thinking: *But, Squirrel Girl, you look great in green!* Thanks, but not every pasty human is so fortunate.

"Um, yeah," he said. "High-security underground lair, you know."

"Also because of all the screaming, sir," a guy at his elbow said helpfully.

"Yes," he said with great authority. "Also because of all the screaming."

"Riiiight," said Squirrel Girl. "Screaming. Ana Sofía, remind me to work on my sneaky skills."

"Uhhhh," said Ana Sofía. She was patting herself all over, as if feeling for any missing parts. Squirrel Girl didn't have a lot of experience in nearly-falling-to-her-death, but she suspected Ana Sofía was going to need a few moments.

She turned back to the Hydra guy, who on closer inspection was wearing a name tag that identified him as "Garry."

"Garry!" she said, super-friendly.

"What?" he said, sounding like a grade-A grump, in Squirrel Girl's honest opinion.

"Garry, you're in charge here. That's so great. I bet you felt like a million bucks when you got promoted to head-Hydra-guy-thing, huh?"

Garry shifted uncomfortably. "Not like I was promoted recently or anything, I've been in a managerial position for *years*," he said, speaking over his shoulder as if for the sake of the guys flanking him. "In fact, I was recently given this brass tentacle pin for all my loyalty and ingenuity and stuff."

"Again with the pin," another agent mumbled.

"I bet this whole mall idea was partly yours?" said Squirrel Girl. "I bet you were an integral part in this clever scheme."

"Well . . . I definitely added to it," said Garry. "I said, there's got to be a fountain, people will rush into a place that might be dangerous as long as there's a soothing fountain, and, you know, they did listen to me and added a fountain into the mall's main massacre plaza."

"Hey, Garry, isn't there a rule against confirming Super Heroes' clever deductions of our evil plans?" asked a guy behind him.

"Totally," said another, pulling a small white booklet from his pocket and flipping through the pages. "Here it is! Article Two, Section Nine, Paragraph One Thousand and Twelve: Under no circumstance should an agent fall for the trap of 'monologuing,' i.e., revealing to a captured Super Hero our devious plans, or to in any way confirm said Super Hero's postulations of said plans—"

"Yeah, yeah," said Garry, "but it doesn't matter now, because they're about to die."

"We are?" asked Squirrel Girl.

"Yep," said Garry.

"When?" asked Squirrel Girl.

"Now," said Garry.

He shifted his feet. He cleared his throat.

"And now"—Garry raised his plasma gun—"you will die!"

"Wait!" said Squirrel Girl, both hands up. "Can't we keep

talking for just a minute? Um, so, you like green, huh, Garry? I like green. I also like shelling and eating nuts. And amateur cobblery. The shoe kind. Well, also the fruit kind. Nothing like a piping hot peach cobbler, am I right, Garry? So . . . what hobbies do you enjoy?"

"Actually," said a Hydra guy, "I really do like peach cobbler—"

"Silence!" said Garry. "There will be no chitchatting. We are Hydra and we will destroy you!"

"Well, I'm a Super Hero," said Squirrel Girl, "and since Hydra is a super-evil organization—"

"Thank you," he said.

"—I am here to take. You. Personally. Down."

"Oh yeah?" he said. "You and what army?"

Oh. Oh! Oh-oh-oh! He said it he said it he totally said it! And, even better, at just that moment Tippy-Toe chittered a plan from one hundred feet up. So Squirrel Girl lifted out her tail and fluffed up its fur, just as one by one squirrels leaped from above, landed on her tail, and with a trampoline-y bounce, shot back up a little ways and landed feetfirst on the floor. Within moments, she was surrounded by two hundred black-eyed, blinkless furry warriors.

"*THIS* ARMY," said Squirrel Girl.

"Ah," he said.

"Yes," she whispered to herself. "YES. Nailed it."

Tippy-Toe jumped onto Squirrel Girl's shoulder and ticked

her tongue at the green-clad gathering. *"Chkt-icky-tickt,"* she said with an eye roll.[73]

"I hear you, Tip," she whispered. "But there *are* a dozen of them. With plasma guns—"

Tippy-Toe chittered something rude about men and their fondness for plasma guns.

"And I don't want Ana Sofía to get caught in the cross fire. Give her a guard, okay? I don't think talking them out of it is going to work here. We'd better—"

"CHKKT!!!" said Tippy-Toe.

She leaped, and dozens of squirrels leaped after her, claws out. They landed on the Hydra agents and began to chew holes into their shirts and cowls.

The agents screamed and fought, plasma guns firing randomly. Ana Sofía ducked. Squirrel Girl was busy dodging Garry's blasts, all aimed right at her.[74]

"These . . . squirrels! They're too much!" shouted one agent. "I toss one off and two more take its place!"

"Impossible!" yelled Garry. "That's *our* thing!"

Tippy-Toe leaped at Garry, gnawing on his helmet. She chittered madly.

"Squirrel-proof armor, you say?" said Squirrel Girl. "There's no such thing!"

---

73 Tippy basically said, "And humans think all *squirrels* look alike?"

74 Garry literally aimed at me and shot plasma bolts! I couldn't believe it! And after our friendly chat. Garry, what a disappointment.

Her favorite character to play in the video game *Ultra Maria Sisters* was a leaper, jumping on top of heads to squish evil fungus men into submission. So, like Savage Princess Maria, Squirrel Girl leaped. Plasma bolts exploded around her, fizzling in the metal walls where she'd just been. She landed right on Garry's head, perched there like a bird. He crumpled beneath the force of her landing.

"That's the spirit!" she said. Mostly to herself, but also to him for gamely collapsing just as she'd hoped he would.[75]

She leaped from the now-prostrate Garry onto the head of the next agent, and the next.

"Sproing," she said with each leap. "Sproing . . . sproing . . ." Behind her they all fell to the ground, knocked out by her impact.

"Oh, man, now I totally want a Squirrel Girl video game. I would dominate! Sorry, Mr. Evil Hydra-Man," Squirrel Girl said, stepping off the shoulders of the Hydra soldier who had just crumpled beneath her.

Another green-suited man scrambled up to her and she readied to pounce, but instead he dropped to the ground beside his unconscious comrade.

"HIS NAME WAS LARRY! *LARRY!*" the newcomer shouted. "AND HE LOVED JAZZ! Jazz . . . and . . . and the sound of monkeys in the rain. . . ."

"Um . . ." Squirrel Girl said, looking around. It appeared as

---

75 So I guess he wasn't *all* bad.

though Larry's friend had been the last of them putting up a fight. A turret-looking thing high on the wall was still randomly shooting plasma around, but it wasn't doing a very good job hitting anything. The last few conscious Hydra people were either pounding on the locked doors, trying to escape squirrels or doing whatever Larry's friend here was doing.

"WHY? WHY? WHY COULDN'T IT HAVE BEEN ME, LARRY?" the man wailed from beside his friend.

"You . . . uh . . . know he's not dead, right?" said Squirrel Girl, as she dodged a plasma bolt from the turret.

The man wiped his eyes with the back of a green-gloved hand. "What?" he sniffled.

Squirrel Girl leaped closer to check Larry's pulse, just in case.

"Nope," she said. "Just unconscious. I was super-careful."

Larry groaned beneath them but did not open his eyes.

"Larry!" the man gasped. "You scared me half to death! How could you do that to me? You're cruel, Larry! Cruel!"

Larry, still unconscious on the ground, lay still as his friend shook his limp body. A plasma bolt struck the ground next to them, scorching the metal floor.

"You know, maybe don't . . ." Squirrel Girl said, climbing up the wall and tearing plasma guns out of the turret. "I mean, he's already down. I think I heard somewhere that it is bad to shake unconscious people."

The agent let go of Larry as if stung. "Right! Of course. Of course. I'm so sorry, Larry!"

The door at the end of the corridor, the one the remaining conscious agents had been pounding on, finally slid open. Beyond the door were dozens more agents dressed in heavy armor. Agent "Larry's Buddy" saw the reinforcements and grinned. He drew a plasma pistol from a holster at his waist, and Squirrel Girl leaped back.

"Whoa!" she said. "Hey now! I thought we were sharing a moment here! You know, poor Larry, let's not shake poor unconscious Larry be—"

He fired.

29

ANA SOFÍA

*T*here was nowhere to hide. Behind them was the metal wall of the chasm where Ana Sofía had fallen. Ahead, a corridor now swarming with new Hydra agents firing plasma guns while fighting off swarms of squirrels, the floor littered with the unconscious Hydra agents downed by the unbeatable Squirrel Girl and her mighty leap.

She watched as Squirrel Girl dodged a direct plasma shot then leaped onto the agent's shoulders, downing him beside his comrades. How long could she keep it up before one found its mark?

Nowhere for Ana Sofía to hide. And nothing to do to help Squirrel Girl. She leaned her back against the wall and breathed.

The only lights came from below—yellow emergency lights in the baseboards shining upward, casting shadows, making their faces look skeletal. There was a low, constant buzzing, though Ana Sofía wasn't sure if it was ambient sound or if all the electrical equipment was reacting oddly with her hearing aids. Or maybe the buzzing was coming from inside her own body. Her stomach certainly felt like it was full of angry waspy butterflies. Her pulse pounded in her temple and shook her vision with every beat. She blinked hard, trying to clear her eyesight.

A couple dozen squirrels had formed a circle completely around her feet. When she stumbled back, they moved with her every step. A furry layer of protection, like socks, once-removed. Their presence made her feel braver.

Note: presence of friendly squirrels increases sense of both safety and belonging.

Ana Sofía took out her phone and began to record. If they didn't make it out of here, she wanted someone to know what had happened, at least. She'd videoed for just over a minute when a plasma shot burned into the wall right by her head. She crouched lower and hurriedly uploaded the video to her TuberTV channel. Now if they died, at least there was some evidence.

At her back, she felt a closed door. Ana Sofía tugged on the handle. Locked.

The squirrels at her feet all stood up on their hind legs as if responding to some warning she hadn't noticed. Reinforcements had arrived: several Hydra agents marching down the corridor dressed in the "squirrel-proof" armor. The intimidation factor of robot-like body armor and full helmet was lessened somewhat by the green color.

Like pea soup, Ana Sofía thought. *Like Abuela's sofa.*

But they still looked pretty alarming. The alarming effect was in no small part due to the horse-size plasma canon they were setting up.

It fired. A huge plasma glob streaked through the dim basement, as bright as deep-sea jellyfish.

In the exact moment the glow-in-the-dark blue ball of fiery plasma shot out, the plasma cannon was knocked awry by several squirrels slamming into the tip, pushing its aim slightly off. Instead of burning a hole right through Ana Sofía's head, the blast hit the door, burning a circle where the door handle would have been.

She stared at the hole in the door as the plasma cannon fired again, the ammo whizzing just above her head.

I should go to there, she thought confusedly.

But thinking seemed to be an entirely different function from actually moving. Her whole body felt made of hard plastic, like a molded toy with no moveable parts. Instinct should make her run. She'd never before imagined that when in great danger, she'd freeze instead.

She looked down at her legs and glared at them, glared so hard they just had to be frightened of her. Glared so hard she got them to shuffle her forward.

Ana Sofía leaned against the damaged door and fell in, away from the blasts. It appeared to be an office—concert posters for Your Racist Uncle adorned the walls, a bouquet of dusty plastic daffodils sat sadly on the desk. And . . . yes! There was a computer. She sat down and got to work.

"You okay out there?" she called as she typed at super-speed, trying to hack her way past the passcode. *Got it.*

Squirrel Girl replied with words she couldn't make out but the tone seemed cheery.

Through the doorway, she could see Squirrel Girl leaping around, landing on Hydra agents' heads, knocking them flat. In her periphery she saw one agent pulled down by so many furry bodies he appeared to be wearing a bear suit. Unless it was a Hydra agent actually just wearing a bear suit, which she supposed wasn't out of the question.[76]

The most recent folder opened on this computer was titled Hate Initiative. The folder locked when she tried to access it without the right password. So she searched for those words in the e-mail program.

From: Team Leader Gamma

To: Undisclosed Recipients

Subject: Hate Initiative

Hey, team!

Great work out there. As we head into our final week before d-day, make sure you keep your squirrel-proof armor at hand, your plasma gun

---

76 There is literally nothing Hydra agents won't do to spread hatred and chaos in their pursuit of world domination, including wearing ill-fitting bear suits. But in this case, he was just covered in attack squirrels.

nozzles clean, and keep working the comments sections of news stories and Friendbook posts. We need to up, up, up the animosity!

Remember to take excellent notes. This is just Phase 1, after all. After the Hate Initiative destroys Shady Oaks, we will be taking it wider. "How wide?" you ask. Why, from sea to shining sea. ;) Easiest way to destroy something is to trick it into destroying itself.

metaphorical hugs,
your Boss

This e-mail message may contain confidential material. If you are not an intended recipient, please destroy all your belongings in a fire and run as far away as you can. We enjoy the chase.

"Oh no," Ana Sofía said aloud. The Hate Initiative? D-day was at the mall tomorrow. And what happened there would destroy Shady Oaks. And then the entire country? This was way, way huger than what a couple of middle schoolers could handle.

A blue plasma ball sizzled through the wall. Ana Sofía ducked a moment too late, and felt the heat of it pass over her head.

"Everything okay?" she called.

She couldn't detect a reply, but she could see squirrels and Squirrel Girl still leaping around out there.

Holy crud. What on earth were they doing? This really was

the real Hydra, and she thought they could somehow take them on? They needed an adult hero STAT!

ANA SOFÍA

Hydra is planning to unleash something called the hate initiative on my town and then the whole country and we don't really know how to stop them? So prolly u shld come to the basement of the mall and save the day before everybody dies?

THOR

Can't come

Presently

Texting between

Punches

ANA SOFÍA

Who is getting punched you or them

THOR

Both

Tis a veritable punch fest

ANA SOFÍA

Ok just thought i'd check

THOR

You and squirrelly friend

Are powerful

You will be vic

Sorry interrupted by punching

YOU WILL BE VICTORIOSAS

ANA SOFÍA

Gracias Thor

Yeah, thanks a lot, Thor. How in the egg-shaped world was she supposed to take care of this? She was definitely not powerful. And sure, her squirrelly friend had the proportional abilities of a squirrel, but what was that when faced with a Hydra army shooting plasma cannons all over the frickin' underground lair?

She searched around through the parts of the Hydra security system that she could access. Both the mall and the basement lair had microphones in the ceilings to pick up voice-activated commands—commands like shutting and sealing all the mall's exterior doors at once. That felt ominous. Also extinguishing all interior lights, setting off fire alarm systems, and turning on disco lights. The code for that last one was "Let's party, bros!" Ana Sofía rolled her eyes. Probably for their victory bash.

Most of the command codes were linked to the voice of an individual marked as *LB*. She couldn't remove the codes entirely but managed to change a couple of words in the commands, for what good that might do.

She peeked her head out the door, wincing in case of plasma blasts. No blasts. All quiet on the basement front.

Several dozen armored Hydra agents were lying unconscious on the floor. Plasma burn holes decorated the metal walls with black craters. Squirrels crouched on various prostrate bodies, breathing hard.

"Whoa. You did it," said Ana Sofía. "How did you do it?"

Squirrel Girl shrugged. "These poo-green jerks needed to be stopped, and I was here, so . . ."

Ana Sofía nodded. Her neck and back ached, and she realized she was hunched over. She'd taken up a permanent crouch posture ever since falling into the basement lair, half-ducked in case of sudden weapons fire.

Párate derecha, she seemed to hear her mother say, reminding her to watch her posture. She had become more slouchy the taller she grew—four inches in just the past year alone—and tended to curl in on herself even when she wasn't in a Hydra lair ducking lethal plasma shots. She straightened. Her spine aligned. She took a deep breath and felt a whole lot more Ana Sofía than she had a minute ago.

Gracias, Mami.

A firm decision began to fill her up. Her mother was working the night shift at the hospital, unaware that her fourteen-year-old daughter was in a Hydra lair. Thor and the Avengers were in space. Who knew if they'd ever come back? But Hydra had to be stopped, and they were here.

She was here. Ana Sofía Arcos Romero was most definitely here. Wobbly knees and all, goshdarnit.

"What now?" asked Squirrel Girl.

"I don't know exactly what Hydra intends to do," said Ana Sofía, "but I know it's bad, and this is their base. So . . . so I guess we need . . ." She cleared her throat. "Squirrel Girl, we've got to shut it down."

Squirrel Girl's smile nearly split her face in half. She looked around at the metallic walls, the shut and locked doors, the control panels with flashing lights.

"Squirrels?" she said.

Hundreds of black, blinkless eyes stared up at her. Squirrel Girl nodded once.

"*Smash,*" she said.

30

TIPPY-TOE

*W*e surged forward like light at the break of dawn, covering the floor, the walls, and everything on them. One of the downed men either screamed or laughed hysterically as we passed. I couldn't tell the difference, and I didn't care.

I am the best there is at what I do. And what I do isn't very nice.

My dear departed uncle, Skiptama Lou, may he rest in trees, always said that a squirrel's body is simply a delivery system for claws and teeth. And claws and teeth, they aren't for being cute. They're for tearing and cutting. For ripping apart.

But my pink bow, that is for being cute. Don't let anyone tell you that you have to be one or the other. You can be both.

Chomp Style ran, gouging chunks out of the wall at regular intervals. Others followed behind, darting into the holes to chew and claw everything within. The walls sounded like a tree trunk with a bad case of borer beetles.

Big Sissy Hotlegs broke into rooms, scampered across desks, slammed into anything not nailed down. As I watched, she kicked a monitor with her back legs. It toppled, crashing to the floor.

A green-suited agent yelped as Chive Alpha poked him with a sparking wire she pulled from the wall with her teeth.

She noticed me watching. "He was quick-snatching for a gun!"

The agent scrambled away, slipping on broken glass.

"RUN, VERMIN!" Chive Alpha chittered at his back. "FLEE FROM YOUR DESTRUCTION! I AM THE FIRE AMONG YOUR BRANCHES!"

"Alpha!"

The young squirrel gave me a look.

"Keep it up," I said.

She gave me a slow smile, and that girl sure looked like she had more teeth than most of us.

There was joyful noise as we worked. Scampering, skittering, chomping, and scratching. The sound of nature being fulfilled and good honest destruction being done. The walls rattled with the passage of my people behind them. Lights flickered, electronics sputtered and died in our wake. The pads that controlled the doors out of the bunker were a shattered, sparking mess.

I surveyed the field of battle, and was hard-pressed not to declare our victory right then. Doreen had left dozens of the green-suited men unconscious on the ground, and those left standing pounded on metal doors that would not open to them, trying to escape the terror of our work.

Those men were overconfident. With their machines and their size and their ignorance, they had forgotten to fear the squirrel.

Behind the hiss and rattle of battle and the screams of terrified men I became aware of a new sound. A wrong sound. The squeal of squirrel fighting squirrel.

Fuzz Fountain Cortez tumbled out of a hole in the wall, wrestling with Wiggy Nubknees. A chunk of Cortez's ear was missing and Wiggy was snapping and scratching like he'd got the mange.

I pounced, anchoring my rear legs around Wiggy's tail and twisting my forepaws under his and back around his neck. I pulled him off Cortez as he struggled crazily.

"Wiggy!" I shouted. "Wiggy!"

"Stink-rot in the walls!" Cortez chittered frantically. "A tube. Wiggy gave it a gnaw and got a snoutful of gas!"

"Die! Die! Die!" Wiggy yelled, finally making some sense. Sort of.

"Wiggy!" I shouted. "You're with friends! This is your nest!"

"DIE," he said, and then fell limp in my arms.

"Is he . . ." Cortez asked.

"Still breathing," I said.

All around me the noises of squirrel destruction stopped, heads turned toward me. Toward Wiggy. We squirrels do fight each other, sometimes. But never like this. Even when warring against other clans, it's about dominance. There's no murder among squirrels. Something had happened. Something wrong.

My cousins eyed each other nervously, and I knew I was not the only one to feel it. Something was in the air. Something was coming. It was like the *click-clack* of dog paws behind you. It was like the smell of a tree on fire. It was like Little Bobby Furflint stealing your first harvest acorn.

And a man was coming. A human man was there, bad air hissing off him in plumes, smelling so strong I could almost see it. Odor of rot and grease and fear fear fear. I turned to attack him, but he was gone. How not there?

Now only *they* were there. All those black blinkless eyes staring. All of *them*, trying to get me, trying to kill me, trying to stop me.

Stop me.

Can't stop me.

Fear! Rage! Will tear, will rend.

Swipe and claw, strike and bite.

Who skulks

no

get you first

I'll chktt

   chktt

      chkit

     kkkktt

31

SQUIRREL GIRL

*H*alf the squirrels stopped mid-destruction, as still as prey in the grass. They all looked over toward Tippy-Toe and those around her. Squirrel Girl paused just before biting a pipe in half to see what had caused the alarm.

The rest of the squirrels were still swiping and biting, breaking and tearing, but now their destruction was not focused on Hydra's base but at fuzzy, adorable each other.

"Squirrels! What in the heck are you doing?" said Squirrel Girl. "CALM THE FREAK DOWN!"[77]

Many of the affected squirrels climbed into holes in the walls—holes most likely created by Chomp Style's stylin' chomps. Others shivered or ran back and forth or curled up

---

77 This particular command has never, ever worked, but I keep trying it anyway, just in case, I guess.

with tails over their eyes and shivered. But Tippy-Toe and Fuzz Fountain Cortez were engaged in full terrifying buck-toothed-and-tiny-clawed squirrel combat.

Squirrel Girl grabbed them by their tails.[78] They continued to writhe and claw at each other. She held her arms farther apart.

"Tippy! What's gotten into you?"

Chive Alpha climbed up to Squirrel Girl's shoulder.

"CHKTT-ITI!" she scolded the two squirrels.

But they didn't seem to hear her, still squealing and twisting.

"I've never seen them like this," said Squirrel Girl.

"I'm afraid their higher brain function is halted. Ha! You know, assuming they had any to begin with!"

She whirled around at the sound of the voice. The squirrels reacted, too, running up her arms to shiver on her shoulders.

A shadow emerged from the dark end of corridor, where berserker squirrels had already destroyed the emergency lights. Slowly he moved into one of the un-squirreled, remaining lights.

"Bryan?"

Bryan Lazardo smiled. He was not dressed in the cargo shorts and T-shirt he'd used in the promo video. Instead he had on a gray-green mottled leather unitard that wasn't quite big enough for him and wrinkled around the elbows, stacking up at the knees over his green galoshes.

---

78 Which is like the number one thing you never, ever do to a squirrel friend, but the situation was desperate!

"Sooo, look, I know this is totally a weird time to ask, what with the fighting Hydra and all and the sudden squirrel freak-out," said Squirrel Girl, "but what, um, what are you wearing?"

He held up his arms to admire his outfit, and the sleeves slid back to his elbows. "This?" he asked coyly. "This is my battle suit!"

"Sweet!" She cinched her hood a little tighter and patted her shoulders. "This is *my* battle suit! We have more in common than you think, actually. Maybe. So we should talk about that, all the things we have in common."

She took a step closer but stopped. Even though Mr. Lazardo didn't look regular evil-guy dangerous, he still worked for Hydra and was probably troubled in some way. A Super Hero had to exercise caution.

"Oh, yeah . . . sorry, but I don't think we're at all alike," Mr. Lazardo said. "What with you being a little princess of, you know, vermin."

"Mixed feelings about that," she said. "On the one hand I'm super-glad you're not one of those bad guys that says 'We're not so different, you and I' while, like, at the same time eating puppies or destroying countries or something. I mean, sure, we're all human and all have our struggles, but eating puppies is in a totally different category—"

"SILENCE!" yelled Mr. Lazardo.

Squirrel Girl jumped. It was just a startled little jump, but when you have legs with squirrel strength, little jumps are like five feet in the air.

"Yow," she said to the marketing executive in the leather jumpsuit. "You spooked me with the way you said *SILENCE!* and pointed and all. It was like you saw something horrible behind me, and either it was named Silence or you were telling me to be quiet so it wouldn't eat me. But that wouldn't make sense because you were yelling and if the monster thing ate noisy people it would eat you first—"[79]

Mr. Lazardo began jogging in place, which was so distracting, Squirrel Girl forgot what she was going to say next.

So she said, "Um . . ."

Now Mr. Lazardo was windmilling his arms, like they tell you to do in gym class to stretch out.

"We don't have to fight," she said. "I said this is my battle suit, but actually I consider it more of an *adventure* suit. So we don't need to exactly do battle."

The man sagged. "Don't tell me you're giving up! What? Already?"

"Well, no. I'm not going to let you keep doing your evil plan or whatever. I just hoped we could talk about it and see if there was another way to make you happy besides, you know, whatever crafty and diabolical plans you have for mall opening day,

---

79 I didn't have a plan here. I was stalling, I guess? Till something about this whole scenario made sense?

which apparently includes killing lots of people? Not cool, man."
Squirrel Girl checked herself. She was supposed to be Building
on Common Ground. "But first let's start off with kudos for
coming up with such a thorough plan, complete with the whole
underground lair! I know it's so hard to stop a project right in
the middle, like this one time when I was building a Lego Ferris
wheel—"

"Oh, I'm not planning to kill anyone," he said, taking a
step toward her. She could see perspiration on his forehead. His
leather one-piece was probably pretty hot, especially with those
little exercises he was doing.

"Good," she said. "We've made progress already!"

He took another step closer. "No, see, this is the amazing
part! *You* will be doing all the killing yourselves. I won't have to
lift a finger!"

Ugh. He was close enough that she could smell him now.
Really smell him. He already smelled like stinky boy and dusty
leather. She could tell that from a distance. But now she could
smell his sweat. And not only was it gross, it was *wrong*. Her
throat involuntarily clenched at the odor, and she coughed.

"There it is," he said. "You're picking up the first whiff of it,
aren't you? How about a more pointed blast!"

His suit had some kind of bellows built into his underarms.
When he flapped his arm, the air that had been inside his suit
puffed out of a spout at his wrist and straight at Squirrel Girl. She

coughed harder. The smell was so familiar. . . . The rally! And the mall T-shirts her parents had been wearing.

"There we go!" he said. "You can't cough it out, though. It's *in* you now."

She took a step back, covering her mouth with the back of a hand. "What?" she asked. "What is in me?"

"My *musk*," he said.

Gross, she thought, and then the world tilted around her.

Wait, *what* was gross? She'd just thought that something was gross but already forgot it. And who was she talking to? Oh yeah, Bry. He was standing right in front of her. How had she not noticed him for a second? He was a bad guy. She should probably do something. But her thoughts felt slippery as wet worms. Her heart pounded. Her chest felt tight, her legs wanted to run. They liked to run. She liked to run. And kick. She wanted to do anything but just stand there. Tippy-Toe and Fuzz Fountain Cortez had jumped off her shoulders. Were they fighting each other again? She couldn't focus enough to look.

Ana Sofía had come out of a nearby room to see what was happening. And Squirrel Girl felt a powerful instinct to kick her.

Kick her, kick her hard, make her go away. Make everything go—
No!

Squirrel Girl looked down at herself, disgusted by these thoughts. Her legs started to tremble beneath her with the effort of staying still.

"Look . . ." Her breath was coming quicker now, erratic. "Mr. Lazardo. Bryan. Bry. You don't have to do this, whatever it is you . . . you're—"

He crept closer. Part of her knew that he was there, that he was getting closer, but he also kept slipping her mind. She started to back away—not from him but from Ana Sofía. That random kicking idea was way disturbing.

"I'm not Bryan Lazardo," he said. "That guy no longer exists."

He flipped a green leather hood over his head. Two large plastic eyes were glued onto it.

They look like Kermit the Frog eyes, she thought, and in her slippery-thoughted confusion she feared this man had killed Kermit and taken his eyes.

"THERE IS ONLY LIZARD BRAIN!" he declared. And then he began to laugh.

She wanted to laugh, too. She liked laughing. But she couldn't. She could only scramble backward. She had to get away. Away from . . . from her friend—what was her name again? Away from this room. Away from everything. She was far, far underground and was suddenly aware of the huge mall above her. She had to get out before it broke through and suffocated her. Who was making her so scared? Who was trying to hurt her? She needed to kick! She needed to claw her way free!

She ran to the nearest wall and tried to climb, her claws scratching the smooth metal surface. She should have been able to climb, but she couldn't. Something was wrong. Something was wrong with her.

She turned back to the source of the wrongness. The Muppet-killer. But he was gone. Wasn't he? She couldn't see him anymore.

Then she forgot what it was she was trying to see.

There was only heat and heart pounding and fear, fear, her breath choking, her limbs shaking and everything angry and afraid.

Claws out.

Tail low.

All fours.

Smell fear.

Smell others.

They will hurt you
    unless you hurt them
        first.

Hurt. Gnaw. Kick.

    Fight.

Flee. Flee. Flee

32

SQUIRREL GIRL

*S*quirrel Girl's thoughts slowly shook themselves awake and began to shiver and stretch and crawl around. The pounding of her heart slowed, and her limbs shook off their shakiness. She tilted her head back and forth, as if to dislodge something stuck to it that was making it hard to think. Hard also to see and smell and hear. And basically just to feel like herself, i.e., the unbeatable Squirrel Girl with amazing squirrel powers. She concentrated on opening her eyes before realizing they were already open. What was the matter with her? For another thing, her nose itched really bad and she couldn't seem to scratch it. Every time she tried, her wrist hurt. Even with cloudy thoughts, she felt certain that itchy nose should not equal ouchie wrist.

Finally she was alert enough to notice the massive iron bands around her wrists and ankles. She was shackled to a wall.

Well, that explained a whole lot.

"Hey there, sport!" said Lizard Brain, leaning over to talk right in her face. "Aha! I see a twinkle in your eye, like you've got some higher brain function going on in there. Your fuzzy pals worked out of it already, but your skinny friend is still curled up and shaking." He laughed. "Sorry, it's just so much fun to see how the musk affects different people! She basically collapsed in a heap, while you were ready to tear your way out of here no matter who got in your way. Even her."

Squirrel Girl gasped and looked Ana Sofía over for signs of injury. Had she hurt her? Because that was the most awful of all awfulness that she could possibly imagine. Ana Sofía appeared intact, but as Lizard Brain had said, she was curled up tight as a fist on the floor, her hair over her face, her body visibly shaking.

"Ana Sofía, it's okay," Squirrel Girl said without hope of her friend hearing. "It's going to be okay. We'll . . . We'll save the day . . . still. Somehow."

Lizard Brain giggled. "See, now I *know* the musk has worn off! 'It's going to be okay,' you say!" he snickered. "No, it isn't! Humans are so good at telling lies to themselves!"

Squirrel Girl pulled on the metal bands, testing their strength.

"Uh-uh," said Lizard Brain. "Not a tremendous idea, nope. And I'll tell you why. Shall I tell her why?"

"Yeah, tell her, Lizard Brain!" answered one of the two Hydra agents flanking the reptile-suited PR manager. They were in full armor, now with gas masks fastened over their nose and mouth.

"I'll bet you can guess why," said Lizard Brain. "It starts with *mmmm* and ends with *ssskk* and you know what's in the middle? *You* are!"

"Your musk," Squirrel Girl said tiredly. "It's your musk. You're threatening to musk me again if I try to escape and then there's a chance I wouldn't be in control of myself enough to keep from hurting my friend, so you know the threat of that will keep me still even if I could get out of these stupid bands."

Lizard Brain frowned. "Well, yeah, but it was really my turn to tell you."

"Sorry, Bry," she said.

He shrugged like it was no big deal even though clearly it bugged him.

Squirrel Girl glanced at Ana Sofía but looked quickly away, her body shivering with panic just at the thought of what she almost did to her friend. What she still might do, with her dangerous squirrel strength. Curse her dangerous squirrel strength! She shivered harder, unable to look at Ana Sofía again.

"Anyhoo," Lizard Brain said, "about my musk. Essentially it reminds people of their true selves and makes them return to it. Primal. Instinctual. No lying to yourself when you're an animal. Groovy, isn't it?"

"Yep," said Squirrel Girl, taking a weak stab at the whole build-on-common-ground thing, though mostly she just wanted to punch him in the face.

"Do you know what your true self is?" Lizard Brain asked.

"What everyone's true self is? Selfishness. You run to preserve yourself. You attack anything that is weaker than you. That's what the mighty musk reveals! Humans are, in their hearts, in their primal brains, *selfish* beings. It's civilization that lies to you that you have to care about anything besides yourself. For example—"

He made a flourish with his leather-sleeved arm. One of the Hydra agents jumped to attention and wheeled in a cart with a cage built of thick chicken wire. At first glance, Squirrel Girl thought there must be some sort of terribly sad llama in there, lying down all miserable to be in such a small cage. But a few tails twitched, and there was a bright pink bow. All the squirrels were lying on the bottom of the cage, looking sluggish, tuckered out, spent, and generally exhausted after their musking and the ensuing flight-or-fight mania.

"Tippy!" said Squirrel Girl. "You okay? Chomps, can you move? Is Gnome Chompsky okay? Please be okay. Cortez, can you check on Gnome? And Shamescuttle? Oh, and Spencer the—"

"Yes, all right, yes, so many squirrels, so many names," said Lizard Brain. "Anyhoo. Fun fact about my musk. Yes, it temporarily clouds higher brain function, turning on the fight-or-flight instinct in creatures, but in order to inflict some real damage, you need to set up ideal conditions. First, an enclosed space."

He gestured to the squirrel cage like a TV salesperson showing off fine jewelry.

"When there's nowhere to run, there's no *flight*, see? There's only *FIGHT.*" He began to giggle again. "And imagine . . . imagine how much worse the fighting—how positively *lethal*—if all the creatures in the enclosed space already kinda despise each other?"

"Like in the mall tomorrow," said Squirrel Girl. "You got Shady Oaks and Listless Pines all mad and hating on each other with that stupid cat versus dog stuff and then when they're all inside the mall you'll lock them in and use the ventilation system to gas them with your nasty sweat odors, which will make them need to fight and they'll kill each other, and the mall security footage will show them doing it to each other as if in a frenzy of shopping mania, so you'll keep opening more malls or other buildings all over the country where you can get people riled up and enraged and then lock them in together and gas them, spreading hate and fear and destruction and death."

Lizard Brain stuck out his lower lip. "Again, it was *my* turn to tell it!"

"Oh!" said Squirrel Girl. "You laced the Team Dog and Team Cat T-shirts with musk, didn't you? When people wore them, they were more prone to fighting. Also, Dog-Lord and Mistress Meow had musk bombs. But they were used outside, and the musk dissipated in the air too quickly to cause any real harm. That's why you need the closed environment of the mall—"

"ANYHOO," he said, "we've worked so hard on this plan,

Squirrelly Girly. I just need to be one hundred percent super-positive that it will go off without a hitch, so here's the sitch: tell me everything you've told the Avengers about this plan, or I musk your squirrel pallies in that confining little cage and you get to watch them tear each other apart, mm-kay?"

Squirrel Girl blinked. "Avengers? What? Who are the Avengers? Oh, you mean the Super Hero people on the TV? I don't know the Avengers, ha-ha, why would you think—"

"'Hey, Avenger pals!'" he read from her phone, which was clearly no longer in her utility belt but in his greasy gloved hand. "'So my best human and squirrel friends believe it really is real Hydra for real setting up a mall for bad-guy reasons. Can any of you come and, you know, avenger them out of my neighborhood?'"

"Crap," she said.

"I've read the texts," said Lizard Brain. "What I don't know is what else you might have told them in phone calls or in person. I assume you heroes all pal around together."

"Totally," said Squirrel Girl with the best straight face she could muster.

"Fine, then talk. TALK! Or the squirrels get the musk."

He pointed his wrist spout at the cage.

"TheAvengersdon'tknow," said Squirrel Girl superfast. "They don't know anything, seriously! Leave the squirrels alone, they didn't do anything to you. Well, except attack all your agent friends and gnaw through half your base, but they didn't do anything to you *personally*!"

"The Avengers don't know where we are or what we plan?" he asked.

"I haven't talked to them," said Squirrel Girl. "Just the texting, I swear."

"I believe her, boss," an agent said through his gas mask. "She seems like a terrible liar."

"True," said Lizard Brain. "Hmm. Good enough, eh, folks? Let's get this Hate Initiative going. What fun! And speaking of fun . . ."

He pointed a wrist spout at the cage and worked his armpit bellows, sending a cloud of visible brownish musk at the squirrels.

"NO!" said Squirrel Girl, pulling on her shackles. She winced, afraid to see the horror that would come next.

The exhausted squirrels began to twitch, again breathing in the musk. But instead of tearing and clawing and biting, they nestled closer, wrapped tails around necks, nuzzled and hid and chittered.

They were afraid. And yet they nested together. Even Tippy-Toe and Fuzz Fountain Cortez, who had attacked each other when first exposed to the gas, seemed to handle it better now, perhaps because they knew what to expect. They lay side by side, their tails entwined.

"Encaged but not enraged," said Squirrel Girl. She looked at Ana Sofía again and felt certain that there was no way, no chance, nohow that anyone, least of all Lizard Brain, could make her hurt her BHFF.

Lizard Brain squirted another puff at the cage. He turned to an agent. "They were fighting, right, Harry? The squirrels? I swear they were fighting each other before."

Ana Sofía had uncurled and sat partway up, the musk seeming to loosen its hold on her at last. She met Squirrel Girl's eyes and finger-spelled words one-handed, down by her side to avoid notice. She was pretty quick and the lighting was dim, but Squirrel Girl thought Ana Sofía was asking if she was strong enough to get loose.

"Maybe," Squirrel Girl finger-spelled back. She turned her head to see if she could reach her wrist with her teeth. She could. Typical non-squirrel-powered villain mistake: they always overlook the teeth. But if she did get free and Lizard Brain musked her again, what if she hurt Ana Sofía? How could she risk it?

"Can . . . Can I say something?" Ana Sofía's voice warbled when she spoke. Either the musk was still thick in her, or else she was just super-afraid.

Yes, say something, Ana Sofía! thought Squirrel Girl. *You are the smartest and the bestest and I know whatever you say will help us win the day and make everything better!*

Lizard Brain looked at her pointedly, clearly still irritated at the lack of violence in the squirrel cage. When she didn't talk, he sighed and said, as if to an imaginary camera, "This is Bryan Lazardo reporting to you live from the Chester Yard Mall basement lair, where some girl apparently has something *super-important* to say from her crouched position on the floor, urgent enough to demand the attention of the mighty Lizard Brain! Go ahead and tell us, trembling girl. The audience at home is waiting!"

Ana Sofía cleared her throat. She said, "Hydra rocks."

Huh. That was not what Squirrel Girl was expecting. It wasn't even close.[80]

"Um, yes. That's true," said Lizard Brain. "Anyhoo—"

"Hydra rocks," Ana Sofía said louder. "Hydra rocks!"

Squirrel Girl was no clearer on what her BHFF was doing. And she felt that she *should* know. Ana Sofía couldn't possibly be sincere in her complimentary exclamation about the evilest organization on the planet. Was this a secret clue Ana Sofía was giving her? Was Squirrel Girl failing a test? And did this mean that they weren't suited for best-friendship after all?[81]

"If you're trying to convince me you're switching sides," said Lizard Brain, "I don't believe it. I'm not giving you a job, so don't even try."

---

80 I was expecting something along the lines of *You're a losing loser who loses* or maybe *Your poo-colored BO will never defeat our sincere and lifelong friendship!* or possibly *Bite me, Turd Man.*

81 If this conclusion was a tad overdramatic, remember that I was shackled in an evil basement lair, so I'm kinda allowed?

"Don't you think so, though?" said Ana Sofía. "That Hydra rocks?"

"I already said I did!" said Lizard Brain.

"Then why don't you say it?" asked Ana Sofía.

"Yeah, boss," said an agent. "Why don't you say it?"

"Yeah, Hydra rocks!" said another, holding up his pointer finger and pinky. "Say it, boss!"

Lizard Brain shifted in his leather suit. "Fine. Hydra rocks."

Tik-tik fffshhhhhh . . . Sprinklers on the ceiling shifted on and began spraying water droplets on their heads. Squirrel Girl had seen no fire, smelled no smoke that would have set them off—

"Ohhhhh," said Squirrel Girl to Ana Sofía. "Earlier you must have hacked into their security system in the awesome way that you do that seems like a legit super power, and set a voice-activated phrase to turn on the fire sprinklers. You chose 'Hydra rocks' because it seemed like something these jerks would be likely to say, but it didn't work when you said it because there must have been a voice-recognition component, so Bry here had to be the one to say it and oh my heck that's so clever!" Squirrel Girl realized she'd been talking really fast, and with the water and all, Ana Sofía likely hadn't been able to read her lips. So she tried to sum up: "You're amazing. I'm really glad you're my friend."

Ana Sofía smiled. It was pretty stellar having a best friend to fight alongside you a hundred feet belowground in a secret evil lair.

"Wait, what's happening?" asked Lizard Brain, pulling his hood forward in a vain attempt to keep his face dry.

"My best friend just cracked your shell," said Squirrel Girl.

"And now I'm gonna eat the pistachio."[82]

"Sprinklers off!" Lizard Brain shouted at the ceiling. Nothing happened.

Squirrel Girl turned to her right wrist shackle and started to gnaw.

"Don't even try to get loose," said Lizard Brain. "Those shackles are squirrel-proof."

The squirrels flicked tails and chittered. The water must have washed away the musk effects for them, too.

"They're laughing," said Squirrel Girl, her mouth full of metal. "There's. No. Such. Thing. As—*squirrel-proof*!"

The shackle snapped under her teeth, and she immediately bent to the one on her other wrist.

"Stop!" said Lizard Brain. "Cease!"

Squirrel Girl pretty much didn't stop or cease.

"I'm warning you!" he said. He pointed his wrists at her and valiantly pumped the bellows under his arms. If his musk was shooting out through the spouts on his wrists, it went nowhere but down in the rain-filled room.

The second shackle broke under her teeth. She bent and pulled open her ankle shackles.

---

82 Aw geez, that wasn't the best line. Next time I go into an evil lair I've got to remember to have some good battle puns ready to go.

"STOP!" said Lizard Brain.

"Nope," said Squirrel Girl.

And she sprang.

First she grabbed her phone from his hand and stuck it back in her utility belt.[83] Then after dodging a couple of plasma blasts she thought maybe getting her phone shouldn't have been step one. But still. It was her phone.

"Rethink your villainous ways!" she said, grabbing a plasma shooter from one agent.

"Find some real friends!" she said, yanking a shooter from the other.

"Contribute in a positive manner to the society in which you live!" she said, opening the side of the cage, releasing the squirrels, and stuffing the two agents into it.

"You can't stop Hydra!" said Lizard Brain. "If you cut one of us down—"

She punched him in the face. He fell down. She watched him for a second, looked around, and shrugged.

"Weird," she said. "I thought two others were supposed to take your place."

He clambered back to his feet and looked at her with great intensity, as if willing his musk to overwhelm her. But the downpour continued to neutralize it, pulling the gas particles into the droplets and down to the puddles on the floor.

---

83 Priorities, amirite?

298

She ran a claw down the back of Lizard Brain's battle suit, ripping the leather open, and then tore it off him so he couldn't gather and spray musk with it anymore. Underneath, he was naked but for tight black swim briefs.

"Gross," she said.

"Shows what you know," he said, his soaked hair dripping water into his eyes. "All the coolest guys are going to be wearing these at the beach this summer. Just you wait!"

"Um, okay," said Squirrel Girl, already feeling a little bad for him, all wet like a lost puppy and sniveling in defeat. He looked about as scary as a wilted carrot.

But still. Take no chances with bad dudes! She hauled him to the wall and snapped his ankles into the unbroken shackles.

"Game over!" said Squirrel Girl. "Final boss defeated. New high score: USGAA!"

"USGAA?" asked Lizard Brain.

"Unbeatable Squirrel Girl," she said.

Two hundred sloppy wet squirrels gathered at her feet, climbed onto her legs, shoulders, head. She smiled.

"*And* army."

33

ANA SOFÍA

"**D**id we win?" asked Ana Sofía, standing up. Even her socks were soaked, and they squished unpleasantly inside her boots. She'd taken off her hearing aids to protect them from the water, and they were dry and safe tucked into a plastic baggie she kept in her jacket pocket for just-in-case-of-rain, and now also for just-in-case-of-heroic-fire-sprinklers-in-Hydra-bases.

Squirrel Girl said something that Ana Sofía didn't catch, so she lifted her wet hair to show her she wasn't wearing her hearing aids.

"Yes!" Squirrel Girl signed. "We saved the day! There is no more day-saving to be done!"

They stood smiling at each other, drops of water plopping off the tips of their noses. Ana Sofía had enacted more smiles since becoming friends with Squirrel Girl than probably the rest of her life combined. Her cheek muscles didn't even hurt anymore.

"Honestly I wasn't too hopeful for a bit there, but WAHOO!" she said in a very un–Ana Sofía way, her fist punching the air.

Squirrel Girl laughed. "You are the best BHFF a Super Hero ever had."

"True. But my cheering was not an invitation to get sentimental, please."

"Right," Squirrel Girl signed. "Sorry. I just love the stuffing out of you, is all."

"Enough."

"Got it. No problem. You awesome, amazing person."

"Aaa!"

Lizard Brain said something, and Squirrel Girl laughed. Ana Sofía didn't hear, but Squirrel Girl told her later he'd asked to be set free, and she'd said, *Nice try, Bry. You're staying here till we figure out what happens after the end of the final boss battle in real life. In video games, this is the part when the game turns off. Ooh, this is exciting!*

Ana Sofía led them all away from the indoor rainstorm, down the corridor they'd come, and into the open shaft room. At last away from the water, the girls squeezed water from their hair and clothes. Ana Sofía replaced her hearing aids.

"Is everybody here?" said Squirrel Girl. "Anyone hurt? I feel like we're shy a few squirrel friends."

Tippy-Toe chittered something, shaking her fur till it started to dry.

"Yeah, I guess you're right, Tip. Wet squirrels take up half the usual space. You all look travel-size. Adorbs! So . . . now what?" Squirrel Girl looked up the shaft and signed, "I don't see a ladder."

Ana Sofía investigated an elevator.

"It appears we did such a good job of destruction that we cut off electricity to the elevators."

"Oh." Squirrel Girl and the squirrels looked around. "Huh. Well, that was some good smashing, squirrels."

And then the roof above the hundred-foot shaft broke, and through it fell Thor. He landed on his feet.[84] Ana Sofía didn't even blink. This was her life now, she guessed. And she liked it.

"And thus I come to save the day!" he said, his hammer held aloft in his mighty arm. "Where are the villainous vermin? They will feel the sting of Mjölnir!"

"Hey! Hi! Great!" said Ana Sofía, suddenly feeling super-embarrassed. "Well . . . this is awkward. We already saved the day."

Thor lowered his hammer. He looked around. "Thou didst?"

"Yep!" said Squirrel Girl. "Like, just now. Literally two minutes ago I said 'The day is saved!' and then you dropped in."

"Oh," he said.

"Sorry," said Ana Sofía. "I didn't mean to make you come all the way from space. I would have texted you not to bother but I didn't think you were planning on it."

---

84 Just like a cat. Or like Thor, I guess. Like Cat Thor.

Thor's shoulders stooped.

"'Tis okay," he said. "The son of Odin had every confidence in thy day-saving abilities. I just wanted to help."

Tippy-Toe leaped onto Squirrel Girl's shoulder and chittered in her ear.

"Oh, hey, Thor! You could be really useful still, though," said Squirrel Girl. "Tippy says when we were . . . um, smashing up the Hydra base, we kind of disabled all the escape routes. The elevators. Even the stairs. You know squirrels," said Squirrel Girl with a shrug.

Ana Sofía didn't quite catch that exchange the first time and asked Squirrel Girl to repeat it.

"Oh! Yeah!" said Ana Sofía. "Elevators and stairs! We're, like, stuck down here! And since you can fly . . . or sort of fly— hammer-fly—can you give us a lift?"

Thor straightened up. He smiled.

They decided to do it all in one trip. Thor held on to Ana Sofía with one arm. She felt like a little kid again, as light as a toddler lifted up by her father—if her father was wearing full- body leather and metal armor. She couldn't help giggling and hoped nobody noticed. Squirrel Girl rode piggyback, batting his long red cape out of her face. And two hundred squirrels attached themselves like tree frogs all over his bulky frame. Amazingly, he had enough surface area to support them all.

With his free hand, Thor whipped his hammer around in

circles, shot it straight up, and suddenly they were *all* shooting straight up.[85]

"Uhhhh . . ." Ana Sofía said before the rush of air stole her breath completely and her stomach seemed to stay behind. The fall up felt faster than the fall down. Thor shot through the hole he'd made and then alighted on the mall roof. Squirrel Girl and squirrels leaped off him, but Ana Sofía still clung on. She looked firmly at the firm ground, and very firmly ordered her hands to let go. They weren't in midair anymore. They were safe. But still her hands gripped Thor's cape and a buckle on his breastplate. She could feel his chest rumble with a laugh.

"I fell," Ana Sofía said. "Earlier, I fell. A long way. Squirrel Girl caught me. But it was—"

SCARY! It'd been really, really scary, and frankly after a fright like that, not to mention fighting all those Hydra agents with their sploidy plasma guns and the horrible, bone-deep, gnawing primal terror she'd felt with the musk, she couldn't convince her desperate, trembling hands that clinging to a large, very strong Super Hero wasn't the best place and only safe space in the entire world, and that once you were there, the wisest course wasn't just to STAY FOREVER.[86]

Ana Sofía felt Thor pat her gently on her head.

---

85 So basically he just throws his hammer really hard, and then hangs on to it so that he goes with it? Not sure if that's physically possible, but I haven't taken Physics yet. I'm still on Biology 1.

86 Dude. I had no idea this was so hard on Ana Sofía. And she still saved the day anyway. Isn't she literally the best in the entire world?

Tippy-Toe climbed onto her shoulder. She wiped her already-dried tail over Ana Sofía's brow. It should have tickled, but instead it was soothing. The squirrel chittered something at her and pointed.

On the ground at Thor's feet, all the squirrels had gathered into a tight red, orange, gray, and black mass. Their tails were fluffed up invitingly.

Ana Sofía glared at her gripping hands until they were ready to obey her. She took a deep breath, and she let go. Two hundred squirrels caught her. It was like jumping into a pile of freshly washed socks, all cozy and soft and surprisingly good-smelling. They slowly released her till she was sitting on the solid roof.

"Someone always catches me," said Ana Sofía.

Squirrel Girl was typing on her phone.

"Black Widow is in space fighting Thanos," said Squirrel Girl, "but I think someone from S.H.I.E.L.D. will be—"

She was cut off by a loud clacking noise that messed up Ana Sofía's hearing aids so much she just switched them off. A sleek black helicopter landed on the roof, and a tall, broad black man wearing an eye patch hopped out.

Whoa, that's Nick Fury, Ana Sofía thought, frankly shocked that after all she'd seen and done with Squirrel Girl *anything* could still shock her.

The S.H.I.E.L.D. commander was followed out of the helicopter by a half dozen men and women in black outfits who immediately rappelled down into the hole Thor had made. One agent carried a long pole with an electric loop on the end, like a high-tech dog catcher. She seemed to know Squirrel Girl, and they exchanged a few words.

"Look out for a guy in swim briefs shackled to a wall—he's surprisingly dangerous!" Ana Sofía called out in case no one else had warned them. "Keep your gas masks on around him!"

There was conversation between Nick Fury, Thor, and Squirrel Girl, which Ana Sofía completely missed until the helicopter blades stopped.

"Nick Fury and S.H.I.E.L.D. will clean up the Hydra stuff," said Squirrel Girl, catching Ana Sofía up when she had switched her hearing aids back on.

"Oh, good," she said. "Just FYI, if there's a way you can do that without blowing up the mall, that'd be great. I mean, everyone was really looking forward to having a mall in the neighborhood. Also for the jobs it would create."

Nick Fury nodded. "I'll see what I can do."

"Thanks," said Ana Sofía. "Even Vin was excited about the mall. He'd mentioned maybe coming here together sometime . . . not that he ever follows through or anything. . . ."

"Who be this Vin?" asked Thor.

Ana Sofía shrugged and wished she hadn't brought it up. Was there a Super Hero who could travel back in time and erase awkward conversations? Because that was a power she longed for.

"Vin Tang is this guy who is sort of friends with us," said Squirrel Girl. "And he—"

Ana Sofía slugged her in the shoulder, but Squirrel Girl kept talking.

"—he kind of asked Ana Sofía out but then he never set a date and never brought it up again, so it's weird, right? I mean, you guys are guys—do you get guys when they do stuff like that?"

Nick Fury's cheeks darkened, and he said something like ". . . I don't have daughters for a reason . . ." before turning away and becoming suddenly very busy with a tablet computer.

"Vin. Tang." Thor scowled. "I will have a word with this Vin Tang."

Thor had certainly jumped right into his tío role, as overprotective of Ana Sofía as her mom's brothers were. Honestly, she'd almost think he was Mexican American instead of Asgardian.

"Don't you dare, Thor," said Ana Sofía. "I mean it. It's seriously not a big deal."

He scowled at her. She glared back. He was a pretty good scowler, but honestly no match for her glare. He broke first, looking away.[87]

"Fine, then. I will probably not visit this Vin Tang and speak to him most sternly."

---

87 He never had a chance. Beware the powerful glare of Ana Sofía!

Ana Sofía sighed really, really hard.

"Well," said Thor, "I suppose I should go back to space now. To fight Thanos."

"If you've defeated Thanos by next Saturday, we're having Marquito's birthday party, and Mom wanted me to tell you she's making a lot of empanadas and also pastel de tres leches."[88]

Thor's brow furrowed thoughtfully. "Saturday. Well, then, I must save the universe by Saturday. I will inform the Avengers of our updated timeline."

With a crack of thunder, he was gone.

"He's such a show-off," said Ana Sofía.

"We should get home," Squirrel Girl said to Nick Fury. "Parents. You know how they are."

"I can offer you a lift," he said, gesturing to the helicopter.

"No thanks!" said Ana Sofía. She climbed down a ladder attached to the roof, her legs trembling until she reached the firm ground below. She began to run toward home as soon as her feet touched asphalt. A squirrel army escorted her all the way.

Ana Sofía Arcos Romero was not a person who collected phobias. She preferred to believe she chose what she did and did not do based on cool-headed reason with no other influences. But maybe, she admitted to herself, just maybe, she had a *thing* about heights.

---

88 Pastel de tres leches means "three-milk cake." It's a light, spongy cake drenched with cream, sweetened condensed milk, and evaporated milk so it's all juicy and yummy and there's no way I'm missing Marco's birthday party.

34

DOREEN

*T*he Monday after the failed mall opening, Doreen woke up to her phone alarm declaring in Hulk's voice, "WAKE UP OR HULK WILL WAKE YOU UP." She immediately regretted downloading that Hulk alarm app. She turned it off and tried to get up, but her tail had other ideas, lying over her head like the coziest blanket in the entire universe. Doreen started to drift back to sleep—

No! She had to get to school early. Squirrel Girl was victorious, but Doreen had an outstanding problem.

She threw on normal clothes, speed-ate three bowls of cereal, stuffed her tail into her pants, and ran to school only slightly faster than humanly possible—at least when anyone was looking.

She arrived just as the doors unlocked, and she bolted up to her homeroom. She was in luck. Her teacher was already there, and the other students were not.

She stared at Ms. Schweinbein's back as the teacher erased the chalkboard.

She's kind of a Todd, Doreen thought. *Laser Lady would totally get me right now.*

Doreen took a big breath and tried to remember what she'd planned to say. Her mind was blank. That talk with her parents on Friday had felt helpful, but to be honest, most of what they'd said she couldn't even remember anymore. She just knew that she had told them everything, and that they'd listened to her. And that she'd felt pretty good about it all—hopeful even. Also the cake. She remembered the cake.

So maybe the most important part of talking it out was not the talking but the listening.[89] She stretched, readied her listening muscles and "I" messages, and then cleared her throat.

Ms. Schweinbein whipped around, startled, and her expression was visibly disappointed when she saw Doreen.

"Yes?"

"Ms. Schweinbein, I feel like maybe you don't like me so much. I was wondering, did I do something that I should apologize for? 'Cause I'm one hundred percent into apologizing."

Then she waited. Trying not to fidget, to show how sincerely she was listening.

Ms. Schweinbein started in on one of her possibly-award-winning sighs, but stopped midway through. "You are the kind

---

89 Or the cake. But I didn't have any cake handy so I was going to have to rely on the listening.

of student, Doreen, that rubs me the wrong way. Your outbursts, your attempt to pace alongside me as if mocking me, your comments about my odor . . ."

Doreen very much wanted to interject with a detailed explanation of why and how and that's not what she'd meant . . . but she shut her mouth and kept on her listening face as Ms. Schweinbein outlined all her faults.

"Teaching is a challenging profession, Ms. Green. And being *mocked* by students is *not* a perk."

Doreen's heart had begun to pound. Sweat gathered on her forehead, feeling prickly and unpleasant. Her muscles heated, her stomach was sick. She inhaled through her nose. No scent of musk. Nope, this was just normal panic. First came the flight option: she should run away and never talk to her teacher again. The fight option perked up, too, by suggesting she had the strength to throw her teacher through a window. No, no, that would not do.

Especially not now, not after she'd seen Ms. Schweinbein at home. She was a real person with a real house and real pets, and an odd and probably illegal barnyard in her basement. That was kind of cool. Maybe Doreen could be the one to have a little understanding.

After rejecting both flight and fight, Doreen discovered a third option, a kindness one, a bonding one. After all, base animal instincts didn't just include flight and fight. There was also building of community: nests of squirrels, packs of wolves, adorable little caveman villages with top-notch cave wall paintings.

"Never mind," Ms. Schweinbein was saying. "I didn't get into teaching to make BFFs, so I'll get over it. So, anyway . . ." She started to go through papers.

"Ms. Schweinbein," said Doreen, "I am really sorry. I didn't mean to mock you, but I totally see that that's how it seemed. I feel awful that I ever made your day worse."

"Oh," said Ms. Schweinbein, seeming surprised. "That's . . . that's okay."

"Also . . ." Doreen pointed to the sign on the wall: WIGGLING IS INAPPROPRIATE HUMAN BEHAVIOR. "Maybe if you thought of us as animals, that would help. Like how when something rolls by a cat, they can't help but want to paw at it? And if something smells interesting, a dog is going to want to sniff it? Well, sometimes human kids need to wiggle. Or say things that aren't just right and perfect, and stuff. If you thought of me as an animal, do you think you could like me bett—"

"YES," said Ms. Schweinbein a little too quickly.

"Oh, good," said Doreen. "Because animals are awesome, which is an opinion that I think we both have in common, and having things in common is good, but anyway I'd love to listen to anything you have to say on that topic as I'm a pretty good listener working on my listening skills?"

"I love animals. In fact . . ." Ms. Schweinbein dabbed the inside corners of her eyes. "When I was little, I wanted to be a goat."

"A goat? Huh. That's really interesting, Ms. Schweinbein. I

never met anyone who wanted to be a goat before. And I just want to say, I think it's really sad when dreams don't come true, but really cool that you're doing your best anyway."

"Thanks, Doreen," said Ms. Schweinbein, sounding like she really meant it.

"And, hey, I was thinking about your . . . um, I mean, you know Squirrel Girl? She asked me to pass along a message to you."

"WHAT." The teacher dropped her papers to the floor.

"I kinda know her, no big deal," said Doreen, gathering up the papers. "But she was thinking, if the mall opens up, it could really use a petting zoo. Not sure what she meant by that *exactly*, since I'm not her and therefore don't have access to all her thoughts, though I'm sure they're grade-A thoughts, but just passing along a random message."

Ms. Schweinbein's eyes twinkled.

For a second there, Doreen thought she might even hug her. But the early bell rang and students started coming in. Doreen took her seat and made a mental note not to comment on how people smell anymore. And one time when she raised her hand, Ms. Schweinbein even called on her.

So Doreen was feeling pretty good when she headed to lunch. She was starving, having run out of the house that morning after only three bowls of cereal with almond milk, and was the first to the Squirrel Scouts lunch table by the frozen-yogurt machine.

Vin Tang arrived second. He looked even paler today than

usual, with dark circles under his eyes. He sat down and stared at his bagged lunch without opening it.

"You okay?" asked Doreen.

Vin startled, then nodded. He leaned closer to Doreen to talk under the noise of the cafeteria. "I . . . Last night Thor showed up at my house. He was holding a hammer bigger than my head. He told me I'd better be nice to girls or he'd know about it."

"Ah, yeah . . . so he's a personal friend of the Arcos Romero family? And Squirrel Girl mentioned to him how you asked out Ana Sofía but then never set a date or called her back—"

"Oh!" said Vin. "I was waiting for her to tell me when. Isn't that how it works? A guy asks a girl to go out and then she takes care of everything else?"[90]

"Um, I don't think so," said Doreen. "Dude, I don't know. But probably you should talk to Ana Sofía about it?"

"Okay," he said, nodding vigorously. "Okay. Hey, so she isn't friends with any of the scarier heroes, right? Like Hulk or Ant-Man?"

"Ant-Man?"

"Ants are *scary*, Doreen! Have you seen them up close? They're like MONSTERS!"

"Yeah, okay, well, just talk to Ana Sofía, okay?"

"Hey, Vin. Hey, Doreen," said Heidi, arriving with her usual entourage of friends. "Since the mall still isn't open, this weekend

---

90 Not that anyone's asking, but this is one reason why I'm not dating till I'm in college, is all I'm saying.

we're getting together at Dennis's pad to talk Squirrel Scout strategy—"

"Hang on," said Dennis, "not everyone's invited, you know."

"What are you talking about, Dennis?" said Heidi. "The party is for Squirrel Scouts, isn't it?"

"Exactly my point!" he said.

"WHAT ARE YOU EVEN TALKING ABOUT, DENNIS?" said Janessa. "Doreen is a Squirrel Scout, isn't she?"

"Oh yeah!" said Dennis. "I forgot that you were! My bad. How come you don't come out with us to fight beside Squirrel Girl?"

"Parents," she said vaguely. "Middle school."

"Dude," he said and gave her a high five. "See you Saturday?"

"Sure," said Doreen.

Her stomach warbled like it was full of wasps and her palms itched and sweated, though she played it pretty cool. She still wasn't 100 percent sure how to be Doreen Green. But she reminded herself that Ana Sofía would be there. It *was* incredibly awesome having a best friend to fight alongside you a hundred feet belowground in a secret evil lair. But it was just as awesome having a best friend to stand beside you as you walked into a middle school party.[91]

---

91 And/or a best friend to leave a party early with you, as we ended up doing. It was an okay party, but too noisy for Ana Sofía, so we went to my house and played video games for hours and ate all the cheese and crackers till we were almost but not quite sick. It was the awesomest.

As the LARPers and Somebodies and the rest of the Squirrel Scouts sat down, Doreen stood up.

"So I spoke to Squirrel Girl," said Doreen.

They all stopped talking and looked at her.

Huh. That line had worked on Ms. Schweinbein, too. She needed to use it more often. "She wants me to tell you guys to calm the freak down."

They nodded wisely.

"That sounds like her."

"Forsooth."

"You guys are getting hurt and being way too violent just generally," said Doreen. "And Squirrel Girl is not hip to it. Like, I know that, uh, *we* all want to fight evil and crime and stuff, but we don't have to be the punchers, right? Let's leave the punching to the girl with the squirrel powers."

That was the speech she'd been preparing, and unlike in her daydreams, there didn't appear to be any fallout. Dennis, who had a sprained wrist from Mistress Meow, was nodding emphatically.

"So we should figure out what being a Squirrel Scout is going to mean going forward?" said Heidi.

"Maybe we need to train more in combat," said Jackson.

"Some of us *are* well trained," said the duchess.

"No, I think we should be more of a fan club, right?" said Dennis. "And cheer for Squirrel Girl and stuff from a safe distance?"

"At least there should be regular parties," said Janessa.

The discussion got going, and Vin live-texted it on the Squirrel Scouts thread so the Skunk Club at the high school could see it as well as Ana Sofía. By the time she arrived, they'd moved on to other topics, and she was well-informed.

Ana Sofía sat beside Doreen and opened up her laptop.

"So we keep talking about me teaching you computer stuff but never do it 'cause there's never free time," she said. "But I don't want computers to just be my thing because if I teach you what I know maybe we can get into the same college one day and major in computer science together and basically just keep being best human friends forever and ever, so how about we just start right now?"

"Heck yes," said Doreen.

She sat across from her, opened up her lunch bag, and tossed Ana Sofía the string cheese her mom had packed for her. She took a handful of raisin-free trail mix, munching while listening to Ana Sofía's in-depth explanation of databases. She hoped no Super Villain chose today to show up in Shady Oaks demanding to fight Squirrel Girl. She was looking forward to a full day of being Doreen Green.

EPILOGUE

*T*hree weeks later, Doreen was back at the mall for the first time since Squirrel Girl punched a bunch of Hydra agents till they didn't want to be bad guys anymore.[92] Hundreds of people from both Shady Oaks and Listless Pines showed up, some in freshly washed Chester Yard Mall T-shirts, but many without. The combined Union High and Listless Pines High marching bands were playing a song they'd rehearsed together.[93] If it didn't exactly create a perfect harmony of love and acceptance, the result could still be classified as "music."

A huge banner proclaimed it OPENING DAY OF COMMUNITY MALL! Beneath the banner, on the dais, Pepper Potts spoke into the microphone. She was a petite light-skinned woman with bright

---

92 Or maybe they're just in S.H.I.E.L.D. jail. But I prefer to believe they woke up from sproing-induced unconsciousness and declared, "Squirrel Girl's awesome punching abilities made me realize I would rather be good and kind and sell ice cream flavors of the delicious variety!"

93 Well, they definitely *played* it together. But after hearing the final product, I'm skeptical about any alleged rehearsals.

red hair, dressed inconspicuously in a blue pantsuit, but her voice was commanding.

"When we at Stark Enterprises heard about the tragic situation here in your community, we saw not only an opportunity to make a great business deal but a chance to help you keep your mall. Your own Squirrel Girl contacted Mr. Stark to ask for his help. Mr. Stark could not be here today as he is currently lending a hand to the Avengers—"

A man in a black suit came up to Pepper Potts's elbow and whispered in her ear, handing her a folded piece of paper.

"Oh," said Ms. Potts, unfolding the paper. "It appears Tony Stark sent a message he wants me to read to you.

"'We at Stark Enterprises are happy to help Shady Oaks and Listless Pines keep their new mall after potential disaster was averted, thanks in no small part to Squirrel Girl. And if she's there, I just want Squirrel Girl to know that a lot of people like how I wear my facial hair. I get compliments on it constantly. And I don't have any reservations about my facial hair choices, nor are they covering up any deep-seated insecurities, just FYI.'

"Okay, so that just happened," Pepper Potts continued, refolding the paper. "In the future, I'm just going to scan Tony's memos to myself before reading them aloud. Anyway, Union Junior student Ana Sofía Arcos Romero has been instrumental in saving this mall and has worked with me personally to find businesses to open shops, including Shady Oaks Shades, Schweinbein's

Petting Zoo, Socks Socks Socks, Somebodies Froyo, Professor Nutty's Nut Emporium, and Burger Frog. I've asked Ana Sofía to say a few words."

Ana Sofía stood up at the microphone. She looked so small up there, squinting out and frowning at the crowd. By now, Doreen was literate in her BHFF's various frowns, and this was her I'm Nervous But Determined frown.

"YEAH, ANA SOFÍA!" Doreen yelled.

The Squirrel Scouts shouted, too.

"Ana Sofía! Represent!"

"That's our girl! Go, Ana Sofía!"

Ana Sofía read from a paper.

"Thank you, Ms. Virginia Potts, CEO of Stark Enterprises and one of my personal role models. *Ahem.* Greetings, people. I'm honored to be here today and first want to convey a message Squirrel Girl asked me to pass along. And I quote: 'Yes, dudes! We totally wiped out those jerks! Hydra is the worst. The literal worst. For real. So let's stop being jerks to each other and enjoy some tasty froyo flavors and play on the escalators!'"

Some in the crowd laughed, some applauded politely. Ana Sofía looked up and folded her paper.

"Look, I've seen the message boards. I know some of you still don't think it was really the real Hydra. Even though I videoed the really real Hydra agents attacking Squirrel Girl with plasma guns in their secret underground lair. It seems super-strange how some believe and pass around the weirdest conspiracy theories and then deny hard, scientific facts and actual evidence—"

Pepper Potts made the wrap-it-up signal with a circling finger and smiled encouragingly at Ana Sofía.

"Anyway," said Ana Sofía. "Squirrel Girl risked her furry tail for you. And I did, too, actually, now that I think about it, only not my tail since I don't have one. *Ahem.* But the least you could do is try to be nice to each other, okay? It's so arbitrary anyway! I mean, yeah some of us live in one neighborhood and some the other, but like Squirrel Girl says, we don't have to be jerks about it! So, thanks, Ms. Potts and Stark Enterprises."

And she promptly walked off the stage. Doreen wasn't sure how much of the sincere and enthusiastic applause her friend could hear. So she lifted her hands in the air, twisting them in the ASL sign for applause.

The Squirrel Scouts around Doreen switched from clapping to the applause sign as well. And the sign quickly spread. Clapping quieted, hands rose, and soon a thousand people in the crowd were signing their applause. Ana Sofía glanced back and her mouth opened. She wiped an eye and hurried off.

Vin was waiting for Ana Sofía as she got off the stage, clapping and smiling. They had a plan to go walk around the mall together. Doreen was going to meet them at the nut shop in an hour.

"Hey, Pepper Potts, read the results from the mascot election!" shouted Heidi.

"RE-SULTS! RE-SULTS!" Dennis tried to start a chant, but

no one else picked it up. He fake-coughed to stop and then ran his fingers through his hair.

"Aye, the definitive results of our civic duty!" yelled the baron.

"Prithee," said the duchess, "announce them to the eager masses!"

Pepper waved and opened the ballot box, scanning the various papers with something that to Doreen looked like a Star Trek device.

"I've tallied the results and we have a clear winner," Pepper Potts said into the microphone. "Most of you chose to write in a candidate, and most of you chose to write in the same candidate. Wow, this is truly amazing. The mascot for your new Community Mall is a SQUIRREL!"

The crowd cheered.

Doreen gasped. She caught Ana Sofía's eye from across the crowd and signed, "Squirrel wins." Ana Sofía smiled. Most people wouldn't be able to tell that she was actually smiling, but Doreen could.

A squirrel! Tippy-Toe was going to be stoked.

Doreen's secret phone buzzed. She ducked out of the crowd to see who was texting her.

SHE-HULK

Hey I'm on the east coast for the weekend but all my friends are apparently in space fighting Thanos. Are you free to go grab a smoothie sometime?

SQUIRREL GIRL

. . .

. . .

. . .

Yep[94]

SHE-HULK

Cool see u soon

SQUIRREL GIRL

Sure no problem since grabbing smoothies with fellow heroes is a thing I totally do on a regular basis and basically the norm for me is what I'm saying

So is there a way to unsend already sent texts?

Anyhoo see u soon fellow hero

SHE-HULK

;)

---

94 Before writing this I deleted several paragraphs of verbal screaming. "Yep" was prolly better.

ACKNOWLEDGMENTS

*W*ill Murray and Steve Ditko created Squirrel Girl for Marvel Comics in 1991. We were thrilled to continue her adventures with this novel. As always, we owe a debt to the giants who came before us, especially the current creators of the *Unbeatable Squirrel Girl* comic series, multiple Eisner Award winners and suspected Inhumans Ryan North and Erica Henderson. You should check out their hilarious graphic novel *The Unbeatable Squirrel Girl Beats Up the Marvel Universe.*

Thanks to Andrea Shettle for her careful reading and wonderful feedback about Ana Sofía, ASL, and hearing aids. Thanks to Cece Bell, who also continues to look after Ana Sofía for us and is, as always, simply phenomenal. (If you haven't read her graphic novel memoir *El Deafo*, you really, really should.) Andrea and Cece, we love you! Muchísimas gracias to Linda Medina Martinez for her help and insight with Ana Sofía and her family. If we erred in any way, all fault is entirely on us.

A shout-out to the US International Council on Disabilities

and the wonderful work they do: www.usicd.org. Also disabilityinkidlit.com is a fantastic resource. Thanks to the writers there who share their time and tremendous experience. Love to thetrevorproject.org and all the Squirrel Scouts who support their lifesaving work.

Thanks to everyone at Disney and Marvel who helped make this book a reality, including Tomás Palacios, Hannah Allaman, Emily Meehan, MaryAnn Zissimos, Sana Amanat, Sarah Brunstad, Emily Shaw, Dan Kaufman, Adri Cowan, Lorraine Cink, Wil Moss, and Charles Beacham.

Special thanks to Deb Shapiro, Barry Goldblatt, Tricia Ready, Max Hale, the Janke kids, Margaret Stohl, and everyone who read the first book and said, "More, please!" This one is for you. And for Max. But also for you.

YOUR FAVORITE MARVEL HEROES ARE HERE!